THE
EMPTY HOUSE

THE
EMPTY HOUSE

Michael Gilbert

PERENNIAL LIBRARY

Harper & Row, Publishers, New York
Cambridge, Philadelphia, San Francisco, Washington
London, Mexico City, São Paulo, Singapore, Sydney

NOTE

The characters in this book are entirely imaginary and bear no relation to any living person. Where an existing institution is mentioned, no reference is intended to the past or present officers or members of such institution. The Bridgetown in the book is imaginary and lies many miles to the north of the real village of that name.

The author thanks Mr. W. B. Yeats, Miss Anne Yeats and the Macmillan Company for permission to quote the verse from "The Stare's Nest by My Window" by W. B. Yeats.

First PERENNIAL LIBRARY edition published 1988.

Library of Congress Cataloging in Publication Data

Gilbert, Michael Francis, 1912—
    The empty house.
    "Perennial Library."
    I. Title.
PZ3.G37367 1988 [PR6013.I3335] 823'.9'14 78-69501
ISBN 0-06-080880-2 (pbk.)

88 89 90 91 92 OPM 10 9 8 7 6 5 4 3 2 1

THE
EMPTY HOUSE

1

Colonel Bob Hay came out of the back door of Rackthorn Farm and started off up the slope toward Culme Head.

It was the first day of July. It had been raining all day, as it had been raining for most of the previous month, signaling the start of the wettest summer recorded in the annals of the West Country for forty years.

The late-evening sun was out now, throwing a slanting light onto the dripping ferns and the lumps of black rock which stood up through the sodden turf.

The Colonel climbed steadily. He was making for the hillock which rose, like one of twin breasts, fifty yards short of the cliff edge. It was crowned by a heap of stones and a wooden post with a curiously shaped iron basket on top. When he reached this vantage point the Colonel turned to look back.

Below him, in the valley, brown and full from the rain, the River Culme ran to its outlet in Rackthorn Bay. The tide was almost high, and he could just make out the ruffle of water which indicated the position of the bar, an arm of sand exposed at low tide and almost blocking the mouth of the bay.

"Dangerous place," he said to himself. "You could

cross it now, and for an hour either side of full tide. You'd come to grief if you tried it much sooner, or much later."

He looked up at the iron basket, visualizing it full of tarred wood and throwing a lurid light across the bay. It had been a favorite device of the wreckers to extinguish the true beacon and light a false one, luring ships onto the needle-sharp rocks at the foot of Rackthorn Point.

"Wicked devils," said the Colonel.

At a point on the other side of the bay where the cliff came down to water level there was a line of parked caravans. A track ran up behind them. From where he stood, the Colonel could follow it as it headed up toward the point and then swung away out of sight behind a clump of trees, emerging lower down and disappearing in the direction of Cryde.

Inland, he could see a mile or more of the road from Cryde to Huntercombe and, almost due south of where he was standing, the point where the byroad from Bridgetown joined it. He watched a car coming up the byroad and wondered whether it would swing right or left. In fact it did neither. It crossed the main road and set off up the track toward the caravan site.

The Colonel unslung the field glasses which he was carrying over one shoulder, and focused them on the car. For the moment it had gone out of sight behind the farm buildings. Now it emerged again. A dark-blue Vauxhall saloon of the old, heavy, four-door type. Impossible at that angle to see who was in it, but he got a distinct impression that the seat beside the driver was unoccupied.

The car passed the line of parked caravans without slowing, and went on up the track, disappearing at the top behind the clump of trees. "Wonder where he's heading for," said the Colonel. "If he's making for Cryde, why didn't he take the main road? There's nothing else up there to stop for. Admiring the view, perhaps?"

When it came, the noise was muted by distance but horribly distinct. For a full five seconds the Colonel stood staring, as though, if he looked hard enough, he could see through the screen of trees. Then he started to run down the hill.

As he reached the farmhouse, a younger man came out, carrying a light sporting rifle. He said, "Something up?"

"A car," said the Colonel. His voice was coming in jerks. "Didn't see it go over. Heard it. I'm going up to look."

As he spoke, he was unhitching the small boat alongside the landing stage.

"Oars," said the young man.

"Can't wait. Use the boathook."

"Any idea who it was?"

"Recognized the car. Couldn't see who was in it. Could be Alex Wolfe. Better get through to Western Command and ask them to send someone over. As quick as you can."

Using the boathook as a makeshift paddle, the Colonel sent the boat skimming across the twenty yards of troubled water. The tide was just making against the current. Judging matters with the skill of long practice, he laid the boat against the landing stage on the other side, threw a loop of rope over a projecting stump, jumped out, and trotted off up the path toward the caravan site. The whole maneuver had taken him less than half a minute. By the time he landed, the young man had disappeared into the house.

A middle-aged man wearing shorts and a bush shirt came out of one of the caravans.

The Colonel said, "If that's your car, I wonder if

you'd help. Run me up the track. I'm afraid there's been an accident."

"Sure," said the man. "I thought I heard something. I was coming out to look. Hop in."

"Steady when you get to the top. Don't want you over, too."

"Don't worry," said the man. "I'm a cautious type. I think we'll stop here, shall we?"

He pulled his car to one side of the track and they got out.

At this point the track ran out toward the cliff, swung to the right some way short of the edge, and then began its bumpy descent in the direction of Cryde Bay. A line of white posts marked the cliff edge.

It was only too clear what had happened.

From the point where the track turned, a line of tire marks showed on the turf. They could picture the frantic braking, but the treacherous ground had offered no grip. One of the white posts had gone, carrying with it a length of rail; another was leaning outward at an angle over empty space.

The Colonel walked cautiously forward and peered over the edge. Two hundred feet below him the water surged and eddied, blue and green and white-crested, between the fangs of rock. With a harsh scream a seagull took off from the edge of the cliff and volplaned down in a graceful curve toward the sea.

There was nothing else to be seen.

The Colonel came back slowly. He found the man sitting in the car. He was looking white.

"Sorry," he said. "Not used to this sort of thing. Makes you feel sick, doesn't it?"

"It's upsetting," said the Colonel. "But there *is* something you can do."

"As long as it doesn't mean going near the edge of that bloody cliff."

"Nothing like that. I shall have to stay up here for a bit. Could you take your car down and stop people coming up here? Just tell them there's been an accident and the police want the place kept clear."

"O.K.," said the man. The prospect of something to do seemed to have cheered him up.

"It won't be for long," said the Colonel. "Some Army people should be here soon. Let them through. Or the police, of course. No one else."

"What shall I say if they want to come?"

"Tell them it's a matter of national security," said the Colonel.

The man looked startled, reversed his car, and drove off.

When he had gone, the Colonel stood for a few moments staring after the car. He had a round and cheerful face, slightly protuberant eyes, and a thick waterfall mustache of the type which had been made fashionable by General Plumer fifty years before.

"Damn this weather," he said.

He was looking at the sun going down behind a bar of blue-black cloud. There was more rain coming. Wind, too. It was dusk already, and would be dark in half an hour. He wanted other people to see the car tracks before a night of storm had smoothed off their edges. He wished he had brought a camera with him.

He squatted down beside the tracks and tried to read whatever message they might hold.

The track up which they had driven was chalk and flint, sunk a few inches into the turf. The point where it swung away from the cliff edge was also the point where it started to go downhill. It was here that the car had broken through the shallow lip of the track and driven straight on to the cliff edge, hitting the post and rail fence hard enough to break through it.

The distance from track to cliff edge was about ten

yards. The tire tracks were clearly marked in the spongy turf. Were they too clear? If, as he had first assumed, the driver had been braking, stamping down frantically on the pedal in a last-moment attempt to halt the downhill progress of the car—and surely that was what he would have been doing—ought not the tracks to show the scrape of locked wheels?

He got to his feet as he heard a car coming. It was a Land-Rover, driven by the young man from the farm.

"Don't come too close, Rupert," said the Colonel. "Park off the track, on the other side. Have you got a torch? Bring it here. I want to show you something. There. What do you think?"

"Looks odd, certainly," said Rupert. "Not a sign of skidding. You'd certainly have seen the marks if the brakes had been on hard."

"That's what I thought," said the Colonel.

"It makes the whole thing look pretty deliberate, doesn't it?"

"It makes it look very odd indeed. Did you get through to Command?"

"I got through, all right. There was a bit of a flap on."

"A flap about what?"

"One of the guards at the Research Station had been reported as missing."

"Which one?"

"Lewis."

"A reliable man. He wouldn't do anything stupid, I'm sure."

"He's not going to do anything stupid now," said Rupert. "He's dead. They found him in a ditch, halfway between the Station and Bridgetown. It looked like a hit-and-run job."

The two men stood looking at each other. The Colo-

6

nel's eyes looked more vacant than ever. Before he could say anything, they heard the helicopter overhead.

"Here comes the Army," said Rupert.

"And the rain," said the Colonel.

2

"It's an odd business," said Mr. Troyte. "A damned odd business. I think it stinks."

"Odd, certainly," said his senior partner, Mr. Phelps. "But then, odd things do happen. We know that."

"Our people don't like it."

By our people he meant, as Mr. Phelps understood, the syndicate at Lloyds for which Messrs. Phelps, King and Troyte, Insurance Adjusters of St. Mary Axe, did most of their work.

"If they don't like it," said Mr. Phelps, "we'd better do something about it, hadn't we? Who did you think of giving it to?"

"I thought of Peter Manciple."

Mr. Phelps pursed his lips. "Bit inexperienced."

"He hasn't had a lot of experience," agreed Mr. Troyte. "He's done two or three good jobs, though. The Palgrave Marina case—"

"Yes. He did a good job there. Didn't he have some family trouble, about a year ago? I seem to remember there was something that upset him badly."

"His father was killed. Might have been an accident. Might have been suicide."

"There was an inquest?"

"Yes. There had to be an inquest. The verdict was accident."

"And you think the jury were being charitable?"

"I don't know," said Mr. Troyte. "I didn't ask a lot of questions about it. It didn't seem to be our business. It upset Peter, of course. But he seems to have got over it all right."

"Very well, let's give it to him. There'll be a lot of leg work involved, get him out of the office. It should keep his mind off his own troubles. Will you brief him?"

Mr. Troyte agreed that he would brief Peter Manciple. He had intended to use him anyway; but he always went through the motions of consulting his senior partner. It was one of the things which made them a good firm.

That conversation took place on Friday morning, two days after the blue Vauxhall car had gone over the cliff at Rackthorn Point. A search by the police, helped by the Rescue Service from Cryde, had found nothing; not so much as a splinter of metal or glass. Nor had they expected to. Don Bisset, the bearded coxswain of the Life Boat, spelled it out to Chief Superintendent Horne of the Devon Constabulary.

"It's deep water," he said, "and there's a backwash under the cliff. You won't get a diver to go down there. He knows he'd be carried in. There's an inlet under the cliff foot. No one knows how far it goes. If ever we did get down there, we'd find a thing or two, I reckon."

"Treasure?"

"Treasure, no doubt. And bones, too. The old wreckers knew all about Rackthorn Point. Anyone who might tell an awkward story would be likely to be pitched over there with a few feet of cable wrapped around his legs. There's a saying in these parts: 'What Rackthorn takes, Rackthorn keeps.'"

The Superintendent put all this into his report, one

copy of which went to Western Command Headquarters at Exeter. It appeared that the only known car in the neighborhood corresponding to the one which had gone over belonged to a man called Alexander Wolfe, a scientist working at the Biological Warfare Research Station near Bridgetown. "These boffins," he said to Sergeant Rix. "They live in a world of their own. Ten to one, he was thinking about some missing equation and drove straight over."

"He's a missing equation himself now," said Sergeant Rix. "And it isn't only the Army who are worried. There's something about an insurance policy. I heard a buzz that he'd insured himself only a few months ago. A hundred thousand pounds, they said."

"Who gets it?"

"There's a sister somewhere. Plays the cello—in one of those London orchestras."

The Superintendent considered this angle of the matter. It didn't make a lot of sense. It was not inconceivable that a man would insure his life and then commit suicide, disguising it as an accident; it had happened in one case he knew about. But that had been for the benefit of a hard-pressed wife and family. Wolfe was a bachelor without known dependents—unless a sister who played the cello could be described as a dependent.

Very odd.

Mr. Troyte sent for Peter Manciple, and while he was waiting for him he got out the policy and studied it again. It was certainly a curious document. Odd in itself; odder still in the light of what had happened. But then, as he had said to Mr. Phelps, odd happenings were part of their trade. Only last year one of the Syndicate's clients who owned a garage which was known to be losing money had insured it against fire in a very large sum indeed. It had been burned to the ground two days later. The fire had demonstrably been started by a flash of lightning. "And unless he had a private line to the Almighty—" said Mr. Troyte. "Come in. Oh, it's you, Peter. I wanted you to have a look at this file."

While Peter Manciple studied the documents, crouched forward in his chair with a lock of fair hair falling over one eye, Mr. Troyte studied Peter.

They had taken him into the business on the recommendation of one of their important clients. When Mr. Troyte had first interviewed Peter, he had been so struck with his apparent frailty that he had insisted on a medical check. The doctor, one of the toughest diagnosticians in the insurance world, had found no fault. "He's unusually tall," he said, "but that doesn't mean that he's a bad life. Quite the contrary. These long, thin streaks are very durable. He was probably a late developer. Most of his early growth went into his height. When he thickens out a little, he'll be all right. Nothing wrong with his heart or lungs."

Events had shown that there was nothing wrong with his brains, either. He had a remarkable gift for filing away and recalling facts. It was something more than mere memory. As a computer will store facts, producing them to order when the appropriate button is pressed, so could Peter absorb, without seeming effort, the contents of endless reports, documents, statements, and accounts, selecting, without any reference back, the facts that mattered and presenting them in a logical sequence. His report on the notorious Palgrave Marina swindle had already become a classic in insurance circles.

"I suppose it's the last clause in the policy that's worrying you," said Peter.

"Right."

"Why did we ever accept it?"

"Look at the premium."

"It's loaded," agreed Peter. He studied the clause

11

again, scratching the tip of his nose with the index finger of his left hand. "What it means is that if there is an *assumption* that the cause of death—or *one* of the causes—was drowning, the insurers are to pay up without actual proof of death."

"Right."

"Did he explain why he wanted such an odd clause put in?"

"Yes. He said that he often had to travel by air, and it might happen that his plane went down over the sea and was never recovered. Or it might only be salvaged years later. Or he might be in a ship that was lost at sea without any evidence of what had really happened to it. It doesn't happen so often now, with wireless and radar, but it's still possible. If the body isn't found, I understand that, strictly, you have to wait seven years before the court will presume death. He didn't want his sister to be kept out of her money."

"Then we shall have to pay up."

"There *is* the usual exclusion clause. If the insured commits suicide within two years of taking out the policy."

Peter stared at him. "Do people really think that?"

"The Army put in a report. A Colonel Hay, a retired officer who was staying in a farmhouse nearby. He was out for an evening stroll. He didn't actually see the car go over, but he heard it, and he was on the spot within minutes. There's a copy of his report among the papers. He says that there was no sign of braking. He and an Army friend who was with him were the only people who saw the tracks while they were fresh. The tracks were more or less washed out by a freak storm that night. But both men are quite positive."

Peter read through Colonel Hay's report before speaking again. Then he said, "What do you want me to do about it?"

"I want you to look into it. The whole thing seems altogether too much of a coincidence to be trusted. Here's this clause. It was drafted by his own solicitors. Their name's in the file somewhere. Six months after the policy's written, Wolfe puts his car over one of the very few places on the English coast where it's probably never going to be seen again."

"Can't they salvage it?"

"Have a look at Coxswain Bisset's report."

When Peter had read it, he said, "If it was suicide, Wolfe was either a saint or a madman. Either way, it isn't going to be easy to prove it now."

"It isn't going to be easy," agreed Mr. Troyte. "It may not even be possible. But there's a lot of money involved, and we've got to make an effort. It's Friday today. Tomorrow you'd better go and see the sister. Lavinia Wolfe, Candlewick Cottage, Sudbury. She plays in some orchestra."

"If she's *the* Lavinia Wolfe," said Peter, "that's a fairly inadequate description. She's leading cellist in the London Symphony Orchestra. I heard a recital she gave at the Festival Hall last year."

"I expect you're right," said Mr. Troyte tolerantly. "I'm tone deaf, myself. When you've got what you can from her, you'll have to go down to Devonshire. Take your time about it. Ferret round. See what you can find. If you dig up anything, let me know at once. If not, let me have some sort of report by Monday week. Right?"

"Right," said Peter. And to his mother, that evening, "It's the maddest thing. I'm not sure whether it's a serious investigation, a cosmetic exercise to please our Syndicate, or a buckshee summer holiday."

"Perhaps it is all three, *chéri*," said his mother. Being a Frenchwoman, she added, "Doubtless you will be able to make a profit from the expenses which you will

13

be allowed. That will be some compensation." She added, without any change of tone, and almost as though it was part of the same train of thought, "I was followed again today."

"Oh dear. Are you sure?"

"Quite sure. It was a small man with a rose in his buttonhole."

"Did you do anything about it?"

"I considered reporting the matter to the police. But on the previous occasion they were *si peu sympathique* that I decided not to do so."

"It must be provoking. Is supper ready? I'm starving."

"Then you must starve for ten more minutes. Time to drink one glass of that abominably sweet sherry which your uncle gave us."

After dinner Peter walked down to the British Legion Club, of which he was one of the many young honorary members. The rain, which had swept up from the West Country on the day before, had cleared off and it was a fresh and sparkling evening.

At the club he found that Fred Dawlish had put their names down for the billiard table. "Time for a pint before this pair finish," said Fred. "They're worse than we are."

They finished their drinks, had an inexpert game of snooker, and took a second pint to a table in the corner of the bar.

"I'm afraid my mother's got them again," said Peter.

"Little men?"

"That's right. This one's got a rose in his buttonhole."

"Makes a change. The last one had false teeth and a squint, if I remember rightly."

"Do you think she ought to see a doctor?"

"I don't believe there's much a doctor can do about it. Would you like me to keep an eye on her? Unofficial like?"

Fred was a detective sergeant at the local station.

"It's very good of you," said Peter, "but if she found herself being followed about by *two* men, she really would blow her top. Better leave it alone. Thanks for the suggestion, all the same."

3

Candlewick Cottage was the end one of six which had originally been built for farm laborers but had gone up in the world. Peter tugged the wrought-iron bellpull and was answered by a mixed chorus of barking—treble, tenor, and bass.

"Quiet, all of you," said a woman's deep voice. "Pipe down, Charlie. I mean it. Sambo, if you jump up again, I'll crown you."

The door was opened, and Peter found himself being inspected by a gray-haired woman with a pleasant face and strong nose, a deerhound, a bull terrier, and a Jack Russel terrier. The deerhound, which was stationed on the right, had its head tilted to the left. The bull terrier and the Jack Russel on the left had their heads tilted to the right. The woman, who was not a lot shorter than Peter, was looking straight at him. This gave the whole group an effect of classical symmetry.

"Miss Wolfe?"

"That's right. I'm not going to warn you again, Sambo. You must be something to do with insurance. I've been expecting you. Mind your head. These cottages were built for a race of dwarfs."

The door opened directly into a sitting room, an untidy place with a large open fireplace, three walls lined with low white-painted bookcases, and a ceiling of carefully uncovered and varnished oak beams. The tops of the bookcases were a clutter of musical scores, loose sheet music, catalogues, greeting cards, and a metronome.

"Watch your head," said Miss Wolfe. "My goodness, you *are* tall."

"Six foot five."

"You'd better sit down before you hurt yourself."

Peter looked for somewhere to sit. The sofa was now occupied by the deerhound. The other two armchairs had been claimed by the bull terrier and the Jack Russel.

"Idle brutes," said Miss Wolfe. "I try to keep them off the chairs, but it's a losing battle. The place for dogs is in the stable." She repeated, "The stable" in a threatening voice. The three dogs looked at her tolerantly. "They know I haven't got a stable." She went behind the chair with the Jack Russel in it and tipped it up, sliding the dog off onto the floor.

"Grab it quick," she said.

Peter sat down. The Jack Russel jumped onto his lap.

"It's all right," he said. "He doesn't worry me. I'm used to dogs."

"It's good of you to say so, but I feel I'm being weak. What I ought to do is to buy a whip. A *large whip*." The deerhound, assuming that he was being talked to, thumped his tail against the arm of the sofa.

"About that policy," said Peter.

"I got a letter about it," said Miss Wolfe. "From the insurance company—I forget their name—and I've lost the letter. Or Sambo may have eaten it. Checks, letters, and banknotes. If you leave them lying about, he gobbles them up at once."

17

"It wasn't a company. The policy was underwritten by a syndicate at Lloyds."

"Goodness. That makes me feel like a ship. And are you a—what is the right word? An undertaker?"

"I'm from Phelps, King and Troyte." He gave Miss Wolfe his card.

She looked at it carefully and handed it back. "What does 'Adjusters' mean?"

"Well," said Peter cautiously, "it's our job to investigate insurance claims."

"And adjust them?"

"If necessary."

"Downward, I'm sure."

"What makes you think that?"

"If you adjusted them upward, no one would bother to employ you."

Peter had to acknowledge that there was some truth in this.

"However," said Miss Wolfe, "there can't be much scope for adjusting this one. It's for a definite amount of money, payable in defined circumstances."

"It's the circumstances that I was asked to look into. One of the clauses in the policy was most unusual. I don't think, in all my experience, I've ever seen one like it."

"Twenty years? Thirty years?"

"What—?"

"You said, in all your experience. The way you said it, it sounded a very long time."

"That was pompous," said Peter. "I'm sorry." When embarrassed, he blushed very easily. "I didn't mean it to be. I've been exactly two years in this job. All the same, it *is* an unusual clause."

"It was drafted for my brother by his solicitor, Roland Highsmith. He'd every confidence in him, I do know

18

that. They were at Oxford together and have been friends ever since."

Peter looked at his file. "That would be Messrs. Highsmith and Westall, Solicitors, of Forebury Street, Exeter."

"Right. But I believe that Westall's an invalid. He's always away sick, or something. Roland does all the work."

"I shall have to have a word with him."

"Why? Is there something wrong with the clause?"

Miss Wolfe put a pair of horn-rimmed glasses onto her strong nose and studied the policy. Peter had realized for some time that her speech and manner were a cloak for a shrewd mind; the sort of mind to be expected of a woman who had made her way to the top in one of the most competitive musical outfits in the world.

"It's the way it's worded," said Peter. "'If there is an assumption that the cause of death, or one of the causes, was drowning.' It seems to have been carefully designed for what actually happened. Does it worry you if we talk about this?"

"I was very fond of Alex," said Miss Wolfe, "and he of me, I think. But we weren't close. We wrote to each other on birthdays and at Christmas, but I hadn't seen him for—let me think—more than three years. Nearly four. You were saying—?"

"If the policy had said, simply, drowning, there would have been an argument that the impact of the car onto the water must have killed him *before* he went under."

"Then you might have wriggled out of it."

"I don't say we would have. It's the sort of argument our lawyers might have put up."

"Clever old Roland. He thought of that one."

"Don't you see, that's what makes it all so odd. It almost looks as if he had this particular sort of accident in mind when he drafted the policy."

19

"Not true. The sort of accident they both had in mind was a plane going down over the sea and being lost without trace. The same arguments would apply."

"Did he do a lot of flying?"

"He used to. A great deal. In the last few years he's usually taken his car across to the Continent and driven about in it. It was easier to shake free of the little men who trailed round after him."

Peter stared at her. He thought of his mother. Surely not a second case of persecution mania?

Miss Wolfe was looking at him over the top of her glasses, which were still perched on her nose. She said, "You don't know a great deal about my brother, I can see."

"Practically nothing. I'd be very grateful for anything you can tell me."

"I don't know the details of the work he was doing. Except that it must have been connected with biological warfare, or he wouldn't have been at that Hell's Kitchen in Devonshire. I'm sure he hated it as much as I did."

"Then why did he work there?"

"He was blackmailed into doing it."

"Blackmailed? Who by?"

"By the government. And if you keep looking at me in that unbelieving way, I shan't say a single word more."

"I do apologize. I do, really. It's just that I was startled. Somehow one doesn't associate governments with blackmail."

"All governments use blackmail. Some openly. Some more discreetly. This was a particularly unpleasant form of blackmail because it was disguised as charity. What my brother specialized in was genetic research, but jobs in that line were few and far between. When he left Oxford, he filled in time for a year or so teaching science at a public school, but always with his chin on his shoulder. Finally he got what he wanted. It was a junior post at the Molecular Biology Research Unit at Cambridge. Whilst he was there they arranged for him to do a spell at the Massachusetts Institute of Technology and he went, on attachment, to Bart's Hospital. They've got a Medical Oncology Unit. He was beginning to be interested in the connection—everyone knows it must exist—between the normal processes of growing older, and the abnormal ones."

"Cancer?"

"Cancer and leukemia are the vicious ones. There are plenty of others. All the knobs and spots and blotches that accumulate as your system gets tired. Like trees."

"It sounds fascinating."

"It certainly fascinated him," said Miss Wolfe. "Do you know anything at all about molecular biology?"

"Not a scrap."

"Well, I don't know much. But some years ago Alex and I had a holiday together on a farm in Wales. Considered as a holiday, it was a dead loss. It rained almost every day. Alex did a lot of talking and I remembered some of it. It seems that everyone has got a personal genetic code. It's carried by his own private arrangement of biochemicals in cells called nuclei, and the important thing is to find out how the chromosomes are packed into them and then to try and read the pattern of information carried by them. Stop me if I'm boring you. This is nothing to do with insurance policies."

"You're not boring me," said Peter. He noticed that, now that Miss Wolfe was talking about something that interested her, she had dropped all affectations.

"I gather that it was like the code-breaking we did during the war. Only, the code they were trying to read was more complicated than anything the Germans ever thought up. It was there that Alex finally lost me. All I can remember is that it was something to do with a

21

submicroscopic thread called DNA. It is chemically the most complex of the five substances which make up a chromosome, and seems to be their intelligence unit. To date, it's been cleverer than any of the people trying to unravel it. There was a woman—I can't remember her name—who Alex said got closest to it. Then she died, and the whole research was put back by years."

"Didn't she leave notes of where she'd got to?"

"You say that as though she was traveling on the Underground and could tell them what station she'd arrived at. When you get to that point in pure research, you're on your own. You're pushing out into the dark. No maps. Not even a star to guide you. It must be the most terrifying and the most exciting thing imaginable."

The terrier on Peter's knees pricked up his ears and gave a single sharp bark. Charlie, the deerhound, unfolded himself from the sofa, padded across to the window, and looked out. From where he sat, Peter could see the road. A car had drawn up, ten yards past the gate. It did not seem to be doing anything in particular.

"That's when the trouble started. Alex wrote an article."

"About his work?"

"Nothing to do with his work. He wrote it after one of his trips to the Middle East. If he hadn't been becoming well known in his own field, no one would have dreamed of publishing it. I wish to heaven they hadn't. It was the sort of mad, infantile, totally apolitical argument that scientists might indulge in while talking over their port after dinner but should certainly never commit to paper. What he said was that a surgeon would remove even a sound organ from the body if the presence of that organ was, on balance, potentially dangerous to the rest of the anatomy. On this analogy, the course of wisdom was clearly to excise the state of Israel. It might be, probably it was, a well-run and peace-loving state. What was wrong with it was that it was *in the wrong place*. Set down somewhere else, it would be harmless. Established exactly where it was, it was a source of infection in the body politic. Can you imagine the reactions?"

"Easily."

"The national press got it, of course. 'Israel a Plague Spot. Move It to the Sahara' was one of the mildest."

"Why did anyone take it seriously? Couldn't they see it was meant as a joke?"

"It's one of the things you mustn't joke about. Like immigration and South Africa. Poor Alex found that out, quickly enough."

"I imagine a lot of people got very angry," said Peter, "but there wasn't much anyone could actually do about it, was there?"

"Was there not? It didn't take long for someone to point out that Alex was doing the sort of job which might, quite easily, lead to important developments in the military field. The public thinks in clichés. Alex was working in a biological research unit. They'd heard of something called biological warfare. One and one make two. Here was a scientist calling for the destruction of Israel, *and he was one of the few men who might be in a position to do it*. You know how television has conditioned people to think of scientists as evil little men with bald heads and steel-rimmed glasses who are plotting to destroy the world. Here was one of them in the flesh. It was nonsense, of course, but the press and the Jewish lobby between them worked up such a head of steam that the government withdrew Alex's security clearance. And that meant, in practice, that no laboratory would accept him. He was so far ahead in his own field that his reputation was already international. And the only job open to him was teaching small boys O Level and A Level science. Now do you see?"

"I'm beginning to," said Peter.

"It was a subtle offer they made him. He could pursue his own line of research, but he had to do it inside a government military institution. The fruits of his research would be covered by the Official Secrets Act, and would be available to the government alone. Subject to that, he was given the run of the most up-to-date facilities, and a free hand. He made two provisos of his own. He would report fully, in writing, but only once every two years. And he was to have as much time off as he wanted, up to four months every year if he felt he needed it. The government didn't like either condition, but they accepted them because they wanted Alex. It was the second condition which worried them most, because Alex used to take those long vacations abroad. As I told you. He shipped his car across to France and simply drove off into the blue. That put them on the spot. If he'd flown, they could have put a man on the plane with him and found out where he was going to. It was driving his own car made it impossible. He hadn't committed any crime. So they couldn't involve the police. The only way would have been to ask for the help of the various foreign intelligence agencies. That would have meant telling them why they wanted Alex traced. And would almost certainly have meant telling them just what line of research he was engaged on. Which wouldn't have made them popular in certain quarters."

"So he just drove off for months at a time, and no one knew where he went to?"

"Right."

"Did *you* know?"

Miss Wolfe looked at him for a long moment, then said, "I didn't know, and if I had, I don't think I should have told you. It's nothing to do with your company."

"I suppose not," said Peter. He thought about what

24

she had told him. It was not conclusive, but it suggested a number of possibilities, most of them disturbing.

He said, "Was your brother the sort of person who would commit suicide?"

"Is there such a sort of person?"

"I think so. I rather think my father did."

"I see," said Miss Wolfe gently. "Yes, I suppose you're right. There are people of whom one would say it was possible. Others, certainly, for whom it would be impossible. I wouldn't put my brother in either category. His head ruled his heart. If circumstances had indicated to him that suicide was the *only* way out, he was capable of planning it in exactly that way."

"In cold blood?"

"He was a very cold-blooded sort of person. Deceptive, too. When he talked to you, you thought that he was telling you a lot, about himself and his hopes and his ambitions. But when you thought it out afterward, you realized that he hadn't actually told you anything at all. It was only on that one holiday that he really unbuttoned himself, and even then—I don't know. I had the impression that there was a certain reserve that I wasn't being allowed into."

"If there is a chance that he organized the whole thing—if you really thought that—could you accept the money?"

"My dear young man," said Miss Wolfe, reverting abruptly to her opening style, "of course I would. I haven't the slightest sympathy for insurance companies or syndicates or whatever they call themselves. That's right, isn't it, Charlie?"

The deerhound agreed with a low rumble. He had no opinion of insurance companies either.

"They're confidence tricksters, that's all. When you work it out, what do they actually *do*? They take people's money, and organize their business so that they're only obliged to give them back part of it. They're like old robber barons. They steal your money and use it to build huge castles, and live in them in the height of luxury and indolence."

Peter understood that the interview was over. He accepted his congé with a good grace, got up, and collected his papers. Miss Wolfe, Charlie, Sambo, and the Jack Russel, whose name he had never discovered, accompanied him to the door.

Miss Wolfe shook his hand in a masculine way. He noted the strength of her fingers as she did so.

The car was still parked ten yards down the road. There were two young men in it, neither of them doing anything in particular.

Peter walked down the long hill toward Sudbury town, whistling softly, a habit of his when he was trying to pin down a recollection. It was something Miss Wolfe had said almost at the beginning. Her brother had put in a few years teaching science at a public school. Surely there had been a master called Wolfe at his own school, Blundell's? It had been before his time, but the oldest boys had still spoken of him, in tones of awed respect unusual in boys discussing their instructors. If that was true, there must be members of the staff who would remember him.

Behind him, he heard the car start up. It cruised slowly down the hill past him and turned into the town ahead.

4

Having discovered that there was no suitable Sunday train to Cryde Junction, and no train of any sort to Bridgetown, Peter decided to ignore Mr. Troyte's suggestion and spent Sunday amusing himself. In the morning he played squash, winning the odd game out of five and exhausting his opponent in the process. His opponent, who was a class player, said, "I don't know how the devil you do it. You must be bloody fit."

"It's not fitness," said Peter apologetically. "It's length of arm. I can get shots back without moving too far."

After a lunch at his favorite pub, he went for a walk. When he got home, he found his mother in a state of excitement and indignation.

"He came to the door," she said. "Right up to the door, and rang the bell."

"A little man?"

"Yes."

"The one with the rose in his buttonhole?"

"I didn't notice his rose," said his mother crossly. "I was too angry to notice anything. To follow me is one thing. To come up to the house and ring our doorbell is quite another thing. However, I had made my dispositions. I was ready for him."

"What did you do?"

"I had my camera in my hand. Before he could start to talk, I had taken a picture of him. Then I slammed the door and said, very loudly, 'In two minutes the police will be here. Be off with you.' "

"What did he do?"

"He ran away."

"Actually ran?"

"Perhaps he didn't run. He walked very fast."

"What are you going to do with the photograph?"

"First, I shall have to get it developed. That will need some thought. They will have warned all the local chemists' shops, and will do their best to destroy the negative. The chemist will apologize, of course. He will say that it was an accident. However, I shall circumvent them. I have a friend who is an amateur photographer. He will develop the photograph for me."

"And what are you going to do with it when it has been developed?"

"What do you imagine I shall do with it, imbecile? Frame it and put it on the mantelpiece? Naturally, I shall send it to the police. They will be embarrassed, but they can hardly refuse to take action when I give them this definite proof."

"My dear old mother," said Peter, putting one arm around her, "who *are* these men who follow you about and come to the door and have enough power to corrupt chemists? Why should they be persecuting you? What's the object of it?"

His mother was silent for so long that Peter thought she was not going to answer him, and might even have forgotten that he was there. Then she said, "It's because of your father."

"What about him?"

"I never meant to tell you this. And you must never, never tell anyone else. Promise me."

"All right."

"Promise properly."

"I promise never to tell anyone whatever it is you're going to tell me now."

"Very well."

His mother moved across to the window, which was wide open to the evening sun, and shut it. Then she came back and composed herself in her chair, sitting upright in it like a square, solemn little judge. She said, "The verdict in the coroner's court was fixed. It was arranged by the authorities. They can, of course, obtain whatever verdict they wish. Your father's death was *not* an accident."

The gray mists which had enveloped Peter at the time were coming back. He started to say, "I was afraid—" but was silenced by his mother. She leaned forward a little, and spoke in a voice scarcely above a whisper.

"I know. You were afraid that he took his own life. Yes? But it is *not* true. He was murdered. Killed, in cold blood, by his superiors in the Secret Service."

"Oh God!" said Peter.

That evening he went down again to the club and found Detective Sergeant Dawlish drinking beer with a group of friends. When he could get him to himself, he said, "I'm afraid my mother's worse. It's not just little men following her. It's the Secret Service."

"That's bad," said Dawlish. "Very bad."

"And I've got to go down to the West Country for a week. Do you think you could, very quietly, sort of keep an eye on her? I don't want her to do anything stupid while I'm away."

"Do what I can," said Dawlish. "Not that there's a lot you can do in a case like that."

At five o'clock on the following afternoon Peter got out of the train at Cryde station and walked out into the town, carrying his suitcase. It was raining, and the streets were full of sulky children and bored parents wearing raincoats and waiting for the sun to come out.

There was a small office in the High Street which called itself "Tourist Information." It had an enlarged photograph in the window showing a group of girls in bikinis sunning themselves on Cryde beach. In the circumstances it might, Peter thought, have been more tactful to take it down.

A girl behind the counter agreed that there was a bus service from Cryde to Bridgetown, but said that the second of the only two buses which ran on Monday had already left. She seemed genuinely sorry about this.

"It's not your fault," said Peter. "Isn't there a hotel at Bridgetown?"

"There's the Doone Valley. It's quite a nice little place."

"Then could you find its telephone number for me? And could I use your telephone?"

The girl thought this would be all right. She also thought that Peter had a nice smile. Shy. Not like some of the terrible youths who came in on the pretense of making inquiries and hung around and made nuisances of themselves.

A gruff voice on the telephone agreed that it was the Doone Valley Hotel. Peter asked if they happened to have a room vacant.

"Would it be just for the night?" said the voice doubtfully.

Peter was not inexperienced in the art of travel. He said, "Oh, no, it's not just for the night. I should want it for at least a week, with full board and that sort of thing. I'd be happy to pay for a week in advance."

The voice, sounding more cheerful, said that it would find out, and came back and said that there was one room left. What name was it? Peter gave his name, spelling it carefully.

"There's just one more thing," he said. "How do I get out to Bridgetown?"

"You haven't got a car, then?"

Peter admitted that he had no car.

"That's a pity," said the voice. "The last bus has gone."

"What I was wondering," said Peter, "was whether there was anywhere in Bridgetown I could hire a car for the week."

"There's Key's Garage. Bridgetown 24. You could try him. He might be able to oblige."

Bridgetown 24 produced Bill Key himself, who said that he had a little Austin which might do. He would bring it over himself so that—what was the name again, please?—Mr. Manciple could try it out.

Bill Key turned out to be only a few years older than Peter. He shook him warmly by the hand and said, "I thought I recognized the name. Tom and I were day boys, but my youngest brother was in School House with you."

"Key Three!" said Peter. "Of course. I knew the name rang a bell. He was my fag."

"An idle young tear-about, I don't doubt."

"What's he doing now?"

"He's still there. Head of the School. Captain of Rugger. Won the Russell. You name it, he's done it."

"Good heavens," said Peter. He was remembering a small, round-faced boy who had conscientiously cleaned the mud off the studs of his rugger boots. "He must be quite old."

"Nineteen in September. He's got a place at Durham. Tom's in the Navy. I inherited the family business. It's quite a business, too, considering it's stuck down miles from anywhere. We do a good deal of work for the Army. It's going to be a tight fit for you."

"That's always the trouble with me," said Peter. "I'm too long."

"We can push the seat back one more notch, but that's it. Great pity you weren't here a week or two earlier. You could have had the old Savoia. There's a car for you! Built for giants. I let Professor Petros have it. He might swop with you, if you only want it for the week. He's a decent old boy."

"Professor of what?"

"Archeology, I suppose. He's doing a dig on Cran Tor. He's pretty well known in his own line, I believe. Fork left here. Do you think you can manage?"

"If I get cramp, I'll let you take over," said Peter.

The left fork had swung them away from the coast and out onto the skirts of Exmoor. There were people who found the steep combes and the sudden gradients, the red soil and the lush vegetation of Devonshire overpowering. Peter was not one of them. He had spent five long and, on the whole, happy years at school there. He felt that he was coming home.

"A pity about all this rain," said Key. "A lot of people have had their holidays wrecked. If it keeps up, we shall have flooding for sure."

The road twisted and then dipped steeply into a combe. As they crossed the bridge at the bottom, Peter could see the brown water running nearly level with the top of the arches.

He said, "You mentioned the Army. What particular bit of it have you got at Bridgetown?"

"It calls itself the Biological Warfare Research Station. Not a very popular outfit. We had a big protest about it last summer. A Peace March. They didn't manage to get in. They camped outside and sang hymns."

"Did it worry the Army?"

"Hard to say. No one likes being unpopular. I suppose it took their minds off protesting against other things."

"Such as?"

"Stag hunting and otter hunting," said Key with a grin which showed a fine set of predator's teeth. "I expect you're anti-bloodsports yourself?"

"What makes you think that?"

"My brother told me at school you had a reputation for being anti-everything."

"I've mellowed with age," said Peter. "These Exmoor sheep are very independent."

"It's no good blowing your horn at them. The only way to make them move is to ram them."

Bridgetown lay in a fold in the ground, overlooked by shoulders of moorland to the south and west, falling away toward the coastline to the north. It looked like a ship anchored in a sea of green waves. As they ran down toward it, the sun looked out for a moment through the scudding clouds and lit up the white walls and red roofs of the cottages clustered around the square gray church.

"Lovely," said Peter.

"Not bad," said Key. "A bit isolated in winter. Last January we were cut off by snow for a week. My place is at the far end of the main street. If you come along tomorrow, I'll see if I can do something about the seat. And that's the hotel. Dave Brewer runs it. Don't be put off by his appearance. He looks like an aboriginal cavedweller, but he's a very nice man really."

Peter was glad he had been warned. The proprietor of the Doone Valley Hotel was a formidable figure, almost as tall as Peter, twice as thick and covered, at every visible point, with hair. He seized Peter's case in one large hand and rolled ahead of him into the hotel.

It was sizable for a village inn. There were eight keys hanging on hooks on a board in the hall. Mr. Brewer selected one of them and led the way up, the stairs creaking under his weight. "Along the end here," he said. "Number eight. It's a nice room. A young man had it last week. An artist. He was planning to stay with us a fortnight, but the rain druv him off. It's all right if you're thinking of walking. A drop of rain doesn't hurt if you're walking."

It was difficult to imagine that rain would have any effect on Mr. Brewer. He looked as impervious to water as an otter. Sensing a question mark at the end of the last comment, Peter said, "I expect I shall get in a bit of walking. It's really business has brought me down."

"Ah," said Mr. Brewer. "Something to do with that accident at Rackthorn Point perhaps?"

"You're right," said Peter. "But how did you guess?"

"When you said business, I thought it must be that. We've had a heap of people through in the last few days. Police and soldiers and such-like. A nasty thing to happen. They ought to put a proper iron fence all along the cliff. Not just a couple of sticks you could break by leaning against 'em. That's the bathroom and lavatory. Come down when you're ready and have a drink before your supper."

Peter unpacked the few things he had brought with him and stood for a moment looking out of the window. He was not sorry that the object of his visit had been so summarily discovered. It would save embarrassment, and might even be helpful. Apart from the obvious move of visiting the Biological Warfare Research Station, where he would probably be told nothing and might not even be admitted, he had formed no sort of plan. The more people who knew what he was up to, the better for him. They would certainly want to talk about it, and he might learn something.

At this point he caught a glimpse of himself in the mirror over the washbasin and burst out laughing. The whole trip was nonsense. If the police and the Army, with their resources, were unable to discover the truth about what had led to a distinguished biologist driving himself over a two-hundred-foot cliff, what chance was there that he, Peter Manciple, was going to do better? He had a shrewd suspicion that he had been given the job as a pretext for a week's holiday. Arthur Troyte might not know the truth of what had happened a month before in a small hotel in Surrey; that was a secret between Peter and his doctor. But Troyte might have noticed the effect which it had had on Peter's work, and decided, in his shrewd way, to do something about it.

Peter washed his face and hands, combed his long, fair hair out of his eyes, and went downstairs. There was only one occupant of the lounge, a middle-aged man with a short, pointed gray beard and gold-rimmed glasses. Peter felt safe in assuming that this was Professor Petros, the famous archeologist. He introduced himself.

The Professor said, in the clear, unaccented English which at once proclaimed him a foreigner, "Our host was telling me that you have come in connection with that sad accident last Wednesday. You would perhaps be connected with the newspapers?"

"Not exactly," said Peter. "I'm connected with the people who carried an insurance policy on Dr. Wolfe's life. They sent me down to—" (What on earth could he say without sounding ridiculous?)—"to have a look into the matter."

The Professor considered this reply, and then said, with a gentle smile, "Yours must be an interesting sort of profession, Mr. Manciple. But tell me, unless I am being indiscreet, what exactly do you expect to find? I believe that all hope has now been abandoned of recovering the car. The body may, of course, be washed ashore, but I am told that even that is unlikely."

"You're an archeologist," said Peter. "I imagine that you often dig holes in the ground without having much idea what you're going to turn up."

"That is a good debating answer. It is true that one has often little idea what one will find. But an archeologist does not dig at random. He relies on a great number of indications and pointers which his experience interprets for him."

"I expect that all investigators get the same sort of instinct," said Peter. "I can't claim a great stock of it yet. Did you know Dr. Wolfe?"

"I have met him. He came here sometimes in the evenings. Accompanied by one or another of his male nurses." The Professor smiled.

"You mean the guards from the Army establishment?"

"There were two of them who seemed to have the particular charge of Dr. Wolfe. One of them, a man called Lewis, was the poor fellow who was run down by a motorist."

"I didn't hear about that."

"It was a sad coincidence. It happened on the same day that Dr. Wolfe died."

"Have they found the person responsible?"

"A policeman was here making inquiries." The Professor smiled again dryly. "He is said to have a clue. Myself, I think it was a passing motorist. The man may never be discovered, but he will suffer from a guilty conscience for the rest of his days."

"Man?"

"Certainly. Did you ever hear of a hit-and-run case involving a woman? It is always a man. Men are such cowards."

"I can see that you are a student of human nature. Can you offer any explanation of Dr. Wolfe's death?"

"Naturally, we have all discussed it in every aspect.

Various suggestions have been put forward. I have my own ideas. Here is our host. May I offer you a drink? I usually take a glass of dry sherry before dinner."

"I'd like the same. Thank you."

"Then two dry sherries. And will you join us?"

"Not just now," said Mr. Brewer. "I've got to lend a hand pushing the Manserghs' car. It's packed up just down the road. I told them if they want to go gallivanting about on Exmoor, they ought to take horses, not a motor car."

"The Manserghs are a charming young couple," said the Professor, "and very adventurous. They spend their time exploring the moor. It is connected with some book. Mr. Mansergh explained it to me, but I did not quite follow it. Here are our drinks. Good health."

"Cheers," said Peter. "Do you want anyone to help with the pushing?"

"I can manage," said Mr. Brewer. He looked capable of picking a car up in one hand. He surged out.

"You were saying," said Peter to the Professor, "that you had your own idea of what happened to Dr. Wolfe."

"It is a very simple idea. Not at all romantic, as some of the ideas I have heard put forward. I think that he suffered from a sudden blackout. Men who sit using their brains all day are susceptible to such attacks. They are not usually serious. They correspond to cramp in the human body. They are a warning that the muscles of the brain are being over-used. It was a sad trick of fate that such an attack should occur at that precise point. You have studied the place for yourself."

"Not yet. But I've looked at it on the map and what I can't make out is why he went that way at all. The track only leads back to the Cryde road. If he wanted to go to Cryde, it would have been much simpler to turn right at the road junction and not go up the path."

"True," said the Professor. "It is a mystery. One to

37

which we are never now likely to know the answer. Here are the Manserghs, I think."

He stood up, moving smoothly out of the deep armchair, Peter noticed. Perhaps he was not as old as he had seemed at first sight.

"Allow me to introduce you. Anna Mansergh, Mr. Manciple."

"That's not right," said the girl. "If you introduce me by my Christian name, you must tell me his."

"A serious gaffe," agreed the Professor.

"Peter," said Peter.

"That's better. What's that you're drinking? I'd better get one for myself. Dave has covered himself with mud pushing our poor old car into the yard. He is a pet. I seem to have got a lot of mud on myself, too."

She looked down at her legs. She was wearing jeans tucked into jodhpur boots, and a windcheater open at the top to show a scarlet polo-necked sweater underneath. Her hair, which came down in a thick wave to her shoulders, was black. Her nose was short and straight. Her eyes were blue and alive. Peter thought that it was a long time since he had seen a more attractive girl.

If she realized that he was staring at her, she seemed unperturbed by it. Possibly she was used to men staring at her. She said, "Dave tells me you're down here to investigate poor Dr. Wolfe's accident. You must tell me about it after dinner. I'd better go and see how Kevin's coping with the car. And I'll have to change. They're not fussy here, but I can't sit down to eat covered in Exmoor mud."

When she had gone, Peter remained standing, staring after her. When he turned, he found the Professor looking at him.

"An attractive girl, don't you think?"

"Very."

"An old Irish family, I believe. You will find her brother interesting, too."

"Her brother?"

"Kevin," said the Professor dryly, "is her brother. Not her husband."

"Oh," said Peter. "I see. Well. Thank you for telling me."

There were four tables in the dining room. One was occupied by two middle-aged ladies who said little and ate with a steady application which implied that they thought they were paying a lot for their meal and were determined to get their money's worth. Beyond them was a couple with a girl of ten who read a comic throughout the meal and let her parents get on with the latest round in what was evidently a running fight. The Manserghs had a table in the window. Peter shared the remaining table with the Professor.

During the course of the meal he introduced the subject of cars. The Professor said, "Certainly I would agree to an exchange. The car that I have is a monster. It devours petrol. I use the car only to take me backward and forward to the site. We will go tomorrow morning to Mr. Key's establishment and effect the exchange. Are you interested in archeology?"

"Interested, but totally unknowledgeable."

"Perhaps you would like to run out and look at the work we are doing. That is to say, if your program allows you time for relaxation."

"Relaxation is one of the things I have come down here for," said Peter. As he said it, his eyes were on the table in the window. The level rays of the setting sun were picking out copper lights in Anna's black hair.

"You must appreciate," said the Professor severely, "that there are fundamental differences between the archeology of the Middle East and that of Great Britain. The Minoan era—"

39

The Minoan era lasted through the savory. When they moved out into the lounge for coffee, Peter maneuvered himself into a chair alongside Anna.

"Your job must be very exciting," she said.

"In what way?" said Peter cautiously.

"In every way. Being a detective, I mean."

"I'm afraid Mr. Brewer has got it all wrong. I'm an insurance assessor."

"It amounts to much the same thing, doesn't it? You go round asking questions and finding things out."

"If you put it that way, I suppose I do," said Peter. "But this isn't really a normal sort of job. Mostly I spend my time sitting in other people's offices, reading their accounts and trying to spot the joins. Here it's different. I have to try and come to some conclusion as to what did happen when Dr. Wolfe drove over that cliff. Whether it was an accident or suicide, or what."

"And how are you going to do that?"

"By talking to people who knew him."

"So *that's* why you're talking to me, is it?"

Peter wanted to say, "I'm talking to you because I think you're the most wonderfully attractive girl I've ever met," but he knew that if he said anything of the sort he'd start blushing.

"Did you know him well?"

"He came in here on one or two evenings. We talked a bit."

"Did he talk about his job?"

"In a general sort of way. We all knew he was working in that place up the road and it must have been something to do with biological warfare—whatever that means. Mostly we talked about other things. Chess, for instance."

"You played chess with him?"

"I couldn't possibly have played him. He'd have been much too good for me. But we talked about it. And about bits of France we'd both been to. And about Exmoor. He was a great help to Kevin in his work."

Kevin, who was helping the ten-year-old girl finish a crossword puzzle, looked up when he heard his name and smiled. He had the same bone structure and the same blue eyes as his sister.

"What work is that?"

"Kevin is doing a book about the Doones. I expect you've heard of them?"

"Certainly I've heard of them. I was at Blundell's and I read *Lorna Doone* twice. The first time as a duty, the second time for pleasure."

"Then you know that the Doones really existed and used to live in a lair in the heart of Bagworthy Forest and ride out in a gang and help themselves to whatever they wanted. Don't you think it's romantic?"

"More romantic now than it must have seemed to their neighbors at the time."

"I imagine they thought about them the way we think about tax inspectors. People you had to put up with as the price of existence. Anyway, I'd rather be robbed by a handsome young man on a horse than by a nasty little creature in a bowler hat."

Peter laughed, and said, "How far has he got with identifying the different places?"

"The great difficulty is to find Plover's Barrows Farm, where the Ridds lived. All it says in the book is that it's two miles above the place where Bagworthy Water runs into the Lynn. The trouble is that there are half a dozen little streams which could call themselves Bagworthy Water."

"That's right," said Kevin, abandoning the crossword puzzle. "And we've been up to our axles in most of them. Do you know what a goyal is?"

Peter thought hard. He was fairly well acquainted

41

with Blackmore's masterpiece. "Isn't it a little valley? Not as deep as a ravine, but with steep sides?"

"Right. And I can tell you something about goyals that Blackmore never knew. If you get into one with a motor car, they're damned difficult to get out of."

The rest of the evening was a delight. The Manserghs were good talkers, and good listeners. It was eleven o'clock when Peter opened his window, climbed into bed, and turned his light out. The rain had stopped, and a full moon was riding in a clear sky. In the distance a nightjar was giving tongue.

Peter lay for a time, thinking about the different theories which had been expressed to him about Dr. Wolfe's death: that it was deliberate, that it was the result of a blackout, that the car had skidded. He ought to have been devoting his full attention to an analysis of these possibilities. Instead, his mind kept jerking back, like the image on a faulty television screen, to a girl with lively blue eyes and hair that was black one moment and golden the next.

It was an exciting idea that she was in bed two rooms away. What did she wear in bed? Pajamas or an old-fashioned nightgown? He believed that some girls, when the weather was warm, wore only a short pajama top. Or even nothing at all.

Did she sleep on her back or on her side? he wondered.

Accident? Blackout? Suicide?

42

5

Professor Petros clearly believed in taking things easily. He had suggested a rendezvous at eleven o'clock at Key's Garage. This gave Peter time for a visit to the scene of the accident.

The rain had been blown out of the sky, and it was a bright, fresh morning. He drove north toward the coast, crossed the Cryde-Huntercombe road, and started up the rough road which led to the caravan site. On his left he could see a bypath leading down to the river and a huddle of new roofs on the far bank which he guessed must be the farm where Colonel Hay and his Army friend were staying.

The road swung up past the line of parked caravans and started to climb. It had degenerated by now into a flint-and-chalk track, and Peter concentrated on his driving. He stopped well short of the cliff edge, climbed out, and walked forward.

The place where the accident had happened was clear enough. The broken paling which marked the cliff edge had been patched, but more as a warning than a protection. The slightest force would send it toppling again.

Peter peered cautiously over.

The tide was almost at low, and fangs of black rock

were showing. Between them the sea lipped and gulped, throwing up bursts of spray, white against the bottle green of the water. There was no sign of shelving. The cliff at that point was slightly overhung, and the deep water seemed to run right up to the cliff foot.

Peter found that he was gripping the upright of the fence so tightly that it was an effort to unclasp his hand and step back. His legs felt unsteady, and he sat down on the other side of the path to recover.

He had come to a conclusion—a conclusion from which he never subsequently departed. No one in possession of his senses could deliberately have driven his car over that fearsome drop. There were things which were possible, if improbable. And there were things which were impossible. This was impossible.

From where he sat, his view inland was blocked, first by an unusually large and thick clump of trees which filled the hollow immediately below him, and then by one of those rounded and shapely knolls which were characteristic of the chalk cliff. He could see a track which skirted the side of this knoll and evidently formed a shortcut back to the road.

He looked back at the track. From the point where the car must have left it, the ground ran downhill in two directions: fairly sharply toward the cliff edge, and rather more gradually down the track itself. The shape of what must have happened was beginning to form in his mind, wanting in detail but clear in outline. He drove back slowly to the hotel.

At Key's Garage the exchange of cars was quickly effected; documents were exchanged and the deposits which they had paid were adjusted in the Professor's favor. The Savoia sixteen, with its driving seat pushed back to the very last notch, accommodated Peter's length. He said, "I'd better go and make my mark with the military. Tomorrow I thought I'd cast round a bit. If your invitation still holds good, I'd like to run out to-morrow morning and have a look at what you're doing."

"Excellent," said the Professor. "The site is not easy to find. We will go together." He drove off, and Peter stood for a few moments watching him go.

Bill Key said, "He's a real old character, isn't he? It's easy to imagine *him* scratching up fossils. But you ought to see his assistants."

"Long-haired students of both sexes, I imagine."

"Nothing like it. They came in last Saturday for a drink at the hotel. They looked like recruits on a battle course. Young, athletic, and polite. You could have fitted any three of them into the front row of the England Scrum."

"Did they explain how they came to be recruited for the dig?"

"They didn't have a lot to say for themselves. As I said, polite but not really communicative. If you're making for the Research Station, it's a small road, second on the left, about two miles down. There used to be a signpost, but they took it down after they had all that trouble with the protesters. You'll spot the turning easily enough, though. It's opposite a piggery. If you don't see it, you'll smell it."

The perimeter of the Research Station was guarded by a double line of wire fence ten feet high, the outer line angled outward at the top, the inner line angled inward. There were overhead lights at twenty-yard intervals. A notice beside the gate said, "Army Property. Out of Bounds to All Unauthorized Personnel." Apart from the fact that it was neat and functional, it bore little resemblance to a traditional Army establishment. As much as it looked like anything, it looked like one of those up-to-date secondary schools where the pupils concentrate on painting, dressmaking, and having a good time. The buldings, solid red-brick-and-glass constructions, all of one story, were spread around in a carefully unorganized manner, hugging the contours of the ground as though to escape attention from hostile aircraft. There was a lot of lawn, and the paths between the buildings were neatly rolled gravel. The only prominent objects were a bulbous construction which looked like a steel egg in a giant eggcup and a mast with two saucer-shaped attachments on the top.

Peter stood in the sunshine staring through the latticework of the gate. It seemed an innocent enough place. He noticed that someone had cultivated a strip of flower bed along the front of the nearest building. There were marigolds and pinks in it, and a floribunda rosebush flourishing in the chalk soil. In the silence he could hear larks singing.

A door in the guard hut beside the gate opened and a military policeman came out. He walked across and studied Peter without speaking. Peter took out the letter which Mr. Troyte had armed him with and pushed it through the latticework. The redcap took it, read the name on the envelope, turned it over to make sure there was nothing written on the other side, then stepped back, wheeled around, and made for the large building on the right of the entrance which Peter assumed must be the reception office. The letter, as he knew, was addressed personally to the officer in charge of the Station and was from a senior official in the Ministry of Defense. One of the secrets of Arthur Troyte's success was knowing useful people in every walk of life.

Five slow minutes passed. The soldier reappeared, unlocked and opened the gate, ushered Peter inside, locked and shut the gate, and led the way into the building, where he handed him over to a gray-haired lady who sat enthroned behind a desk inside the door. He contrived to do all of this without speaking a word. Perhaps he was dumb? Peter remembered a story he had once read about a mad scientist who was served by slaves all of whom had had their tongues cut out to prevent them revealing his secrets. Was it possible—?

No, the gray-haired lady still had her tongue. She said, "Colonel Hollingum may have to keep you waiting a few minutes, sir. Would you like a cup of coffee?"

Peter said he thought this would be a very good idea. The gray-haired lady spoke down the telephone. But when the door at the far end of the hall opened a few minutes later, it wasn't the coffee. It was a small Indian in a long white coat. He came up to Peter, placing one neatly shod foot in front of the other as softly and precisely as though he were practicing a new dance step. He said, "You must be Dr. Vinograd. I am so pleased to meet you."

"Well, no," said Peter. "My name is Manciple."

"You are not Dr. Vinograd? I had a feeling he would be somewhat older. Do not take that as a reflection on you. Youth is a priceless asset. Not something you need apologize for. What is to be your function here?"

"It isn't exactly a function. I'm here in connection with the death of Dr. Wolfe."

"Dr. Wolfe? Oh. Yes. I have not introduced myself. I am Dr. Bishwas. Dr. Wolfe was my colleague. It was very sad."

There was something behind this which Peter found it hard to fathom; a feeling of more meant than was said. He wondered whether perhaps it was because the conversation was taking place within earshot of the gray-haired woman.

"If you knew Dr. Wolfe well," he said, "perhaps there is somewhere we could talk in private."

"I am afraid—I am very much afraid—that there is nothing private I could tell you. Will you be with us for long?"

"As long as I have to."

47

"I see, yes. You are staying locally? In Bridgetown perhaps? You are in the good hands of Mr. Brewer. An interesting example of Dravidian survival."

At this point the coffee arrived in a plastic cup carried by a sergeant. Dr. Bishwas smiled apologetically and departed as softly as he had come. As Peter was finishing the coffee, a bell sounded. The gray-haired lady said, "That is Colonel Hollingum. He can see you now. The last door on the left."

Colonel Hollingum, who rose from behind his desk to greet Peter, looked more like a doctor than an Army officer and more like a civil servant than a doctor. The long white overall which he was wearing could equally have concealed service dress or a black coat and striped trousers. He said, "I hope we shall be able to deal with this matter fairly quickly, Mr.—um—Manciple. This is one of our busy days."

"I hope so too, sir," said Peter.

"I am not clear from this—um—communication exactly what it is I am expected to tell you."

"We wanted to see if we could get any sort of lead as to how—or why—this very odd accident should have happened."

"An unhappy accident. But I do not understand quite why you describe it as odd. Dr. Wolfe's car ran off the track and went over the cliff."

"Well, there were one or two odd things about it. The fact that there were no skid marks, which would seem to indicate that he made no attempt to brake after going off the path."

"That would be quite consistent with his having had a blackout."

"Yes, I suppose so. I was hoping that you might be able to fill in the background for me."

"You realize that I cannot discuss the work he was doing here."

"I do realize that. What I meant was the factual background. How long he had been here. What sort of life he lived."

"He joined us nearly six years ago."

"I suppose he worked very much on his own?"

"Almost entirely."

"So that until you got his report every two years, you really had little idea what point his researches had reached?"

Colonel Hollingum stared at him. Then he said, "Has some member of my staff been speaking to you?"

"Nothing like that. I happened to be talking to his sister."

"It was indiscreet of Dr. Wolfe to discuss his work with his sister. And if he did choose to tell her anything, she should not have passed it on to you."

Peter saw that they were getting off on the wrong foot. He said, "She didn't know anything about his work. I doubt if she'd have understood it if he had described it, and I'm quite certain I shouldn't. The last science I did was making gunpowder at my prep school. It wasn't even very good gunpowder. It didn't explode."

"I see. Then what—?"

"The sort of things I wanted to know were whether Dr. Wolfe was in normal health and spirits last week. Was he worried or upset about anything?"

"You must appreciate that I had very little to do with Dr. Wolfe personally. He went his own way. I had categorical instructions not to interfere with him."

"He was well known in his own line?"

"He was the most distinguished genetic biologist we have ever had in this establishment. My job was to see that he had the best possible working conditions and total lack of interference."

"Did he go outside the camp much?"

"When he was working here, very little. Sometimes

he went out fishing. And he went occasionally into Bridgetown in the evenings for a glass of beer at the Doone Valley Hotel."

"And one of your men went with him."

The Colonel looked at him stonily. He seemed, Peter thought, to have a list divided into two columns: items which could be discussed and items which could not. Peter was aware that he had again approached the dividing line.

The Colonel said, "You misunderstand the position. I was responsible for Dr. Wolfe's—um—comfort and well-being inside the camp. When he left it, he came under a different jurisdiction. Lewis and Bateson were neither of them my men."

"Lewis was the man who was hit by a motorist?"

"Yes."

"That was on the same day that Dr. Wolfe had his accident?"

"Yes."

"Would he have known about Lewis' death?"

The Colonel considered the matter. Evidently the answer was on the permitted side of the line. He said, "We had the news about Lewis in the course of the afternoon. It was widely discussed. I imagine Dr. Wolfe heard about it before he left."

"And when was that?"

"Shortly before nine o'clock that evening."

"Might he have been upset at the news?"

"He might have been. We should not necessarily have known that he was. Dr. Wolfe was not a man who exhibited his feelings in public."

There was a short pause. It seemed to be the end of the conversation. Dr. Wolfe had left the camp at nine o'clock in the evening. His car had gone over the cliff at Rackthorn Point shortly afterward. Finish. Peter could think of nothing else to say; of no question he could ask to which any helpful answer could be given. He was on the point of rising to his feet when the Colonel spoke again.

He said, "There is something I must say to you before you go," and paused.

During their brief conversation Peter's opinion of the Colonel had been changing. He knew, of course, that he was not dealing with a fool. He now realized that the Colonel's stiffness and taciturnity were not the result of official obstruction or hostility. Colonel Hollingum was worried. He was anxious to put something across, and was uncertain how to go about it.

"I wonder if you realize that your car was picked up on our early warning system when it turned off the main road. It was recognized as coming from Key's Garage, and we were finding out about you from Bill Key before you had got out of the car. The few minutes we kept you waiting outside the gate were spent in telephoning the writer of that letter. Fortunately, we caught him at his desk in the Ministry. If we had failed in either instance, you wouldn't have been allowed inside the gate."

"I realize you have to be careful," said Peter.

The Colonel went on as though he had not heard him. "There is an infantry platoon on permanent duty here. One section is on red alert. The other three sections are ten minutes' notice. We have an open radio-telephone link with Western Command, and another with Whitehall. I mention these precautions to give you some idea of the priority accorded to the work which is going on here. Whether I approve of that work or not, it is my job to see that it goes on uninterrupted. You understand me?"

Peter nodded.

"You mentioned the fact that Dr. Wolfe reported on his own work, in writing, at the end of the second and fourth years. Those reports did not go to me. They went to the Joint Services Scientific Advisory Committee, which, in turn, reports directly to the Cabinet. I know roughly what was in them, but not the details. Nor, of course, do I know the policy decisions which were based on them. I expect it was thought better that I should be kept in the dark."

The Colonel smiled briefly, and Peter caught sight of a human being behind the official mask.

"It can be very trying work. During the time I have been here, we have lost three scientists. The first disappeared five years ago, when he was on leave. When I say disappeared, I mean that, literally. He might be anywhere, above the earth or under it. He has not been seen or heard of since. The second one failed to turn up for breakfast one morning, and I went over to his quarters to look for him. He was in his bath. He had cut his own throat the night before. It was not a pleasant sight."

Peter nodded again. The room seemed to have become stuffy and airless.

"I am telling you these things so that you will listen very carefully to the advice I have to give you. Go back to London. Write your report. Say that it is quite impossible to decide whether Dr. Wolfe took his own life or whether it was an accident. Whatever the truth of the matter, one fact is certain. He is dead."

6

By the time Peter got back to the hotel, lunch was under way. Anna was alone. Detecting the faintest hint of an invitation which might or might not have been there, Peter walked across to her table.

Anna said, "Come and keep me company. Kevin has gone to Cryde to see if he can hire a Land-Rover. He's tired of pushing us out of goyals. How have you been spending the morning?"

"I've been changing cars, too. I've got one more suited to my length of leg. Then I went over to the Research Station."

"Did they let you in?"

"After checking everything down to the date of my birth and my size in shoes and gloves."

"It's a terrible place. In Old Testament times it would have been visited by fire from heaven. I don't suppose they let you look at any of whatever it is they're doing, did they?"

"Certainly not. I had a chat with the boss, and was told a few things about Dr. Wolfe, most of which I knew already. I got the impression that he was a very private sort of person."

Anna considered the point, sitting up in her chair

and straightening her back as she did so. The movement brought her breasts very slightly forward inside the thin shirt she was wearing that morning. Peter lowered his eyes and became engrossed in filleting the grilled trout on his plate.

"He wasn't private in the sense of being stuffy," said Anna. "He was easy to talk to, and interesting. He knew about a lot of different things. Music—I suppose from his sister. He talked a lot about her. And rock climbing and sailing, and the connection between music and chess and mathematics. He was fun to talk to. But when it was all over, you did realize that you hadn't got one inch past his outer defenses."

"Do you mean that he was hiding something?"

"Not exactly. I mean one got the impression that he was leading two quite different lives, or maybe even three. And he could switch from one to the other whenever he wanted. No, Dave, I simply couldn't. *Treacle pudding*, in this weather? I'll just have some cheese."

"Cheese for me, too," said Peter.

"What are you going to do with yourself this afternoon?"

"I thought of exploring the country behind Rackthorn Point."

"Work or pleasure?"

"A bit of both."

"Can I join in the pleasure part?"

"By all means," said Peter. "We'll take my car to the caravan site and do the rest on foot."

"Is this where it happened?" said Anna.

"I think it must be. And that's the place where the fence was broken. For God's sake, watch it."

Anna had walked to the extreme edge of the cliff and was bending forward, looking down. "It's quite a drop," she said. "Do you think anyone could have gone over it with his eyes open?"

"No," said Peter, with a shudder. "I don't. Please come away from the edge. You're making me feel wobbly inside."

Anna came back and sat down beside him. She said, "Different things frighten different people. I've never minded about heights, even when I was quite small. What I can't stand is squishy places. Bubbling marshes and bogs and quicksands. I used to have a regular nightmare about being sucked down, very slowly, into a marsh. First my mouth went under, then my nose. I can remember saying, 'If you try hard enough, you can breathe through your ears.' "

"What happened then?"

"It seemed such a funny idea it made me giggle, and I woke up. Where do we go from here?"

"Straight down towards the wood. There must be some way through it. You can see the path going up on the other side."

There was no difficulty about it. The wood was unfenced, and was not particularly thick. They pushed their way through and climbed the knoll beyond. Standing on it, they could see across the valley, from the line of the Cryde-Huntercombe road to the levels of Exmoor running away, fold behind green and purple fold, into the distance.

"That's where you think he went, isn't it?" said Anna.

"It's possible," said Peter, considerably startled.

"First having pushed his car over the cliff. Could he have done that?"

"I think so. He'd drive it off the path, leaving it pointing downhill. It's a fairly steep slope. The turf was wet, but it wasn't soggy. In fact, it was probably rather slippery. One good push and I think the car would have gone over, all right. Particularly if he'd broken the fence first. After that, he'd just have to walk down the way we came. It was already getting dark. There was the whole night ahead of him."

"How are you going to prove it? Always supposing you're right."

"The only way of proving it would be by finding Dr. Wolfe."

"There'd be no argument then," agreed Anna.

"Don't, please, say anything about this to anyone else."

"Certainly not."

"Not even to Kevin."

"All right. Not even to Kevin. Though I share most secrets with him."

They walked down the hill toward the road. In a curious way Peter felt that the last few minutes had broken down all restraints between them. It seemed perfectly natural that they should find a sheltered dip in the hillside and sit down in it. He had no wish—or no immediate wish—to do anything but talk.

"Is Kevin your twin?"

"He was born five minutes after me. In a lovely, decrepit old mansion house in the north of Donegal, under the Derryveagh Mountains. It's a peaceful corner of northern Ireland even now, so I'm told, though we haven't been back in the last five years. Don't you think it's a mistake to go back to somewhere where you've been very happy?"

"Yes," said Peter. "Yes, I do."

"My mother died when we were born. Perhaps the local midwife wasn't very clever. I don't know. It must have upset Father badly, but he never let it worry us. We had a succession of women who were called housekeepers. I think Father slept with most of them. It didn't worry us at the time and it doesn't worry me now. It was an eighteenth-century sort of household. Father taught us the important things, like how to ride properly and handle a gun or a fly rod. We went to school later and hated it. I ran away three times."

Peter willed her to go on talking. She was lying back, propping herself on her elbows. The shirt she was wearing was made of some thin material which looked like cheesecloth. It was biscuit colored, with a thin blue stripe.

"Father never seemed to worry about anything. Certainly he never worried about money. There was enough, that was all that mattered. I gather it came from a family brewery which his father and his uncle had set up. Money was made for spending, not keeping. What would have happened in the end, I don't know. He was killed out hunting, and lawyers took over and looked grim and talked about insolvency and the workhouse, but it didn't happen, because that very year they found enormous deposits of bauxite on our property. That's really all there is to tell. Kevin and I are a hopeless pair. We've not been trained to do anything useful, so we wander round enjoying ourselves. Now tell me about your life."

"It won't be nearly as interesting as yours."

"I hope it was happy, because I don't really enjoy gloomy stories."

"Then I'll tell you about the happy part. It was when I was ten and my older brother was twelve. We had a bungalow on the Thames at Laleham. That's a little place about fifteen miles outside London. We were both at boarding school, but we spent all our holidays there, winter and summer. In some ways the winter was best, when the river was high and there weren't too many people about. We became real water rats. We had a punt and a dinghy and a canoe, and we took them out in all weathers. There wasn't any trick of watermanship we didn't know and improve on. Once, for a bet, I took

57

a canoe across the river standing up in it and using a punt pole, and if you think that's easy, you ought to try it. Of course, it wouldn't have mattered if I had fallen in, I was only wearing bathing trunks."

Anna laughed and said, "I can see you, Peter, looking like a long, skinny spider."

"I *was* rather skinny. Another thing we used to do was take the punt upstream, dive out of it, and let it drift down empty, with us swimming behind it and almost underneath it. People would see it was adrift and get very worried and come out to catch it, and we used to pop out of the water like seals and grin at them, which made them furious. And sometimes we'd come home blue with cold, and Mother would make us have a hot bath and cook great plates of porridge for us. It was a lovely time. Later we went back to live in London, and things weren't such fun any more. Jonathan, my brother, was sent by his firm to New Zealand and got married and decided to stay out there."

He wasn't going to tell her about the other thing.

Anna said, "Something happened which made you very unhappy."

"Yes."

"Then don't talk about it. Only think about nice things. Jumping in and out of the water like a little frog, and eating porridge."

She was half lying, propped up on her elbows. Her left hand was quite close to Peter's right hand. As he moved it cautiously forward, Anna shivered suddenly, jumped to her feet, and said, "Let's go back to the car. All that talk about porridge. It's made me feel hungry again."

When they got back to the hotel, they found Kevin, very pleased with himself. He had managed to hire an old Army-surplus Jeep with a winching attachment which he was demonstrating to Dave Brewer.

"You just hammer one of these pickets into the ground, fasten yourself to it, and wind yourself out backward."

"You get yourself bogged down to rights," said Mr. Brewer, "and you won't get out with no winches. Only one thing'll pull you clear. That's a team of cart horses."

"We'll see," said Kevin. "We'll see."

It was at ten o'clock that night that the telephone call came.

"For me?" said Peter. He had not yet told even his head office where they could find him, although he should certainly have done so.

"It's you he asked for," said Mr. Brewer. "Mr. Mansipple. Didn't give his name."

The telephone was in a dark, triangular recess under the stairs. By bending his head and stooping forward from the waist, Peter was able to get at the instrument, but by no contortion could he have managed to shut the door behind him.

"Mr. Manciple?" said a voice which he thought he recognized.

"Yes," said Peter.

"It is Dr. Bishwas, from the Research Station. I have something I wish to tell you. It is of great importance that we should meet."

"I'd be only too glad. Do you want me to come to your quarters?"

"That would not be a good arrangement. No, I shall come out and have a word with you."

"It's kind of you to take the trouble. Where do you suggest, and when?"

"Now, as soon as possible." The note of urgency in Dr. Bishwas' voice was unmistakable. "If you will take your car and drive out on the road, as you did this morning. But do not turn down the side road which leads to our front entrance. Go beyond it, and take the next turning. It runs along the outside of our boundary fence. Follow it to the end of the fence, and I will be waiting for you at the corner and will guide you from there."

"That seems clear enough," said Peter slowly. "Shall I start now?"

There was a pause. Peter got the impression that Dr. Bishwas might be consulting someone; perhaps only his own conscience?

"No. I shall not be able to get away immediately. Could you be there at eleven o'clock, please?"

"Very well," said Peter. "Is that all?"

"That is all, for the moment."

Peter extracted himself from the recess and stood for a moment in the hall thinking. He would have to mention the matter to Mr. Brewer. Otherwise he could well find himself locked out when he got back. He found the landlord shepherding the last of the drinkers out of the public bar.

"That's all right," he said. "I'll let you have a key. I'll leave the light on in the downstairs passage. Turn it out when you come back." He seemed uninterested in the reason for this midnight excursion.

Peter went up to his room. There was time before he need start. He got out a pad of paper, sat down in the chair beside his bed, and tried to compose his thoughts. Superficially, he had made little progress and had almost nothing to report. Nevertheless certain nebulous ideas were already forming in his mind: shadowy possibilities, the children not of logic, but of instinct. It seemed essential to get them down on paper. A Latin tag, learned and forgotten in his schooldays, came into his mind: "*Litera scripta manet.*" That was true. Words spoken floated away on the breath that uttered them, but the written word endured, for better or worse.

Half an hour later the first part of the report had been

written, placed unsealed in an envelope, and addressed to Arthur Troyte. He put it away in his briefcase. He could finish it in the morning. There were still a few minutes left. He took out another piece of paper and wrote on it: "I am going out, at his invitation, to meet Dr. Bishwas of the Biological Warfare Research Station, at the southwest corner of the perimeter fence. I have no idea what he wishes to tell me." This note he also sealed up in an envelope and propped it up against the looking glass on the shelf above the fireplace, where it would be obvious to the first observer. Then he went out, locked the door of his bedroom, pocketed the key, and went quietly downstairs.

There were voices in the lounge. He could distinguish the pedantic tones of Professor Petros and he heard Kevin say something in reply. As he slipped out of the door at the back, he thought he heard Anna laugh.

He found the turning which Dr. Bishwas had indicated. It was a roughly macadamized track running between high banks, and there were signs that its most recent users had been a herd of cows. After a few hundred yards it opened out and he could see, on his left, the boundary lights of the Research Station. When he reached the corner of the fence, he saw Dr. Bishwas standing beside the track.

The Doctor came across as he stopped, and said, "Might I suggest that you turn out your headlights? There is sufficient light for us to see. We have only a short way to go. Thank you. If you drive straight along the track, you will find a building. It is, I fancy, a barn for the cattle, but in this weather they stay out all night. We shall not be disturbed." The Doctor gave a disconcerting giggle, and Peter realized that he was in a state of extreme nervousness.

They drove on in silence until a darker patch in the darkness around them indicated the position of the barn. Peter switched off the engine and they both climbed out. The Doctor went ahead and pulled open the door of the barn. He had produced a flashlight, which he shone into the interior of the building.

"Come in, Mr. Manciple," he said, "and dispose yourself. What I have to tell you may take some little time."

7

The barn was warm with the stored heat of a summer day. Peter sat on an upturned crate inside the door. Dr. Bishwas perched himself on the edge of the half-floor above him and sat there enthroned and grave, like a teacher preparing to discourse to his disciple.

"I assumed," he said, "from the length of time you were together this morning, that Colonel Hollingum told you very little."

"He spent most of the time giving me a number of reasons why he could tell me nothing."

"He is a good man by his own lights, although his lights are not mine. He sometimes seems to me"—Peter could tell that Dr. Bishwas was smiling in the darkness —"like a master who has been left in charge of a class of children who are cleverer than he is. He wields the physical power, but knows that mentally his charges are beyond him. He is a simple soldier. In so far as he understands what is going on, he disapproves of it, or so I think. But a soldier does what he is told. That is a comfort to him. Also, perhaps, he can persuade himself that what he is doing is not aggressive. The object of the research is defensive: to prepare countermeasures against the possibility of attack by others. Between the wars—did you know?—your country produced some of the most virulent poison gases in the world. The establishment which perfected them was known as the Anti-Gas Warfare Station at Winterbourne Gunner, near Salisbury. Anti-gas—you appreciate the subtlety."

"And they were none of them used."

"They were none of them used, for the same reason that the normal products of biological warfare will never be used. Because both sides possess them. Because their effects are too immediate, and therefore ultimately irremediable. And because they invite the most unpleasing reprisals."

"That's a comfort, anyway," said Peter.

"It would be a comfort, if it was the whole truth."

In the silence which followed, Peter could hear tiny sounds. A bird shifting its position on the rafters above him. Some small animal moving in the hay. The comfortable normal sounds of life going on. If all human and all animal life was destroyed, would sound cease too? Would an empty planet revolve in silence around the sun?

"If you are to understand what I am going to tell you —and I would shortly make it clear to you, I hope, why it is important that you *should* understand it—then I shall have to assume in you some knowledge of biological structures."

"Until a few days ago," said Peter, "you would have assumed wrongly. Recently I was given a short lesson on the subject. I now know that everyone has a personal genetic code which is carried by a private arrangement of biochemicals in cells called nuclei. What geneticists try to do is to decipher the pattern of information carried by the nuclei. Oh, and I remember, too, that chromosomes play a part in it. They are made up of five different substances, and the most important is called DNA, whatever that may be."

"Deoxyribonucleic acid. From whom are you quoting?"

"From Dr. Wolfe's sister."

"He spoke often of her. I was not aware that he discussed the technical side of his work with her."

"Only once. They were on holiday in Wales and it rained and he was bored."

"You have a visual memory?"

"Something like that. Why?"

"When you spoke just now, you were visualizing the words which Miss Wolfe spoke to you, as though they were written down and you were reading them. Does it afford you total recall?"

"Not total. Selective."

"Interesting." Dr. Bishwas sat swinging his neatly pointed feet. Now that Peter's eyes had become adjusted to the half-darkness, he could see Bishwas more clearly.

"If you are to appreciate what I am going to tell you, we shall have to start a little further back. You realize that the human body is entirely composed of cells? Every last part of it, flesh, blood, skin, muscles, and nerves. It is a miraculous living entity, the cell, complete in itself. We can dissect it and destroy it, but we cannot reconstitute it. If we could do that, we should indeed be gods. We could create life."

Dr. Bishwas paused, and Peter could again hear the night breathing around him. In seven days created He the world and all that is therein. How long to destroy it?

"Each cell, you must understand, is composed of two parts. The outer part, the cytoplasm, is the work force. It absorbs food, converts it into energy, and keeps the factory going. Inside the cytoplasm is the nucleus. If we call the cytoplasm the body, we could call the nucleus the brain. It is a minute but immensely complex structure made up of threads of DNA composed of nucleotides. You can think of them as tiny beads on a thread.

65

Until recently we have only been able to study them by biological staining. Very recently the Molecular Biology Research Unit at Cambridge succeeded in reproducing them in the form of microscopic crystals."

Peter had been sitting quietly, body and mind relaxed, as he did when he wanted to imprint facts onto his memory. Now he said, "I suppose there are only a limited number of people at any time at work in this field."

"There are not more than a handful of men in any country who are capable of comprehending it. People who can comprehend the ground gained and advance from it into the unknown are fewer still. When they die, the rest of us are thrown back. We can only follow in their footsteps and hope, with patience and good fortune, to reach the point from which they are stepping off and advance a few steps more into the darkness before we, too, die."

An owl outside said, "Hoo," and Peter jumped. Dr. Bishwas said, "I became dramatic, I apologize. Let us return to our cells. You must understand one further fact about them. Some cells are static. That is to say, they increase in size, but do not divide. The cells of the nerves and the muscles are of this type. Other cells, such as blood cells, are in a constant state of subdivision. But this is the important point, Mr. Manciple, and it is one to which you must give particular attention, for it is the objective of my whole discourse. You remember that each cell has in it a nucleus, and that this nucleus contains the genetic code which governs your whole development. It dictates not only external characteristics such as the shape and growth of your body and the color of your eyes and your hair, but internal matters as well. Your mental capacity, your predisposition to certain derangements such as hay fever or color blindness. The speed with which your arteries harden in age. It may even, although this has not yet been proved, effect a predisposition to cancer. You understand what I am saying?"

"Yes," said Peter. "I understand what you are saying."

"Very well. Then you will appreciate the importance of the fact that when a cell divides, the nucleus of the daughter cell *must* correspond *in every particular* with the nucleus of the parent cell. This is achieved in a series of six steps, each of which has been noted by geneticists and separately identified and named, by which the nucleotides attach themselves to the daughter cell in a correct and prearranged order, thus ensuring that the genetic code is reproduced accurately. Sometimes, by accident, this does not happen. This is what we call a mutation. The logical sequence of the body's development is interrupted. The results are almost always catastrophic. The loss of resistance to disease. Mental inequilibrium. Freakish growths, unrecognisable as human beings, ranging from the moron whose body grows but whose mind remains that of an infant, to those poor creatures who, if they live, may be exhibited for gain in circuses. More usually, and mercifully, they die and are preserved for the instruction of students in the museums of our teaching hospitals."

"You spoke of this being the result of some accident. Has anyone discovered what *sort* of accident is involved? I mean, what causes the accident?"

"Until recently there has been very little knowledge but a great deal of speculation. The work of Dr. Daniella Rhodes at Cambridge, which I mentioned to you earlier, has led to advances in the search for reasons, but whole areas are still in darkness. The *results* of lawless development, on the other hand, have long been noted. Cancer is only one of the more obvious. Some of the predisposing factors are also known. Radiation, for instance. It is now realized that in its earliest applications the incautious use of radium probably caused more cancerous growth than it cured. The inhalation of fumes can be another predisposing cause. But the fundamental cause, the trigger which actually sets the mutations into motion, is still a mystery. It is a mystery to the solution of which the researches of leading geneticists in all countries are being applied. Because if it could be determined, we might be able to find out how to control it."

"And this is what Dr. Wolfe was working on?"

"He was working on it, almost continuously, for the whole of his time here. It was a natural development, you see, of the work he had been doing before he came. The papers which he wrote at the end of his second and fourth years, and which I was privileged to see, demonstrated how far he had advanced."

"And in the last two years?"

"During the last two years, and more particularly recently, I could not help noticing a change in Dr. Wolfe. It was not apparent to everyone. He was a very controlled man. A man who planned his own actions meticulously. I will give you a small example. He kept a bag with spare clothes and other necessities ready packed in the back of his car. In this way, no one could tell, when he drove out of the camp, whether he was going down to the Doone Valley Hotel for a drink or was leaving for a four months' holiday. In the same way that he regulated his actions, he regulated his speech. He would tell you what he wished you to know. *He would make the exact impressions on you that he wished to make.* I alone, I think, who knew him very well, was in a position to identify the change which had come over him. But recently I realized the truth. He was afraid."

"Afraid?"

"It seems a remarkable word to use of such a man. But yes. He was afraid. Something, I am certain, happened to him during his last vacation. He was away for nearly five months in the middle of last year. He came back in September. One could not help noticing the scar. It was nearly healed, but quite distinct."

Dr. Bishwas put one hand up to his own face.

"It started underneath the left ear and ran down almost to the point of his jaw. A sensitive man might have grown a beard to conceal it. Dr. Wolfe was not sensitive about it, but he was not communicative either. No one liked to press him for an explanation. It was after he returned, at the end of last year, and in the first months of this year, that I noticed the change. Sometimes as I watched him working in the laboratory by day, or glimpsed him, through the window of his room in the evening, writing or perhaps just sitting in his chair and thinking, I got the impression—you may laugh at this —of a scientist of medieval times. We make fun of them now, Friar Bacon and Duns Scotus, but they *were* scientists, you know. Indeed, they were men of great mental power and wide-ranging imaginations. All that they lacked was the infrastructure of scientific knowledge on which we build today with such blind confidence. Can you not visualize such a man seated alone in his library at night, surrounded by books full of curious learning, delving deeper and deeper into the half-understood mysteries of life and death, of good and evil, of white magic and black magic, until at last he felt, almost within his grasp, round the next corner, on the next page, the answer to the ultimate question? Was it God or the Devil who ruled the universe? Might they not be afraid—would *you* not be afraid—to turn that page?"

Peter said nothing. A car which had been coming down the main road slowed and checked for a moment. Was it going to stop? No, it had gathered speed and was moving away. If Dr. Bishwas had heard it, he gave no sign. He was swaying very gently backward and forward on his perch, and Peter thought, though he could not be sure, that he was smiling.

"You find such thoughts fanciful," he said at last. "They are no more fanciful than the truth, which I learned, quite by chance, four weeks ago. The Colonel will have told you that Dr. Wolfe very rarely left the camp. He had one relaxation: that was fishing. Near the coast the rivers are too deep and too swift, but a few miles inland, on the moors, there are stretches where you can get good sport. Dr. Wolfe had an arrangement with one of the farmers—a place called Watersmeet. He would sometimes take his lunch and spend the day out there. On this occasion, most unusually, he suggested that I should go with him."

"You think he was nervous about going alone?"

"He did not seem to be nervous. I should have been small protection had he been attacked. I am not pugilistic. No, I think he had been making up his mind for some time to confide in me, and he saw this as a good opportunity. It was a better opportunity than he had conceived. At midday the rain commenced. We spent much of the afternoon in a hay barn.

"I will explain as simply as I can what he told me that afternoon. He had concluded that the orderly process of cell division was governed by a factor—he had named it the H-factor since it was connected with the hemogloblin. It was *only* when this factor was disturbed that mutations occurred. He was still a long way from discovering how the H-factor carried out its complex work, which he described somewhat in the terms of the conductor of an orchestra. But he had come to one conclusion, and it was the implications of this conclusion which were terrifying him. He had concluded theoretically—there was absolutely no clinical work, you understand, to support his theories—that the H-factor could be arbitrarily disrupted by an additive to the bloodstream, taken in through the stomach and the gut in the ordinary way, just as alcohol, for instance, enters the bloodstream. *It was an additive which could be mixed with water without losing its potency.* Do you see what this meant, Mr. Manciple? Do you observe its implications, in practical terms? Can you visualize what would happen if a suitable quantity were added to the water supply of a small country? The effects would not be immediate, so that no countermeasures would be taken. Or they would not be taken until it was much too late. It would take years for the full effects to be apparent. But in a single generation you would have destroyed a whole people beyond any chance of repair. Perhaps destruction is too kind a word. You would have produced, out of sound stock, a generation of mindless freaks, sports of nature, useful only to be exhibited to the curious in tents."

Peter said, under his breath, almost as though speaking to himself, "Can such a vile thing possibly be true?"

Dr. Bishwas said, "There is no final proof. Dr. Wolfe explained his reasoning to me that afternoon. It took him several hours to cover the ground, and you must remember that we speak the same language. With me he could use scientific shorthand. With anyone not trained in that particular discipline, the explanation would have taken a week—perhaps many weeks. I can only tell you that, at the end, I was convinced."

"If it is true—if there was any possibility that it might be true"—Peter found that he was almost stuttering—"could Dr. Wolfe—could any responsible scientist have suggested it as a possible weapon of war? Would he even have committed his conclusions to paper? Suppose they got into the wrong hands."

"I can answer only the second of your questions. All of Dr. Wolfe's conclusions, and the date and calculations which supported them, were microfilmed. The paperwork was then meticulously destroyed. Thus, the totality of his records could be carried in a small briefcase, which never left his possession. He even brought it out with him when we went fishing."

"And you think it was with him in the car when he left the camp last week?"

"I am sure of it."

"And is now at the bottom of the sea, off Rackthorn Point?"

"If that is where Dr. Wolfe is, yes."

Peter let that go. He wanted an interval to get his breath back, to assimilate objectively what he had been told. Finally, he said, "If the record of his work over the last two years is lost, does that mean that the work stops? Or does someone else start, two years back?"

"Not even two years back. When one man has trodden out a path, it is easier for the next man to follow."

"But would this particular line of inquiry necessarily *be* followed?"

"Certainly."

"Even if you knew it would lead to such an unthinkably horrible conclusion?"

"Science is not concerned with the use made of its discoveries, only with discovery itself."

"And look where that led us. Straight to the atom bomb."

"The last war produced the atom bomb, true. It also produced penicillin and other antibiotics, which have saved more lives, Mr. Manciple, than the war itself destroyed."

"All right," said Peter. "All right, I'm not going to argue. It's a futile argument, anyway. But there is one thing I must know. Why are you telling me this?"

"For two reasons," said Dr. Bishwas. He was leaning so far forward that he seemed almost to be falling on top of Peter. "The first is that if anyone is asked to continue Dr. Wolfe's work, it will almost certainly be me. I was his principal assistant. In much of his work, his only assistant. It is known that I was in his confidence."

"And you would not refuse?"

"I *could* not refuse. But, equally, I shall be in a position to know when this research has reached a point where it might leave the laboratory and come into the arena of field usage. It is at that point that the possible consequences of this horrible weapon *must* be explained to the world. I cannot do so myself. I am bound by the Acts and by the terms of the many undertakings they exact from all of us before we are allowed to work here. If I were to attempt to publish anything, it would be immediately, and effectively, repressed, of that I can assure you. But you are a free agent, Mr. Manciple. You could not be stopped from obtaining publicity for these matters."

"Yes," said Peter slowly. "Yes, I should be able to do that." He thought of the various organizations concerned with pacifism and human rights, of all of which his mother was an enthusiastic member. "There shouldn't be much difficulty about that. How would you get the stuff to me?"

"It would not be difficult. They cannot keep us under lock and key, although they supervise our movements and our contacts as closely as they can. I was allowed out tonight without any trouble because it is known that I sometimes sleep with a girl in the next village. Such relaxations are thought to be good for us, and to bring us refreshed to our work in the morning."

"They ought to introduce it into schools as a substitute for PT," said Peter. But he was not devoting the whole of his mind to Dr. Bishwas. It was on a lot of different things. The car which had stopped at the end of the road. He wished that he were safely home in bed. He wished that he had not come out.

"You realize, of course," said Dr. Bishwas, "that we must have no further personal contact. If it were even suspected that I have talked to you, that would place you in a most ambiguous position."

"Yes," said Peter. "And now—if you don't mind—"

"You are fatigued. I am not surprised. If you will give me a few minutes' start, I shall make my own way back to the camp on foot. Goodbye, Mr. Manciple."

"Goodbye," said Peter.

He heard the light footsteps dying away in the distance. Then he went out and sat in his car, summoning the courage to move.

"If there is any trouble," he thought, "it will be at the end of the path, where it joins the main road."

There was no trouble. Ten minutes later, he was back in his bedroom. The letter was still on the mantelpiece. As he picked it up, he felt that it was not exactly as he had left it. There was nothing obviously wrong with it. It was still firmly sealed. There was something which his sense of touch was trying to tell him, but which his brain was too tired to interpret. He was on the point of tearing the letter up and depositing it in the wastepaper basket when he changed his mind and put it, unopened, into his briefcase. Then he undressed and climbed into bed.

Usually, he found it difficult to get to sleep for the first night or two in a strange bed. On this occasion, as soon as his head touched the pillow, he seemed to pitch head foremost into a land of dreams; dreams which started with the innocent fantasies of Alice in Wonderland, where rabbits talked and turtles sang, but which changed to horror when he saw that the animals were really people; children with elephant trunks and children with flippers instead of hands, children who moaned and howled and trumpeted through their grotesquely elongated noses.

It was a scream which broke the nightmare. A scream so loud and close that it jerked him upright in bed. It was some seconds before he realized that it was he himself who had screamed.

8

"Looks like a change in the weather," said Dave Brewer. "Most mornings we've had a bit of sunshine first thing, then down comes the rain."

"Fine before seven, rain before eleven," agreed Kevin.

"Now we've started with a nice bit of mist. We might get a real scorcher. More toast, Miss Mansergh?"

"You're such a terrible tempter," said Anna. "More toast, more cream, more potatoes. I believe you're trying to turn me into a roly-poly pudding."

"Becoming fat," said Professor Petros, "has very little to do with what you eat. What matters is what happens to the food once it is inside you. If your mind is constantly under stress, food can pass straight through your body without being ingested at all. This was demonstrated in the Chindit operations in Burma, where men died of malnutrition although they were apparently eating adequate quantities of food."

"Is that so?" said Kevin. "Then I must be a very stressful person, because I eat what I like and never get any fatter. What about you, Mr. Manciple?"

"I'm much the same," said Peter. "When I was at school, I was so thin you could hardly see me if I turned sideways, and I certainly ate an enormous amount. Most boarding schools starve their pupils, but we had an exceptionally nice housemaster. He was a bachelor, of course."

"Why do you say 'of course'?" asked the Professor.

"When a housemaster is married, his wife economizes on the food. Look at Mrs. Squeers."

"Mr. Key from the garage tells me you were both at Blundell's School," said Kevin. "I'd like to talk to you about that sometime. I've always thought that there must be a lot of autobiography in the opening chapters of *Lorna Doone*."

Peter said doubtfully, "By the time Blackmore himself was at Blundell's, I think it was a little more civilized than it was in John Ridd's time."

"Did the bigger boys still throw the little ones into the River Loman?"

"Not when I was there."

"What about fights?" said Anna. "You must have had fights."

Peter thought hard. He would have liked to oblige Anna, but he couldn't honestly recall that two boys had ever fought in any formal manner.

"Scuffles," he said. "Nothing like *Tom Brown's Schooldays*."

"I should surmise," said Professor Petros, "that boys' schools are a great deal softer now than they were a hundred years ago."

"They're not exactly soft," said Peter. "Just more grown-up. The only ordeal I can remember was a terrible race called the Russell. It was all across plowed fields and it was about a hundred miles long."

"A hundred miles?"

"It seemed like it. And the course had been artfully designed so that you had to cross the Loman six times. It was usually in flood."

"I believe you enjoyed it," said Anna.

"Only in retrospect."

"The sun is beginning to come through," said the Professor. "If you'd care to follow me in your car, I could show you something of the work I'm presently engaged in."

"It's very good of you to take the trouble," said Peter. He looked hopefully across the table. "There's plenty of room in the car if both of you would care to come along."

Anna grinned at him and shook her head. She said, "We're going to be busy today. We're looking for the Wizard's Slough."

As she said this, she shuddered. It was partly an artificial gesture; perhaps not entirely so, Peter thought.

Four miles out of Bridgetown on the Cryde road, the Professor, driving the little Austin, swung to the right and, a mile later, sharply right again, up an unmarked, roughly macadamized track. The big Savoia negotiated this turn with some difficulty. The track climbed steadily, between high banks, emerging at the top onto the moor itself. Peter had walked on both Dartmoor and Exmoor, and he loved them both; but it had not taken him long to recognize the difference between them. Dartmoor was the man, rugged, stark, honest, sometimes friendly but more often disobliging. Exmoor was the woman, soft, undulating, superficially attractive, and full of unexpected depths and dangers.

The Austin turned again, this time through an open gate in a wire-mesh fence, and Peter saw that they had arrived.

The living quarters consisted of three caravans, parked in a neat row. There was a large hut of the sort you could buy in sections and put up in five minutes with a spanner and a bit of luck, and a barn which had clearly been on the spot when the diggers arrived. Behind the caravans was an Army-style marquee, and behind the marquee a stove was smoking cheerfully.

"You're well set up here," said Peter.

"There is no premium in being unnecessarily uncomfortable," said the Professor. He led the way into the hut. There was a trestle table, with neat piles of files on it. One wall was taken up with a plan and a cross-section of the dig.

The Professor said, "This will give you a rough idea of what we are doing. We obtained access through the kindness of the Exeter Archeological Society. It is the known site of a Roman villa with a small village settlement. The owner of the villa was probably a magistrate. His dependents and slaves were housed in the village. It is unfortunate that we have not been permitted to open the whole site. The owner of the western end—" he demonstrated on the map—"is apparently opposed to any form of investigation. I am unable to tell you why. It is thought locally that he may have fallen into one of the trial excavations when the site was first explored."

He smiled, and Peter smiled back cautiously. Sometimes he found it difficult to decide whether the Professor was joking or not.

"However, we are opening up the portion of the site which is available to us, east of that red line on the plan, and we have made some interesting discoveries. If you look at the sectional drawing, you will see that we have cut through the perimeter wall which no doubt acted as protection to the village, and into the fosse which was dug when the wall was built. Ditches are always worth investigation. Then as now, people were apt to throw unwanted artifacts into ditches. I will get one of my young men to show you— Ah, here he is. Stephen, this is Mr. Manciple, whose name I mentioned to you yesterday."

A young man had come in quietly. He was wearing

an open-necked shirt and shorts, was about four inches shorter than Peter but a lot broader, and looked fit to tackle any item in the Olympic decathlon without further training.

"I see that there are papers here which I shall have to attend to. Would you show Mr. Manciple round?"

"I should be pleased to do so. Come with me, Mr. Manciple."

Although he enunciated the words correctly, he was clearly foreign. Peter wondered if Stephen might originally have been Stefan.

"We will look first at the work in progress, yes?"

"Fine," said Peter.

They followed a path which led around a shoulder of the hill to a place where there was a trench some twenty yards long and six feet wide in the chalky soil.

"That must have taken a bit of digging," said Peter.

"We have an enthusiastic team," said Stephen.

Peter could hear cheerful voices some way away on the far side of the mound.

"They are commencing a trench at right angles to this one. When we have finished, we shall have divided the area into four sections. This is known as the cruciform method of excavation. We then remove the soil carefully—using trowels, not spades—from each section in turn, starting at the center and moving outward. If you will follow me, I will show you."

Peter stepped forward to look, and felt himself slipping. A muscular hand grasped him by the arm and pulled him back.

"It is better to remain on the duckboards," said Stephen. "The ground is still very slippery." He glanced down at his wristwatch.

"I'm afraid I'm keeping you from your work," said Peter.

"Not at all. But I think we have seen all that is of

interest here. We will return and I will show you some of the results of our labors."

The barn had been fitted up as a showroom. Overhead lighting had been installed, and a line of shelves put in. On the shelves was a variety of different objects, each with a numbered card beside it. There was pottery, from small fragments up to nearly complete bowls and dishes. They were all of the same orange color, and on the larger pieces Peter could make out designs in relief. The one he was looking at showed a lion which seemed to be chewing off a man's head while a second man, armed with an ax, attacked it from the rear. A name in the top corner possibly identified the artist.

As well as the pottery, which formed the bulk of the exhibits, there were a number of flint arrowheads and some curious square stones with a hole in each corner.

"What on earth could they have been?" said Peter.

Stephen consulted a numbered list which he was holding. He read out, "They were wrist guards used by archers. There would be thongs threaded through the holes which would attach them to the forearm."

Peter could think of no intelligent comment to make. He moved back toward the door, reflecting that it was very difficult to go on being interested in something about which one knew absolutely nothing.

Beside the door, in the lefthand wall, was a smaller opening which had probably led to an inner storeroom of the sort where a French farmer would have kept his wine casks. It had been fitted with a stout door, and Peter wondered what treasures were kept in it. On a bench by the door were arranged trowels, shovels, and sieves, all clean and all arranged with the neatness which characterized the whole outfit. He picked up one of the trowels idly and put it down again. As he left the hut, he saw Stephen rearrange it so that it was exactly in line with the other trowels.

The Professor emerged from the office and waved a dismissive hand at Stephen. "You have seen it all. What do you think?"

"I think it's most impressive," said Peter. "I had no idea of the amount of organization involved."

"Archeology today is business. It is no longer a matter of enthusiastic amateurs digging at random. You have seen the finds we have made so far? They have attracted much interest. Hardly a day passes but we have people coming in. Usually, I try to show them round myself."

"It's very public-spirited of you."

As he bucketed down the lane in the Savoia, something was nagging him. It worried him so much that when he reached the macadam road he stopped the car and sat for a moment making a systematic effort to locate the trouble. It was the same instinct which had drawn his attention to a minor item in the accounts of the Palgrave Marina Company, and he expended a like degree of effort in identifying it.

It was nothing to do with the excavation itself or the objects which had been extracted from it. It was—yes, that was right—it was the trowel he had picked up. It had a strong wooden handle, a metal tang, and a pointed blade. The tang was attached to the blade, as he had seen when he had turned it over, by three metal rivets.

He was going to have to do some telephoning.

He studied the map. The road he was on was a secondary one which would take him out onto the Dulverton-Corfley road and so into Exeter. As he was putting the map away, he spotted a name: Watersmeet Farm. A very minor road was marked, leading to it and to nothing much else. Peter thought he might have a quick look at the place where Dr. Wolfe had done his fishing. Ten minutes later he was beginning to wonder if he had been wise. The road had deteriorated into a cart track.

The Savoia rode the ruts gallantly, like a big ship in a cross sea. The moor stretched on either side, bare of fence or hedge, green and seductive. When he topped the last rise, he found he was looking down onto a shallow basin which held the headwaters of the River Culme.

The farm buildings slept in the sun. When Peter knocked on the door, a dog started barking. Footsteps came shuffling up the passage, and the door was opened by a very old woman. Peter said, "I understand you have some fishing to let."

The old woman blinked up at him. Her mouth opened slowly. She said, "You're very tall."

"Six foot five," said Peter.

"My name's Horridge."

"I was asking about the fishing."

"Dan is my boy. He's mowing just now. When the sun comes out, you've got to take advantage, haven't you?"

Peter smiled. The old lady smiled back, revealing a single tooth, lone survivor of the long campaign of life. She waved one hand to indicate a track which led down through meadows to the river.

Dan Horridge was driving a tractor towing a gang-mower. He stopped when he saw Peter. "Saw your car," he said. "You'll have been talking to Mother. I expect you had some trouble there, didn't you?" He smiled, too. They seemed friendly people. "She's stone deaf, but she won't admit it."

"I'm afraid it's a long shot," said Peter, "but I'm staying at Bridgetown, and Mr. Brewer mentioned that you had some fishing here."

"Dave Brewer?"

"That's right."

"Well, I do and I don't, if you follow me. I have a stretch of water here, but I'd let it to that poor gentleman who went over the cliff. I expect you heard about it, didn't you?"

In fifteen leisurely minutes Peter heard a lot about Dr. Wolfe.

"He was a very clever gentleman, so I understand. But you'd never have guessed it, not to talk to him. When the river wasn't right for fishing, on account of there being too much water in it or too little, why, he'd come right into our kitchen and talk to us by the hour. Anything you mentioned, he'd have something to say about it. Mother took to him at once. So did our old dog, Blackie. He's a suspicious brute, for the most part. Of course, you need a guard dog in a place like this. But he made friends with Dr. Wolfe at once. He used to talk to him, and Blackie seemed to understand what he was saying. That's what made it so funny."

Mr. Horridge stopped to spit politely over the far side of the tractor.

"Funny?" said Peter.

"Odd. Mind you, I'm not superstitious myself. But there's no denying it was odd. The night it happened— last Wednesday, that was—he couldn't settle down at all. Then he started barking. I went and had a look outside, but there wasn't nothing to be seen, so I came in and gave him a piece of my mind, but I could see he was upset about something. Afterward, when I heard about what had happened to Dr. Wolfe, well, I did wonder. They say dogs can feel things that human beings can't. Do you think he might have sensed what had happened?"

"What time did he start this barking?"

"What time? Why, it would have been about four o'clock in the morning. Just before it got light."

"How far would you say you were from Rackthorn Point?"

"By road, or coming across the moor?"

"Can you come straight across?"

"Easy enough. All you've got to do is stick to the riverbank and follow it up. How far, you were asking. It might be twelve miles or maybe a bit more. Say fifteen if you didn't rightly know the shortcuts."

"Yes," said Peter. "I see."

He thought that Mr. Horridge, who was no fool, was beginning to cotton on, too.

9

"Coincidences," said Roland Highsmith, "are forbidden in fiction, but happen quite frequently in real life, particularly in our profession. I had a client who came in not long ago and asked me, 'What happens if my wife and I die at the same time?' I had to explain to him that, in the law, two people couldn't die at the same time. And then, what do you think?"

"Airplane crash?" suggested Peter.

"As a matter of fact, no. He killed his wife and took his own life."

"I'm not sure, sir, that I should exactly call that a coincidence."

"Wouldn't you?" said Mr. Highsmith. He considered the point. "You think he may have been meaning to do it all along. I'm afraid your profession may be turning you into a cynic." Roland Highsmith was spherical rather than fat. A lot of his weight was spread around his hips, giving him the low center of gravity invaluable to a racquets player or a boxer. At forty he was beginning to go thin on top, but looked both shrewd and cheerful —qualities very necessary to a man running a one-man solicitor's practice.

His desk had been placed so that he could see, over a

line of intervening roofs, the tall tower of Exeter Cathedral. He was staring at it now, as though he derived comfort from its square and stony strength.

"The case of Alex Wolfe was different," he said. "You might, I suppose, call it a sort of coincidence, but it didn't start out that way. He had read too many accounts of airplanes going down into the sea or into some remote part of the Arabian desert and not being found for years or perhaps not at all. That was the sort of contingency he was guarding against and was prepared to pay an extra premium to avoid."

"Did he fly much in those parts?"

"In the early years, when he was at university and afterward, he learned to fly, and flew a lot. He had at least one narrow escape when the plane he was in, a Piper Cub, missed the landing ground at Muscat in a sandstorm and then lost its way. Mercifully, it came down on the foreshore and not in the sea."

"Recently, I gather, he took most of his holidays by car, in Europe."

"They started in Europe. Where they finished up was a mystery. He was a good driver, and enjoyed driving for its own sake. He could also navigate and handle a small boat."

"Then the whole world was his parish," said Peter. "He sounds a remarkable sort of man."

"I wouldn't quarrel with that assessment," said Mr. Highsmith. "With good eyesight, sound nerves, and a first-class mind, he could apply himself to acquiring any technique which attracted him. When we were at Cambridge together, I taught him to play chess. It took him exactly three months to move right out of my class."

"I suppose you knew him better than most people."

"I think perhaps I did."

"Then can you suggest how a man with sound nerves

87

and good eyesight could have driven his car accidentally over the top of a cliff?"

There was a moment of silence. Peter could hear three typewriters being belted, two of them in synchronization, one in counterpoint.

Mr. Highsmith said, "Blackout?"

"It's been suggested, but do you really believe it?"

"Can you think of any more likely explanation?"

"Yes," said Peter, "I can."

"And what is that?"

All three typewriters stopped together, as if they, too, were waiting for his answer.

Peter said, "I don't think Dr. Wolfe went over Rackthorn Point at all. I think he manhandled his car over the cliff."

"Singlehanded?"

"It wouldn't be too difficult. Once the car is off the path, there's quite a sharp downhill run to the cliff edge. He'd have broken the guard rail beforehand, of course."

"I see. And what do you suggest he did then?"

"If I'm right about the first part, I *know* what he did next. He walked straight down into the wood. It was getting on for dusk. Possibly he stayed in the wood until it was quite dark. Then he walked fifteen miles across the moor, keeping the Culme stream at his right hand, and arrived at Watersmeet Farm at four o'clock in the morning. I imagine he spent the whole of that day tucked away in a barn, sleeping and eating the food he'd brought with him."

"I suppose someone saw him arrive at the farm?"

"No one saw him arrive. But the dog at the farm, who was an old friend of his, heard him and tried to tell the farmer about it."

"A difficult witness to produce in court."

"Agreed."

"Can you suggest any reason why Dr. Wolfe should have pursued this—this extraordinary course?"

"Yes. I think I can guess, too. He'd been preparing to get out for some time. I understand that he kept a spare kit permanently in the back of his car. What gave him the actual signal to do so was when one of his personal guards was killed."

"A hit-and-run accident, it was assumed."

"I think Dr. Wolfe may have seen it in a different light. The work he was doing was beginning to make him a fairly obvious target for attack."

"For attack by whom?"

"By people who didn't approve of the work he was doing. There must have been plenty of them. Particularly when you remember that he once advocated the complete removal of the state of Israel."

Mr. Highsmith said, "That was a monstrous attack. A piece of unscrupulous propaganda. Anyone who troubled to read that comment in the context of the article as a whole must have realized that it was no more than a pedantic joke." For the first time in their talk he seemed to be both angry and personally involved.

"Maybe the people who might have been on the receiving end didn't see it that way."

"All right..." Mr. Highsmith was still angry. "Let's get on with your story, shall we?"

"There isn't a great deal more to it. A second night's walk, rather an easier one, would have brought him to one of the stations of the main London-Exeter line. By taking an early train from there, he could have been anywhere in England by that evening. Or out of it."

"After two nights' tramping and a day in a barn? The stations between Exeter and Tiverton Junction are not large or busy. Surely someone would have reported such an odd and unkempt sort of passenger."

Peter said, "You knew Alex Wolfe well?"

"Yes."

"Then why should you imagine that he would be unkempt? On the contrary, he would have been freshly shaved, his hair would be neatly brushed, he would be wearing an inconspicuous raincoat, possibly carrying a rolled umbrella in one hand and a briefcase in the other."

"A briefcase?"

"I'm not sure about the umbrella. But a briefcase, certainly."

"So?" said Mr. Highsmith. "What then?"

"It crossed my mind that he might have come to Exeter with the idea of calling on his solicitor."

There was a long silence. Then Mr. Highsmith said, "I'd like you to take a look at what's on the wall to the left of the door."

Peter climbed obediently to his feet and walked over. It was a framed document.

"As you will see," said Mr. Highsmith coldly, "that is the certificate permitting me to practice as a solicitor. In other words, as an officer of the court. If you are seriously suggesting that I allow myself to be party to a fraud on an insurance company, then I can only suggest that you repeat the allegation in writing and I shall know what to do about it."

Peter came back slowly and sat down. He had not been many years at his job, but he had had occasion to interview a great many people, some of whom he had suspected, and one or two of whom he had actually accused of fraud. He was beginning to be a connoisseur of their reactions. Mr. Highsmith, he was reasonably certain, was acting out a sham of anger. He said, "I'm sorry. I didn't say that he got here. I said it might have been in his mind to call on you. But then he, too, would have realized that he couldn't involve you in anything dishonest. If that was his conclusion, then he'd have gone to London, or maybe directly to Portsmouth or Plymouth to catch a boat."

"If he had been stupid enough to come here," said Mr. Highsmith, "he'd have been unlucky. According to your ingenious timetable, he'd have arrived here—let me see—on the Friday morning." He was turning the pages of his appointment diary as he spoke. "On that particular day I went straight from my house to Taunton and was busy in the County Court all day. I've no objection to your checking that with my staff if you wish."

Peter got up. He said, "Certainly not, sir. I'm totally prepared to take your word for it. And I apologize once more for a stupid and ill-considered remark."

Mr. Highsmith, who had also got up, said, "There's one thing I'd like to know. Am I to take it that your company proposes to dispute the validity of Mr. Wolfe's claim under the policy?"

"On the basis of anything I have discovered so far," said Peter, "I very much doubt whether they *could* dispute it, don't you?"

"I don't believe any court would listen to you."

"In fact, the only thing which would convince them would be the production of Dr. Wolfe in person."

"I agree," said Mr. Highsmith. He seemed to have recovered his good temper, and shook Peter warmly by the hand as he showed him out.

After Peter had gone, Mr. Highsmith stood for a few moments in the middle of the room, listening.

When he heard the street door close, he walked across to his desk, opened his left hand, and dropped something into the wastepaper basket. Then he rang the bell to summon his head clerk and gave him instructions which, used as he was to Mr. Highsmith's idiosyncrasies, startled that elderly man.

10

Once clear of the outskirts of Exeter, Peter pulled his car off the road. He needed to do some thinking, and he wanted to do it while the events of the past hour were fresh in his mind.

One of his gifts was an acute perception of the moods of people he was talking to. He was able to measure the tightening and relaxing of tension with almost mechanical accuracy. Arthur Troyte had once described him as a walking lie-detector.

During the time he had spent with Roland Highsmith there had been two perceptible changes of gear.

At the onset the solicitor had been easy. He had produced the line of patter appropriate to a conference with a fellow professional. The first change had not been unexpected. It had occurred when Peter had suggested that Dr. Wolfe might have faked the accident. No more cordiality. A succession of brief and uncompromising questions. Behind it, anxiety concealed by occasional splutters of anger. All natural enough.

It had been the second switch which had been so interesting. It had occurred—yes, that was the point—it had occurred when Mr. Highsmith had forced Peter to get up and walk across to examine the framed certificate. From that point onward he had been no kinder, but he had recovered his confidence.

So what had he been up to while Peter's back was turned?

One point was clear: he had not moved out of his chair. Therefore, whatever he had done was somehow connected with his desk. If he had opened and closed one of the drawers, Peter felt certain he would have caught some hint of the movement. Deduction from that? It was something actually *on* his desk.

Visualize the desk.

An appointment diary; a matching pen-and-pencil set; a cylindrical black ruler; a blotting pad with clean pink blotting paper in it; a small silver frame containing a photograph of a woman and two tough kids; three telephones; beside the telephones a pad used for making notes.

Something on top of the desk had been changed while Peter's back was turned, and he was becoming more and more certain what it was. When he had first seen it, there had been a number of jottings on the pad. By the time he got back to the desk, the pad was clear. Therefore, Mr. Highsmith had torn off the top sheet and disposed of it, probably in the wastepaper basket. And once it was gone, his self-confidence had miraculously returned.

Interesting. Very interesting indeed.

Visualize the pad.

Peter had been sitting beside the desk, and the pad had been under his eye for some time. Subconsciously he must have photographed what was on it more than once. Three entries, all in black ink, no doubt made with the pen out of the pen set. The top one was a reminder to telephone either Mary or Maria (the final letters were confused). The second was a note: "Confirm appt. Jul. 9." Nothing suspicious about that, surely?

The third one was a number, preceded by two letters. No difficulty about the number: 16384. To a mathematician the appearance of a prime number raised to the power of fourteen was as memorable as a rufous warbler to an ornithologist. It was the letters which he was finding it difficult to fix. The first one had been D. That was for sure. But what was the second one?

A lorry rushed past with a clatter and a cloud of diesel smoke.

Think.

Ten minutes later Peter opened his eyes, looked at his watch, and shivered. A lengthy effort of concentration seemed to leave him as tired as if he had packed a day's work into half an hour. He sat staring at the road. The long drive back over moor roads to Bridgetown seemed unattractive. Also, he had a lot of telephoning to do and he remembered the small and awkward telephone booth at the Doone Valley Hotel. Once inside, it was impossible to shut the door. The calls he had to make demanded total privacy and quiet.

There was a signpost a few yards ahead of him. The sight of it made his mind up for him. He had his night bag in the back of the car. The Stanhope Arms in Tiverton was exactly what he wanted. He hoped that old Knight would still be in charge. When his father had come down to see him at Blundell's, he had made a point of staying at the Stanhope Arms and had had endless arguments with his host about the morality of staghunting. Curiously, it was Knight, the countryman, who had opposed it and Peter's father who had supported it. Sometimes they had forgotten young Peter, sitting solemnly in a corner, and had nearly come to blows. But the evenings had always ended in alcoholic amity.

Mr. Knight was there, and recognized Peter. "You've

filled out a bit," he said. "How's your father? I hope he's keeping well."

"I'm afraid not. He died last year."

"Did he, now? I'm sorry about that. We'll all come to it sooner or later." •

"I was wondering if you could fix me up with a room."

Mr. Knight looked doubtful and ran his finger down the register. He said, "It's the County Agricultural. We're all very full. However, you're in luck. There's one room. Last-minute cancellation. Thirty-four. It's in the annex. If you wouldn't mind looking after yourself? I'm a bit short-handed."

Half an hour later Peter was strolling down the High Street toward the bridge at the bottom. On his right was the flat Elizabethan frontage of Old Blundell's, with the octagonal light on the top and the letters P. B. in stone outside the gates.

Here John Ridd had passed his schooldays, studying with reluctance, fighting with uncommon determination. Here generations of West Country worthies had sent their sons, to learn to stand up for themselves in a country which respected physical courage as the queen of all the virtues. Could it be true, as the Professor had suggested, that boarding schools had gone soft and were producing boys of first-class intellectual accomplishments and no guts? Was that why the real leadership of the country was falling into the hands of men who had fought their way through the jungle of rough, ill-equipped secondary day-schools? "If the salt has lost its savor, wherewith shall it be salted?"

A girl passing on the pavement looked at him curiously, and he realized that he must have spoken out loud. He turned quickly to the left and hurried down the well-remembered stretch of road which led out of the town toward the new school, a mile out on the Halberton road.

The first person he saw when he got there was a large young man who grinned, seized him by the hand, and said, "Manciple, my ex-master."

"Good God," said Peter. He looked again and saw that it was not a young man but a very large and well-constructed boy. "Key Three."

"The very same."

"I can't say I should have recognized you."

"Well, I expect I have grown a bit in the last five years. You look almost exactly the same."

"I know," said Peter. "Thin, dopey, and untidy. Your brother told me. I ran into him out at Bridgetown."

"He said he'd met you. Come and have a word with F.B. He's always talking about you. He says you are the only natural mathematician the school has ever turned out."

"He won't want to be bothered. He's probably up to the eyes in end-of-term reports."

"Nonsense," said the boy. "He'll never forgive me if I let you slide off without seeing him."

He steered Peter under the red stone tower and down the passage, through a crowd of boys who stood aside respectfully to let them through; the respect, Peter guessed, being more for his guide than for himself.

They found Mr. French-Bisset in a deck chair on the lawn. He was completing the *Guardian* crossword puzzle and seemed untroubled by end-of-term reports or by anything else.

Peter had always got on well with his housemaster, an angular bachelor with red hair, a sharp tongue, and an educated taste in claret. He jumped up, shook Peter by the hand, and said, "Now, isn't that a nice surprise! You'll stay to supper."

"Well—"

"Of course you will. The house monitors are all having supper with me. You remember? It's an ordeal I subject them to at the end of each summer term for the good of their characters. You'll be able to meet them and decide how far they've gone downhill since your time. Bring your car round and park it in the drive."

"Actually, I walked up."

"Then you won't want to walk all the way back again after supper. I can easily give you a bed for the night."

"I haven't any things with me."

"My dear Peter, you're talking to an experienced bachelor. I always keep a spare pair of pajamas and shaving kit for people who drop in."

"Well—" said Peter. It was an attractive and a nostalgic idea. Also, he remembered the annex of the Stanhope Arms, which was on the corner of the High Street and caught the full blast of the through traffic. "It's very good of you. I shall have to do some telephoning."

"My study is at your disposal."

The first person Peter spoke to was Mr. Knight. The landlord seemed more relieved than disappointed. He said, "I've had two applications for that same room since you left and the third just come in. A commercial gentleman. I'll tell him he's lucky. No, that's quite all right. We'll keep an eye on your car for you. You can come and pick it up in the morning."

The next person he wanted was a man whom he addressed as Theo. He missed him at the British Museum, but caught him at home.

"It's odd about the trowels," agreed Theo. "Are you certain?"

"Quite certain. The ones I saw were all the same."

"Not welded?"

"Not welded. Riveted. I happened to remember an article I read. It was in one of the Sunday color supplements. Perhaps you remember it?"

97

"If it's the one I'm thinking of, it was written by my boss at the B.M."

"It said that you had to have a special sort of trowel for archeological work. If you used an ordinary gardening trowel, the rivets got worn flat in no time and the handle came off."

"If your Professor was an experienced man, it certainly sounds odd. Tell me more. What had he found?"

"The usual sort of things. There were a lot of pots, and some flint arrowheads—and oh, yes, archers' wrist guards."

"Flat, square things with holes in the corners?"

"That's right."

"What period?"

"I don't know exactly what year it was. The site was thought to be a Roman magistrate's villa with a small settlement round it."

"That makes it a bit difficult to understand the flint arrowheads. Quite the wrong period. What about the pots?"

"They looked genuine enough. They were a rather nice sort of orange color with pictures on them. At least, they were not exactly pictures. They were sort of stuck onto the clay."

"What were the pictures? Fights and banquets?"

"That sort of thing."

"Did you happen to notice the name of the craftsman?"

Peter thought about it. He said, "Yes. There were names on two of them. Part of a name on one: M. PERREN—. The rest was missing. And TIGRANIS. That was inside a sort of wreath on the other."

"And you want to know if these are pots which could have been found in a West Country Roman settler's villa?"

"That's exactly what I want."

"I haven't got the reference books here. I'll have to look them up tomorrow morning. If it's urgent, I'd better telephone you."

Peter gave Theo the number of the Stanhope Arms Hotel, rang off, and sat thinking for a few minutes. All right. Suppose Professor Petros was a fraud, was that fact of the least importance to his investigations? He felt, as he had done at the beginning of more routine assignments, that there were a number of uncertainties, some of which might be relevant; others would certainly be irrelevant. But the faster he cleared away the irrelevancies, the sharper would the truth appear.

He dialed another number. Roger had reached his home and was relaxing with his pre-dinner drink. He listened in some astonishment to what Peter had to say.

"Nutty as ever."

"Who?"

"You are. Only you would ring me up with a question like that."

"It's very important."

"I hope so. I charge double for advice given out of hours. Say it again."

"DS 16384."

"It can't be a motor-car number."

"I'd deduced that."

"Why do you suppose I'd be likely to know what it meant?"

"Because you're a solicitor. And I found it in a solicitor's office."

"Then why didn't you ask him what it meant?"

"That wouldn't have been practical."

"Up to your games again, are you?"

Roger's firm did a lot of work for Phelps, King and Troyte, and was resigned to being asked to undertake unusual investigations for them.

"What it sounds most like," said Roger at last, "is a

Land Registry number. Where was this particular solicitor's office?"

"In Exeter."

"Well, that makes it even more likely. Because DS is the symbol for all registered titles in Devon and Somerset."

"Isn't there some index, so that you can find out which property it refers to?"

"There is an index. But it's not open to the public. Only to the owner of the property and someone with some legitimate reason for consulting it. An intending purchaser, someone like that."

"Couldn't you pretend to be acting for a purchaser?"

"Sooner or later you're going to get me struck off the rolls."

"I'm sure you'll manage it somehow."

"It'll mean someone going down to Tunbridge Wells. That's where they keep the records."

"Send someone down tomorrow. Charge it to us, of course, and give me a ring at Tiverton 496. It's the Stanhope Arms. Before lunch if you can, but I'll hang on as long as I have to."

"The Nelson touch," said Roger. "Close with the enemy. Lose not an hour. And look where it got him. One arm, one eye, and a hero's funeral."

Dinner that night was by candlelight. Afterward, Peter remembered the three boys who came down with Key by their appearances more than by their names. There was a big, fair boy, a small, swarthy, twinkling boy, and a thin, serious boy with glasses. To start with, they were quiet, formal rather than nervous, but a second glass of their housemaster's claret loosened them up.

A twist in the conversation brought it around to the question Peter had been asking himself that afternoon.

"Softer?" said Mr. French-Bisset. "No, I don't think

that's the right word. Boys nowadays work harder. They have to. There's more competition for university places every year. And I think they play just as hard. The thing is, they don't take it so seriously. When I was a boy here—that was in the forties—rugger was still a religion. Even if you weren't good, you had to pretend to be very keen about it. Nowadays I don't suppose a boy would actually be lynched if he said he thought it was a stupid game and he preferred something more intelligent—"

"Like croquet," suggested Key.

"Croquet's a terribly rough game," said the dark boy. "My young sister once hit me with her mallet. I've still got the scar."

"What's made the most difference between then and now," said the fair boy, "is having a room to yourself."

The others agreed with this.

"It's an innovation since your time," said Mr. French-Bisset. "Being a bachelor, I don't use nearly as much of the private side of the house as my predecessor did. We've reorganized a whole wing into small single rooms for the ten senior boys."

"Bliss," said Key.

"It makes all the difference," agreed the fair boy. "Pigging it with thirty others in the day-room when you first came was bad enough. But being forced to share a room the size of a large cupboard with someone you didn't really like—"

Everyone laughed. There was some joke here that Peter didn't understand.

"It's not that we're soft," said Key. "We're just more grown-up. Old Garland used to rattle on about the days when he was here. It must have been about sixty years ago, but it sounded like *Tom Brown's Schooldays*. New boys being made to sing solos in the prep room on Sunday evening and have boots thrown at them. What good was it supposed to do them?"

"Useful if you were planning to be an actor," said the dark boy. "First-night nerves would never seem so bad again."

Peter said, "Surely old Garland can't still be here?"

"He retired last year. He lives at Ilfracombe and spends his time composing crossword puzzles and double-dummy bridge problems."

"He'd remember Alex Wolfe, I expect."

At the mention of the name, all the boys looked up together. Peter realized that they must know all about it, and must have heard (How? Through Key Senior via Key Three?) that he was connected with it.

The dark boy said, "Can you tell us what really did happen?"

"If you want me to protect you," said Mr. French-Bisset, "you've only to say the word."

"No, that's all right," said Peter. "I don't know what happened. Not yet. But I am trying to find out. I expect you read about it in the papers."

Key said, "My brother used to talk about Mr. Wolfe a lot. And that's odd, when you come to think about it, because none of us Keys have ever had any brains—"

"Tell us something we don't know," said the dark boy.

"Pipe down," said Mr. French-Bisset. "Go on, Key."

"It wasn't even as if they were here together. Mr. Wolfe left a year or more before my brother arrived. But boys were *still* talking about him. I think they realized he was something special even then."

"I expect it was because he was normal," said the fair boy. "Most science masters are freaks."

The thin, serious boy, opening his mouth almost for the first time, said to Peter, "You don't really think Mr. Wolfe's dead, do you?"

"I rule," said Mr. French-Bisset, slowly looking at

102

Peter, "that that question is out of order. I wonder if I dare offer you all a glass of port."

"That depends what port it is," said Key reasonably. "If it's the 1963, it ought to go quite well with the claret."

As Peter lay in bed that night listening to the wind whispering among the tops of the tall trees outside his window, he was not thinking about the problem of Dr. Wolfe. He was thinking that he liked Mr. French-Bisset a lot; more than he had done when French-Bisset was simply his housemaster, because then he had not understood him so well. He wondered if people realized what lasting effects, for better or worse, schoolmasters had on the boys they taught. Particularly in boarding schools. For ten of the most impressionable years of their lives, schoolmasters were much more important to boys than their parents. Sometimes you were lucky, sometimes quite definitely not. Peter remembered one housemaster, when he had been there, who had been a clergyman—

He drifted off to sleep.

It was almost exactly this moment that Mr. Birnie's nightmare began.

A click, which half woke him, as the lock of his bedroom door was forced back. Then soft hands, which lifted the bedclothes. Others, less soft, which held him down. A hand which clamped a cloth over his mouth to stop him whimpering. The sharp prick of a needle in his arm. Then merciful nothingness.

11

The rain clouds rolled up again during the night and it was through a gray world that Peter trudged down to the town next morning.

He found the Stanhope Arms in an uproar, and old Mr. Knight as nearly worried as he had ever seen that stolid Devonian.

"Lucky you've turned up," Mr. Knight said. "We'd have had to send and fetch you."

"Who? Why? What's up?"

"It's the police. They'll tell you." He indicated the door of the private bar. "You go along in."

The private bar still smelled of the beer which had been drunk there and the cigarettes which had been smoked there the night before. Seated behind one of the tables was a small, stout man whom Peter had never seen before. On each side of him sat a uniformed policeman.

Mr. Knight said, "This is Mr. Manciple. You were asking about him."

The larger of the two policemen, who had the stripes of a sergeant on his arm, said, "Sit down, Mr. Manciple. Perhaps you can help us."

"Perhaps I can," said Peter, "if you tell me what it's about."

"I ought to be in hospital," said the stout man.

"Mr. Birnie here had an unfortunate experience last night."

"Yes?" said Peter. He examined the stout man, who looked as if he had dressed in a hurry and had then crawled through a hedge. His cheeks and all three of his chins were unshaven, his eyes were red-rimmed, and there was a white crust around his mouth. Peter thought that Mr. Birnie had had a severe shock, or was suffering from a record hangover.

"It would appear," said the Sergeant, consulting his notebook, "that Mr. Birnie was abducted forcibly from his bedroom last night, drugged, taken away by car, subjected to intimidation and questioning, and then abandoned by the roadside at an early hour this morning. Fortunately, a passing motorist saw him and brought him back here and we were informed."

"I'm very sorry for Mr. Birnie," said Peter. "A most unpleasant experience. But why—"

"What's it got to do with you? you were going to say. The fact of the matter is that he was occupying your room."

"I'm going to be sick," said Mr. Birnie.

"Even so—"

"And Mr. Knight hadn't altered the register, you see."

"There wasn't much time last night. I'd have altered it this morning."

"No one's blaming you, Mr. Knight. I'm just stating the facts. Anyone coming in during the evening and looking at the register—it's kept open on the ledge of the reception office, I understand—they'd have read your name and assumed it was you occupying room thirty-four, you see."

"I suppose they would."

"So it looks as if it was you they were after."

"Why do you say that?"

"As soon as they found out it wasn't you, they didn't have no more interest in Mr. Birnie. They didn't even rob him."

"They turned out my pockets."

"Yes, sir. But that was just to make sure you were telling them the truth—about who you were."

At this point a doctor arrived. He examined Mr. Birnie and said, "There's nothing that six hours' sleep won't put right. I'd recommend a hot bath, too."

"I shall protest to my M.P."

"That's right. You do that," said Mr. Knight. "You can have the same room and I won't charge you for the extra night, as long as you're out by four o'clock."

When Mr. Birnie had been led away, the Sergeant said, "I don't know what your plans are, Mr. Manciple, but I'd be obliged if you'd stay on until the Inspector gets here. He's in Exeter at the moment, but he's coming right over. He'd like to have a word with you, I do know that."

"All right. I've got to wait here for two telephone calls anyway."

"Well, that's quite convenient, then, isn't it?"

"You make yourself comfortable in the coffee room," said Mr. Knight. "There won't be anyone else in there. Not during the morning."

The first call came at eleven o'clock. It was Theo. He said, "I've been having a look at our catalogues of terracottas. I located both your chaps in Walters' *Ancient Pottery*. Marcus Perrenius crops up a lot. He seems to have been the owner of a factory at Arezzo which turned out Arretine ware. It's very similar to the stuff we call Samian, or Terra Sigillata, which was manufactured in central Gaul. Tigranis was one of the craftsmen, probably a slave, employed at Perrenius' factory.

His name and the name of another slave, Xanthus, are two you find quite commonly on pottery from that particular workshop."

"Then they are genuine finds?"

"From your description, they certainly sound like genuine Arretine ware. Which makes it all the more curious."

"Why?"

"Because Arretine ware is never found in Britain. At least, it's never been found yet. Samian, yes. Arretine, no."

"Then that means that Professor—that the man who showed them to me—is a fraud?"

"It doesn't mean he's not an archeologist, although no one at the B.M. remembers his name. It simply means he's been salting the mine."

"Come again?"

"If he gets a lot of people looking over the site, he might want to have a few impressive pieces to show them. Unethical, but understandable."

"Wouldn't he risk discovery?"

"Only if he was stupid enough to show them to someone with X-ray eyes like you. Do you want me to do anything about this? I could come down myself next week and have a look, if you like."

"I think we'd better leave it alone, for the moment. Thank you very much, Theo. I'll let you know if anything comes of it."

Detective Inspector Horne of the Devon Constabulary arrived as Peter was ringing off. He was an unalarming man with a brick-red face and white hair and a fatherly manner.

He said, "When I got a report from Sergeant Rix, I thought I ought to have a word with you. It seemed to me that the circumstances wanted looking into. They seemed odd."

"Very odd," said Peter. "And if they really were after me, very alarming."

"Somewhat alarming," agreed the Inspector. "So what we have to ask ourselves is why these men should have wished to attack you."

"I've been asking myself the same thing ever since I heard about it."

"And did you come to any conclusion?"

"I suppose it must be something to do with the job I'm down here on."

"Which is what? That's to say, if it's not confidential."

"There's no secret about it. I've been sent down by the insurers to look into the accident that happened to Dr. Wolfe."

The Inspector said, "Yes?" He said it in a neutral voice which might have meant that he knew about it already, or might have meant that he was digesting the information. "Bridgetown? You'll be staying at Dave Brewer's place, no doubt."

"That's right. You know him?"

"Everyone knows Dave Brewer. He's what you might call a character. However, it doesn't get us much for-rader, does it? Why should the fact that you're looking into Dr. Wolfe's death provoke these people to attack you?"

"It's much odder than you think," said Peter. He explained, with the omission of certain details, his movements on the previous day. "So, you see, no one can possibly have known that I was planning to spend the night here."

"Could you have been followed?"

Peter thought of the long, empty moorland roads. "No," he said. "Quite impossible."

"And you're sure you didn't mention to anyone that you were coming here?"

"I couldn't have mentioned it. I didn't make my own mind up until the last moment."

"Then that makes it odder still, doesn't it?"

"It's quite mad."

"The men who did this weren't mad, sir. They were professionals. Three of them, we think. They picked the lock of the annex door and the lock of the bedroom, and they didn't make enough sound, getting in or getting out again, to disturb an old lady in the next room who suffers from insomnia."

While Peter was thinking about this, the Inspector added, "You said just now that you supposed it must have been something to do with the job you're on down here. You might be right. I just wondered why you assumed it."

"Well," said Peter, "I lead a peaceful sort of life, as a rule. Most of my work is done with books and calculators, sitting behind a desk. I seem to have barged into something rather unusual down here. Colonel Hollingum—he's the man at the Research Station—"

"Yes, sir. I know Colonel Hollingum."

"He gave it to me straight from the shoulder. Leave it alone. Go home. That may have been sound advice, from his point of view. But we couldn't just drop it. It would have meant that the insurers would have to pay up, without any real investigation being made."

"I understand that Dr. Wolfe's sister was to get quite a substantial amount."

It occurred to Peter that Inspector Horne was curiously well informed. He said, "Are you involved in this yourself?"

"Yes, sir," the Inspector said. "I *am* involved in what's been going on at Bridgetown. It was a bit beyond the local talent, so we were called in from Exeter. That was convenient, because Western Command Headquarters is at Exeter and we were able to cooperate with them."

Peter had a sudden picture of machines beginning, very slowly, to move into action; of gears engaging and wheels turning; ponderous machinery which, once started, would not be easy to stop.

He said, "You realize that I am not concerned with anything more than to make absolutely sure that Dr. Wolfe is dead."

The Inspector said, "I could wish that our job was as simple as that. We've another problem on our hands now. We'd like to know what has happened to Dr. Bishwas."

"Good God," said Peter, "has something happened to *him*, too?"

As soon as he had spoken, he realized that the Inspector had led him to the edge of the swimming pool and pushed him in at the deep end. It had been very neatly done.

"Then you did know Dr. Bishwas, sir?"

Policemen always added "sir" when they thought they had got you in a corner.

"Yes," said Peter. "I'd met him."

"And when was that, sir?"

"He spoke to me in the reception hut when I was waiting to talk to Colonel Hollingum."

"And was that the only occasion, sir?"

"No," said Peter. "It wasn't."

It seemed pointless to lie about it. It would have to come out sooner or later. He told the Inspector all that he could remember of their meeting, leaving out only the technical details of their conversation. The Inspector was more interested in things that had happened than in things that had been said. Where exactly had Dr. Bishwas been waiting for him? How long after they had started talking had he heard the car stop? What direction had Dr. Bishwas moved off in?

"When did they first miss him?"

"At breakfast next morning. He didn't come back to the camp at all. They made inquiries down in the village. It seems there was a girl."

"Yes," said Peter. "He told me about her. She was his recreation period."

"Whatever she was, she's in the clear. There are plenty of witnesses that he never went near her house that night."

"So where did he go?"

The Inspector didn't answer that. He was looking out of the window, at the cars jostling each other in the street and the pedestrians hurrying out of the way to avoid being splashed. In the end, he said, "Could you tell me what you were planning to do? Give me some rough idea of your movements?"

"I'm waiting here for a telephone call."

"And then?"

"A lot will depend on what I learn from that phone call—if I learn anything at all."

"You couldn't be a little more precise than that, I suppose?"

"I can't tell you what I'm going to do until I know myself."

"I suppose that's reasonable," said the Inspector. "But when you do make your mind up, I think you ought to let us know."

"Oh," said Peter. "Why?"

The Inspector took his time over that one. Then he said, "Those men last night who snatched poor Mr. Birnie. He must have seen them quite clearly, but, do you know, *he wouldn't give us any sort of description of them*. I would guess they'd told him what was going to happen to him if he did. The state he was in this morning, it wasn't so much a hangover from the drug they put into him. It was a hangover from being more frightened than he'd ever been frightened in his life before. A sort of delayed shock, you might call it."

"So?"

"If it was the same people, or friends of theirs, who picked up Dr. Bishwas, and they had the whole night to work on him, I expect they'd have got out of him what he'd been doing and what he'd been talking to you about. And if they did, it seems to me you ought to be a bit careful. If you follow me."

"I follow you perfectly."

"Of course, I may be putting two and two together and getting quite the wrong answer—it happens sometimes." The Inspector heaved himself to his feet and made for the door. "But you will bear it in mind, won't you?"

"I'll bear it in mind," said Peter.

The call he was expecting had not come by lunchtime, and after lunch he sat in the coffee room for a long time, watching the raindrops form on the windows, join up into tiny rivulets, amalgamate with bigger streams, run down and disappear.

At four o'clock Mr. Knight brought him two cups of tea and settled down for a chat.

He said, "I wouldn't have mentioned your father, not if I'd known he'd gone. Tactless of me."

"That's all right," said Peter.

"He was an interesting man. I enjoyed talking with him. I always meant to ask what he did."

"He was an actuary."

"If he'd told me that, I wouldn't have been any wiser."

"An actuary's job is to evaluate things. He has tables which show you how long you can expect to live. That sort of thing."

"Interesting," said Mr. Knight. "I'd like to have a peep at mine sometime."

112

"One of the first things I can remember him telling me was that the average man will live six times as long as his dog, five times as long as his cat, three times as long as his horse, and half as long as a giant turtle. For weeks after that I was plaguing him to show me one."

"A giant turtle?"

"An average man. In my own mind, I'd pictured him walking down the street, leading a horse and a dog and carrying a cat, with the giant turtle waddling beside him."

Mr. Knight laughed and said, "Children do say strange things. The other day my granddaughter asked me— Hello, this looks like the call you've been waiting for. Better take it in the office."

Roger's voice came thinly over the wire.

"I've got the information you want," he said. "DS 16384 is the title number of a house at Cryde Bay. The address is number eight, the Chine. The title was first registered in March of this year, so it's impossible to tell how long the previous owner had had it. The present registered owner is Roland Thomas Highsmith. Does that mean anything to you?"

"Yes," said Peter. "That makes sense, and thank you."

"You're welcome," said Roger.

Peter went to find Mr. Knight.

"Certainly you can stop on," said Mr. Knight. "No one wants to start a motor run at this time of day, not in this sort of weather. I'll let you have a room next to mine, in the private part. You'll have no trouble there. I've got a dog called Butcher sleeps in the passage. Half Alsatian, half Doberman, and all the worst characteristics of both."

"It's extraordinarily kind of you," said Peter.

"Well, I wouldn't do it for everyone. But I was fond of your father. And I remember the first time you came here with him. You can't have been more than twelve or thirteen; and you said, in that funny squeaky voice of yours, *'Isn't* this a nice hotel!' I've never forgotten that."

Comforted by the snuffling of Butcher outside his door, Peter fell asleep quickly. When he woke up, he guessed that it was between four and five in the morning. The gray light was beginning to show through the uncurtained window. The silence was absolute. It was an hour when dangers seemed many and comforts few; but he was in a curious mood of resolution. He was the average man. His years were numbered in the records.

There had been a morning, at about the same cold hour, also in a hotel bedroom, when his courage had altogether failed him. He had imagined that he held the keys of his destiny in his own hands and he had been wrong. He was not going to make the same mistake again.

12

Next morning Peter drove north, following the winding and wooded valley of the Exe almost to its headwaters, topping the watershed at Wheddon Cross and descending by the Avill Valley toward the coast.

The sun was shining bravely as though apologizing for the previous day, and the countryside, between the noble tower of Dunkery Beacon to port and the Brendons to starboard, was a sight to gladden the eye. Most of Peter's thoughts were on his car, which was behaving oddly. He knew nothing about the internal-combustion engine except that it absorbed regulated doses of petrol, oil, and water. He hoped that it would carry him safely back to civilization.

He only just made it. The engine finally died as he was descending the last steep hill from Dunster to the coast road. His impetus carried him to the road junction, where he saw a garage sign and coasted in.

"A bit of luck," he said.

"Something wrong?" said the mechanic.

"Something is undoubtedly wrong," said Peter. "The engine has been making protesting noises for the last five miles and has now gone on strike."

The mechanic, a gnomelike man dressed in greasy

overalls, disappeared head first into the engine and emerged to report a cracked distributor.

"No good trying to patch it," he said. "Soon break up again. Needs a new part."

"Oh dear," said Peter. "Will that take very long?"

"Pick it up today at Carrick's in Minehead. Could have her ready for you tomorrow morning, with a bitter luck. Day after, if they have to send to Taunton for it. Lovely machines, these Savoias." He stroked the car on the nose as if it had been a horse. "Temperamental, though. Where are you making for, might I ask?"

"I was hoping to get to Cryde Bay."

"No trouble. Take the train."

"Train?"

"Dunster station. Straight ahead of you, about half a mile."

"Oh. Fine," said Peter. He got his small overnight bag out of the back of the car. "I'll be staying the night in Cryde Bay if I can find someone to put me up, and I'll give you a ring from there tomorrow."

"Might be difficult to find a place. Be impossible next week, when the school holidays start. Fills right up then."

Peter thanked him and strolled down the deep-banked lane which led to the station. Small, fluffy clouds were chasing each other across the sky, and the birds were singing. He felt that he was entering one of his lucky periods. How gallantly his car had carried him! How easily it might have let him down on a wild and deserted stretch of Exmoor!

These feelings survived even the discovery that he had an hour and a half to wait for the slow train which stopped at Cryde Bay. He had seen from the map that this was a modest-sized coastal resort about five miles to the east of Cryde and serviced by a switch line.

When he got there, Cryde Bay railway station was

asleep in the sun. The only sign of life was an aged taxi cab parked in the forecourt. The driver, too, seemed to be asleep, but looked up when he heard the sound of Peter's approach. When he detected that Peter was not a potential fare, he went to sleep again so decisively that Peter hardly liked to disturb him, and wandered past him and out into the town.

On the promenade he found a more helpful inhabitant, a brisk lady with a shopping bag, who said that she knew all the guesthouses were full up, but he might try the Seven Seas because she'd heard that it was only just opening for the season.

When he got to it, Peter liked the look of the Seven Seas. It was tucked away at the far end of the sea front at a point where the road started to run up the cliff. There were steps leading down from it to a shiny beach and an old jetty with a cabin cruiser moored on the far side. He marched up the front path and rang the bell.

For a long time nothing happened, but there were certainly sounds of movement at the back. He leaned on the bell. This produced an oath from the interior, followed by footsteps. Then the door opened. The proprietor of the Seven Seas Guest House and Peter Manciple inspected each other. Neither seemed displeased with what he saw.

"Anderson," the man said. "Known by all as Captain Andy, though I never was captain of anything more than that cockleshell down the steps."

He was a man of middle size with a brown and open face and a bald patch on the back of his head. Peter introduced himself.

"You're the first swallow that makes a summer," said Andy, "and I hope it's going to turn out a bloody sight better one than it's been so far. You haven't got any children with you?"

"No children."

"That's all right, then. We're not exactly organized for children as yet."

He led the way down the passage and into what was going to be a dining room. At the moment the tables and chairs were piled against one wall and painting was in progress.

"Peach emulsion paint on the walls, and ivory white on the strips of wood between. It should be tasty, don't you think?"

"Very tasty," said Peter. He eyed the brushes wistfully. "I suppose I couldn't—"

"Why not?" said the Captain. "That wall's dry, you can start on the wooden bits."

The rest of the morning passed pleasantly. They knocked off for a late lunch, cooked by the Captain and eaten in a very well-equipped kitchen. Over lunch the Captain, feeling perhaps that some explanation was due, said, "I wasn't really intending to open up until Monday week. But I thought you looked like a chap who doesn't mind roughing it a bit."

Peter, his mouth being full of bacon omelet, nodded to signify that he didn't mind roughing it.

"I got left this house by my aunt. I used to come and stay here when I was a kid. It was too nice a house to sell, but I couldn't afford to give up my business—I run a catering firm up in Luton. So I came to this arrangement with my partner. He takes charge of the business from Midsummer Day till Michaelmas. I come down here and open up for the school holidays. Always have a crowd of children. Noisy little bastards, but fun to have around. We've got regulars by now, come year after year. The first lot aren't due till Monday week, so we'll be quiet enough till then. Were you thinking of staying for long?"

"For a day or two, anyway," said Peter. "My plans are

118

a bit unsettled. Is there anything I can help you with after lunch?"

"I was planning to run a buffer over the floor of the lounge and wax it. It's a one-man job, really."

"Then I'll take a stroll around the town. By the way, do you know a place called the Chine?"

"It's at the other end of the front. A sort of split in the cliff. There are one or two nice old houses tucked away in it. You weren't thinking of buying one of them, perhaps?"

"You never know."

"Because if you are, you ought to have a word with Highsmiths."

"Highsmiths?"

"The solicitors."

"I thought they were an Exeter firm."

"So they are now. But they started here. Young Roland Highsmith was born and bred in Cryde Bay. I knew him well in the old days. He opened his first office on the promenade here. Of course, there wasn't enough work to keep him here. As soon as he got going, he moved up to Exeter, but he kept the office here. There's one of his assistants, a Mr. Quarles, looks after it. He knows all about the local properties. You have a word with him. Mention my name."

Peter promised to do that. Even though he had no intention of buying a house, it occurred to him that it might pay him to have a word with Mr. Quarles.

"Captain Andy sent you?" said Mr. Quarles. "Very happy to help if I can. It isn't an easy place to buy a house. They get snapped up as soon as they come on the market."

"He did mention that there might be one in the Chine."

"There *was* a house going in the Chine. The one at the far end. It belonged to old Mrs. Mottistone. A real old dragon she was. It's been sold now, though. I rather think our Exeter office handled it. If you do see anything you want, we'd be glad to help."

Peter thanked him, and made his leisurely way along the front. An offshore breeze was slicing the tops of the little waves in the bay and he could see one or two small boats taking advantage of it.

The Chine was a natural fault in the cliff which cut off the west end of the town. To the right it ran straight down to the sea, making a deep-water inlet flanked on the near side by a thin strip of shingle. To the left it was serviced by a small and badly made-up road which twisted away out of sight between banks covered with fern and heather.

Houses had been built, higgledy-piggledy, wherever there was a flat space large enough to hold one. At the far end the road turned sharply to the left. Peter had counted seven houses, and reckoned that Number 8 must be the one which was just coming into sight. He wondered whether it was wise to show himself. But, after all, why not? Casual strollers must come up the road from time to time. He turned the corner.

If Mrs. Mottistone had been a dragon, she had chosen herself a dragon's lair. Number 8 was not an attractive house. It was larger than the others he had passed, built of red brick which time had darkened to the color of stale blood, and was so wedged under the lips of the Chine that it must be in shade for three quarters of the day. The windows at the back could get no sunshine at all. The windows which faced the road were, all but one, shuttered.

Peter took in the details at a glance and without slowing his pace. He had seen two other things. The single unshuttered window, to the right of the front door, was a few inches open at the top, which seemed to argue human occupation. And there was a flight of steps, leading up at the far end of the Chine, which suggested a useful alternative way of approach.

The strip of garden in front of the house was rank grass backed by an overgrown bed of Aaron's rod and a creeping plant with long, fork-shaped leaves which Peter thought might, appropriately, be dragon's-tongue. He walked past and climbed the steps. These brought him out onto a cinder path which ran alongside an abandoned stretch of railway line. This must be the line which had once continued along the coast toward Porlock.

In due course, the path took him back to the station forecourt. The single taxi still stood there, and the driver still seemed to be asleep. Peter found a café on the front which sold him a cup of coffee for a price which would, a few years before, have bought him an entire meal. He then located the post office in a back street, and telephoned his mother from one of the two callboxes outside it.

His mother cut short his explanation of where he had been and what he had been doing. She said, "I advise you *not* to mention the place you are telephoning from."

"Why on earth not?"

"This house has been under day and night surveillance since you left."

"Oh dear."

"And I think it very probable that our telephone has been tapped."

"Do you really think—?"

"I am not sure. But every time I lift the receiver to answer a call, I hear a distinct click. Your father once told me that this was a clear sign that the call was being intercepted."

"All right," said Peter patiently. "I won't tell you where I am, beyond saying that it's somewhere on the

North Devon Coast, and that I've found a very pleasant place to put up for a few nights."

"When will you be home?"

"It might be quite soon."

"You have done what you set out to do?"

"I think so," said Peter. "With any luck I'll know for certain by tonight. Look here, Mother, if you're really worried, why don't you go to the police?"

His mother said, "You can hardly realize how stupid that suggestion sounds. When will you understand? *The police are on the other side*. They know what they are doing. They are assisting them."

"All right," said Peter with a sigh. "Look after yourself. I'll be back as soon as I can."

"Not what you might call much night life in Cryde Bay," said the Captain when Peter told him that he meant to take a walk around the town after dinner. "There's a cinema, or there's a pierrot show in the Palais de Danse. I went last week, but I couldn't understand half the jokes. The audience seemed to like it."

Peter chose the Bijou Cinema, and sat through a film he had already seen in London. It was nearly eleven when it finished and he walked out into a clear, cool night. The moon was not yet up, but there was a luminous quality which he had noticed at other seaside places and which seemed to be the light off the sea reflected into the black and starlit bowl of the sky.

The station forecourt was deserted. Even the taxi driver had departed to continue his sleep at home. The path by the railway was easy to locate, and Peter padded along it quietly. He had worked out a rough plan of action. When he got to the Chine, he avoided the steps, which would have taken him to the front of the house, and moved instead to the right, feeling his way along the upper slope, knee deep in ferns and already damp with dew.

In the quick glance which was all that he had allowed himself when passing the place that afternoon, he had noted that the descent at the back of the house was not really precipitous. If he took his time, he had no doubt he could clamber down it. As long as there was no dog in the house, he should be quite safe. If he was spotted he had two possible exits. He could circle the house and decide at the last moment whether to bolt up the steps or down the Chine.

It took him longer than he had anticipated, because, when he was halfway down and fully committed, he ran into a wire fence buried among the tall ferns. To climb over it would be difficult and would make a noise. In the end, he lay flat on his back and scraped a sufficient hole in the sandy soil to wriggle under the bottom strand. Once he was clear he rolled over onto his face, held the wire with both hands, stretched his long legs out, and let himself slither down the last few feet onto the stone-flagged path. Here he stopped to shake some of the sand out of his clothes, and to listen.

At that moment a light went on in one of the back windows. Peter cowered. It was a few breath-stopping seconds before he realized that the light had nothing to do with him. The occupant of the house had come into the kitchen and was moving about in an unhurried way which indicated no alarm.

Keeping well back in the shadow, Peter raised himself cautiously.

The man was standing behind the table, half facing him. He was using an old-fashioned can-opener to attack what looked like a can of soup. He was of middle height, and Peter put his age at about forty. The only remarkable thing about him was his beard. It looked to be exactly the sort of beard which a moderately hirsute man might have succeeded in growing in the space of

123

ten days. It already concealed both sides of his face from the cheekbone down to the point of the chin.

The can-opener slipped and the man bared his teeth.

Peter edged slowly backward into the darkness. He had seen all that he'd come to see. If, as he suspected, the man was alone in the house, this would be a safe moment to make his exit by the front.

He had circled the house and was on the point of making a dash for the front gate when he heard footsteps approaching. Someone was coming up the road, not strolling but walking in the purposeful way of a man who is making for a definite objective. Peter drew back into the shadow of the house and waited.

His instincts had been correct. The newcomer turned in through the front gate and approached the house. Here he paused, and Peter, who was not more than five yards away, could see that he was fumbling in his pocket for—yes, no question. It was keys.

The opening of the front door let out a thin fan of light and confirmed Peter's suspicions. The visitor to Number 8, the Chine was the Exeter solicitor Roland Highsmith.

As soon as the door had closed, Peter was on the move again. He wanted to get away from the house as quickly and as quietly as possible. Five minutes later he was back on the sea front.

The thin rind of the new moon was showing over the horizon. He walked slowly, listening to the sea lipping the shingle. He was trying to sort out the events of the last few days and put them into some sort of perspective.

He had no doubt at all that he had found Dr. Wolfe. He did not give himself overmuch credit for it. The long chain of coincidence which had led him to Cryde Bay was too thin and too fragile for self-congratulation.

What he was in no position to appreciate at that point was the full extent to which blind chance had helped him. He had no idea that there were three different organizations anxious to keep track of his movements; and that he had side-stepped all of them. For the moment, he was off their screens. They scanned for him in vain.

He was in limbo.

13

"Ilfracombe?" said Captain Andy. "It'll take you all of two hours. Along the coast road most of the way. Porlock, Lynton, Combe Martin. A very nice run. As long as the weather holds up."

"It looks all right at the moment."

"It looks very nice at the moment," agreed the Captain, casting a speculative eye out of the window. "Almost too good. We had a week of rain and storm. Now we get a few bright days. Like the eye of the hurricane. Worse to come."

"The wireless said 'set fair.'"

"They'll say anything. The government pay them to keep people happy."

A telephone call to the garage at Dunster had assured him that his car was ready. When he got there, it seemed to him that the gnomelike mechanic was worried about something.

"She *is* all right, isn't she?"

"The car? Surely. She's right as rain. It's your friends I was wondering about. Perhaps I did wrong."

"My friends?"

"Turned up an hour after you'd left. Two young

men. Foreign, I thought. When they saw the Savoia, they started asking about you."

"Did they give any names?"

"No. Just said they were friends. Motoring down the coast on a holiday. They said they recognized the car. It's not a common make. They wondered if it belonged to their friend Manciple."

"But—" said Peter.

"But," agreed the mechanic. "I knew, because you told me, you'd hired it from Key's Garage at Bridgetown, so I thought 'funny.'"

"Very funny," said Peter, with a cold feeling in the pit of his stomach. "What did you tell them?"

"I said they were quite right, it did belong to Mr. Manciple. I said as how you'd left it here for a proper overhaul. Might take several days. You'd told me you were taking the train back to Taunton so you could switch onto the main line for Barnstaple, where you were planning to stop until the car was ready. After they'd gone, I did wonder if I'd done right. Maybe they *were* friends of yours."

"You did absolutely right," said Peter, "and I can't tell you how grateful I am."

"Well, they were foreigners, see, and telling lies. I didn't like the look of them. I should keep clear of them, if I were you."

Excellent advice, thought Peter, as he drove the car, now purring happily, through the wooded hills of the North Devon Coast toward Lynton. Excellent advice, but how did one follow it? How could one keep clear of enemies who followed your car with unseen eyes, never more than an hour behind it? When he reached a point near the top of Kipscombe Hill where the road ran out from under the trees, he turned into a rutted lane, drove on for fifty yards, stopped, and walked back to the main road.

Three cars had passed him in the last half-hour. None had overtaken him. He sat down, hidden among the heather at the roadside, and waited. A baker's van passed him without stopping. Ten minutes later two girls on bicycles, with large rucksacks on the carriers, came toiling up the hill in the other direction. After that, nothing except the singing of the birds and the humming of bees.

A loud and insistent humming, growing in strength. A helicopter swung into view from the south—no bee this, but a surly cockchafer. It passed almost directly over where Peter was sitting and continued out over the sea. It had the look of an Army machine.

Peter walked back to the car and continued on his way. He was giving only half his mind to his driving. The other half was trying to recollect whether a helicopter had come over him when he had parked his car outside Exeter four days before. He had stopped there for a considerable time and had been so deeply engrossed with private speculations that he would probably not have noticed if a wing of heavy bombers had flown over him. The characteristic square-cut top of the Savoia would have been easy to pick up from a helicopter at three or four hundred feet. . . .

A horn blared, and he realized that he had strayed absentmindedly onto the righthand side of the road.

At Ilfracombe a policeman directed him to the address he had been given. It was in the southern part of the town, well away from the boardinghouses and the hotels. It was where the residents lived, retired folks for the most part, happy to spend the evening of their lives in the small, detached houses, each with its small, neat garden.

As soon as Peter lifted the latch of the gate, a curtain twitched in the front window and a face appeared. By the time he reached the door, it was open and Mr. Garland was standing there glaring at him. Peter was not worried. The glare, as he knew, was a preliminary defensive gambit, developed by Mr. Garland in his dealings with generations of schoolboys.

He said, "I don't suppose you remember me, sir. I'm—"

"Wait," said Mr. Garland. Peter could see his lips moving as though in prayer. "Mathematics Manciple. Correct?"

"Correct."

"I have to employ these little mnemonics. It would be difficult, otherwise, to recall the names of more than a thousand boys. Sometimes they are obvious. Pimples Pirie. It's the first two letters which are significant. There was a boy with a bad stutter. By happy coincidence, his name was Stutchbury. Before your time, I think. Come in, come in. I am always glad to see old boys. Quite a few of them come to visit me."

He led the way into the front room. There was a large table in the middle at which a curious game of bridge without players appeared to be in progress. The cards, larger than life size, were mounted on wooden stands, so that they could be moved onto different parts of the table, which was squared like a chessboard, except that there were thirteen squares on each side. Two of the walls of the room were covered by bookcases. Most of the books seemed to be dictionaries or encyclopedias.

"Ingenious, are they not?" said Mr. Garland. "You purchase the shelves in sections and screw them together. Soon I shall have sufficient to cover the third wall also. I collect books for my old age as a squirrel collects nuts for the winter."

He looked like an old gray squirrel. A cheerful old gray squirrel with a large hoard of nuts and a safe hole to keep them in.

"And what are you doing in this part of the world, Manciple?"

Peter had been wondering as he came along exactly how he was going to broach the proposition which he had in mind. He said, "I expect you read in the papers about Dr. Wolfe."

"Alex Wolfe." Mr. Garland turned away toward the sideboard. "Yes. I wonder if you would care for a glass of light sherry."

"Well—"

"I usually have one myself at about this time. You'll join me? Good."

By the time Mr. Garland had turned around again, his face was as expressionless as usual. But Peter had not missed the sudden change, the flash of almost savage interest.

"Alex Wolfe," he said. "Yes indeed, I read about it. He was a brilliant man. The country can ill spare people of that caliber."

"You knew him well, sir?"

"I might say so, yes. We shared lodgings together in Tiverton for the whole of the three years he was at the school. One gets to know a man when one lives and works with him. In much the same way that I got to know your father."

"My father?"

"Certainly. I hope this sherry is to your liking. Some people find it rather light."

"It's very nice. Would you mind telling me—"

"When I worked with your father? Did he never tell you himself? No, I suppose he would hardly have done so. He was bound, like myself, by the fetters of the Official Secrets Act. But since it is now more than thirty years in the past, I hardly imagine—" Mr. Garland snuffled happily—"that I shall be imprisoned in the Tower of London if I tell you. It was during the war. We

130

worked together for—let me see—it must have been nearly four years at the Decoding Center at Bletchley Park. His training as an actuary was of great assistance to him. While I have always been interested in puzzles and conundrums. Or ought one to say conundra? The point had never occurred to me before."

He pottered across to the bookshelf and took down a volume of the *Greater Oxford Dictionary*. It seemed to be a well-used book.

"No," he said. "Conundra would be incorrect. But here I am, deviating onto quite a different topic to the one you introduced—"

And cleverly done, too, thought Peter.

"You mentioned Alex Wolfe. Do I gather that your visit to the West Country is in some way connected with his unhappy demise?"

"I have been looking into it."

"An official investigation?"

"Perhaps I should explain."

If he was going to get the old gentleman's help, it had to be the whole story. Or almost the whole story. There were certain things which could be left out. As he spoke, Peter was conscious of a change in Mr. Garland. He had dropped his normal mask of donnish affability. The signs were small, but could be observed by a careful watcher. A slight tightening of the mouth, a fractional closing of the eyes. During the whole of the recital, he hardly moved in his chair. Even his hands, folded in his lap, were still.

At the end of it, he said, "That is a very remarkable story, Manciple. I imagine that you are telling it to me for some reason."

"I am telling you because I want your help. I want you to come back with me and pay a call on Dr. Wolfe."

"Yes. Why?"

"Because, in spite of the beard he has grown to hide the scar on his face, and any other small changes he may have made in his appearance, I am certain you could identify him. And because, if he were prepared to tell anyone what he was up to, I imagine he would tell you."

"Your first surmise is correct. I should know him at once. Your second surmise might be correct. We were very old friends. Nevertheless, I fear I must decline to help you. Alex never did anything without good reason. He must have very cogent reasons for what he is doing now."

"There will be other people who could identify him, but they would be official people and bound to take an official line. I thought that if you— Well, it would leave our options open."

"Possibly," said Mr. Garland. But he did not say it in the tone of voice of someone who is changing his mind. "Although I should have thought that you, personally, had *no* option in the matter. Whatever your personal feelings, you surely have a paramount obligation to your employers to tell them, if no one else, what you have discovered."

"I suppose so."

"You sound unhappy about it. You are torn in two directions? It is certainly a problem. But not, I fear, a problem which my books will help to solve."

As Mr. Garland said this, he snuffled again. It was a signal that he had reverted to the innocent old schoolmaster. Peter recognized the finality of the change. He accepted a second thimbleful of sherry, discussed a number of mutual acquaintances, and wandered out into the sunlight of Ilfracombe. He was puzzled, and worried; but mainly puzzled.

His puzzlement continued as he drove out of Ilfracombe. It came to a head as he reached the exact place at which he had halted on the way out. He said, "Helicopters be blowed. You'd need a fleet of helicopters to keep track of a car in these lanes."

He drove the Savoia into the same rutted lane, got out, and sat down beside it.

"There's something about you, old lady," he said, "which allows people to follow you at a distance. It can hardly be a sense of smell. You've had some gadget attached to you." A second line of thought presented him with a cross-reference. "And I know when it was put on."

It explained something which had been worrying him before. If Professor Petros was a fake, and up to some mischief, why had he allowed Peter to visit the dig? Peter, it was true, had assured him that he knew nothing about archeology, but why take the risk at all?

"That's when it was fixed," said Peter to himself. "When Stephen took me for that tour of the trenches. I caught him looking at his watch. He had been told to keep me out of the way for a specific time. It must be quite a simple gadget to fix. And quite easy to find."

It was a black metal box, about six inches square, spot-welded onto the frame inside the back panel of the trunk. No tools that Peter had would remove it, but the front panel of the box was only held by a thumbscrew. Peter opened it and examined the complicated contents with interest.

"You're a talkative little bastard," he said. "But you shall talk no more." Using a pair of long-nosed pliers, he extracted the miniature valves and broke the tiny connecting wires. Then he screwed back the front of the box, got back into the car, and drove off happily.

14

Next morning Peter was awakened by bells and realized that it was Sunday. He found a note: "Gone to Mass at St. Barnabas' Church. Eggs on the dresser, bacon in the fridge." He had cooked and eaten his breakfast by the time the Captain got back.

Peter said, "Would it be all right by you if I wanted to stop on here for the rest of the week?"

"No problem," said the Captain. "If you're hard up for something to do, you can help paint the other bedrooms. We want to be shipshape by next Monday."

"What I must do first is drive out and collect my stuff, and make my peace with Dave Brewer. I've paid for the week in advance, so he won't be the loser."

However, it was not Mr. Brewer who opened the door of the Doone Valley Hotel to him. It was Detective Inspector Horne, who said, in his placid West Country voice, "We'd been hoping you'd put in an appearance, Mr. Manciple. You've been what I might call off the map lately, haven't you?"

"I've been—" said Peter, and was stopped, at the last moment, by an absurd recollection of his mother saying, "When will you understand? The police are on the other side." He changed it at the last moment. "I've

134

been touring round a bit. Have there been some developments here?"

"You might call it a development, yes." The Inspector led the way through the hall and out into the yard at the back. "Perhaps you'd care to have a look at something we've got here."

He opened the door of what had once been the dairy, and Peter followed him in. With no presentiment of what he was going to see, the shock was uncushioned.

Where the milk churns and butter crocks had once stood lay little Dr. Bishwas. His body was covered by a blanket, but his face was exposed. His mouth was half open, and his lips had drawn away from his teeth in some convulsion of agony in the seconds before death had released him.

As Peter put out his hand to the blanket, the Inspector said, "No, sir. I wouldn't look, if I were you. The body's not in a very pleasant state."

"I was going to cover his face," said Peter with a shudder. "Where did they find him?"

"He was found half in, half out of the Culme, way out on the moor. It's a place where the water comes down fast, among the rocks."

"You mean he was drowned?"

"We haven't had the autopsy yet. But no, sir, I don't think he died by drowning. Nor I don't think he fell into the river by accident. Both his legs were broken, you see. Snapped across the shin. Hold up, sir. You'll feel better outside."

He steered Peter out into the yard. Peter fought down his nausea, and said, "Have you any idea how—or who—"

"That's two questions. Three, really. How, who, and why? That's why I was glad to see you, being perhaps the last person who spoke to the poor gentleman before this happened to him."

135

"Yes, I suppose I was."

"You told me about it when we spoke at the hotel in Tiverton. In outline, as you might say. I wondered if you could fill in some of the details. The best way would be if we ran over the ground. We could go in my car. Perhaps that would be more comfortable."

The Inspector's voice was fatherly, but Peter was beginning to tune in to the undertones. He realized that he had been subjected to a carefully prepared shock in order to loosen him up, and the realization went some way to restoring his balance.

As they drove past the Research Station, he answered the Inspector's questions slowly. Yes, he had had a telephone call that evening. He had picked up Dr. Bishwas at the corner of the boundary fence. Yes, just about here. Bishwas had been waiting for him, had got into the car, and they had driven along the track.

He could see the barn ahead of him, and a section of the track which had been marked with white tapes.

"We'll keep over to the left here," said the Inspector. "We've hopes we may be able to pick up some tire marks. The ground was still pretty soft."

"You'll certainly find *my* tire marks."

"We were thinking of the other car, sir. The indications are that the Doctor was brought back here after you'd gone. It'd be a handy sort of place if they wanted to question him. If you'd step out now, we'll have a look inside and you can go on with your story."

There was a very faint smell in the barn. It had not been there before. Was it blood or sweat? Or was it fear?

Sergeant Rix was in the barn. He greeted Peter as an old friend. "Funny how things always seem to start moving when *you* turn up," he said genially. And to the Inspector, "I found these bits of rope in the hay. The cut ends look quite new. And this."

It was a rolled-up ball of handkerchief.

"Could be blood on it."

The Inspector produced a cellophane bag and said, "Pop it in here, Sergeant."

They might have been two boys clearing up after a picnic.

"I imagine this was the place you had your little talk, sir."

"Yes," said Peter. "Dr. Bishwas sat up there. On the edge of that sort of manger thing. I was down here."

"Would you have been sitting down, too?"

"Most of the time I stood up. Part of the time I sat on that bale of hay. Is it important?"

"I was wondering whether anyone standing outside—at the back of the barn, say—could hear what you were saying."

"I imagine they could hear every word."

"You said something about a car stopping."

"Yes. I heard a car check at the end of the lane. It didn't actually stop."

"When would that have been?"

"About a quarter of an hour after we'd started talking. Maybe a bit more."

The Inspector was examining the inside of the barn with impersonal curiosity. Maybe he was seeing it as a photograph illustrating the book of the crime? To Peter it was a place of horror. A place where a little creature had been roped to the hayrack, gagged with his own handkerchief, and tortured to death. When would that fatuous Inspector and that oafish Sergeant stop pottering around, peering into things which no longer mattered? Come to that, why couldn't he just say, "To hell with you" and walk out?

He could hear a car coming up the track. The Sergeant looked out, and said, "It's the Army, sir." They went outside, the Inspector closing the door carefully behind them, as if to prevent the escape of any clues which he might have overlooked.

The new arrival was a light utility car with Army markings. The man who got out, though not dressed in uniform, had the look of a soldier. He had a round, weather-beaten face, protuberant eyes, and a gray waterfall of a mustache.

He said, "I'm Bob Hay. You must be Peter Manciple." He shot out a brown hand and Peter found himself shaking it. "If you've finished with Mr. Manciple, Inspector, I'd like a word with him."

"That's all right, Colonel. I think he's told us all he can. For the time being, that is."

"Jump in," said the Colonel. "I'll drive you back to the hotel." During the drive he said nothing. Peter studied his face, but it said nothing, either. It was the sort of face a young soldier started to cultivate at Sandhurst, adding a line here and a fold there as rank and experience increased, until at the end it was as perfect a piece of protective covering as the bronze masks behind which warriors of old had hidden their thoughts and fears.

As they were getting out, the Colonel said, "There seem to be a lot of people about. Is there anywhere we could have a little pow-wow?"

"The best place would be my bedroom."

When they got there, the Colonel annexed the only chair and Peter sat on the end of the bed. The Colonel said, "There's no need to go over everything you told Inspector Horne. I've read your statement. It seems quite staightforward. But there's one thing that puzzles me. That rendezvous you fixed with Dr. Bishwas. You drove straight there, I suppose? The opposition seemed to pick it up damned quick. You didn't tell anyone where you were going, by any chance?"

"I told Dave Brewer I was going out. I didn't say where."

138

"No one else? No one at all?"

"No. But I did leave a message."

"Oh. Who for?"

"For no one in particular. I thought the whole thing might be some sort of trap so I wrote a note explaining where I was going and who I was going to meet, and left it propped up on that mantelpiece."

The Colonel got up, examined the mantelpiece, and then walked across to the window. He said, "Never seen a room quite so easy to burgle. Asking for trouble. Do you realize the outhouse roof runs up to within two foot of your windowsill?"

"I suppose someone could have got in," agreed Peter. "But even if they did, they didn't read the letter."

"How do you know?"

"Because it was still unopened when I got back."

"And how do you know that?"

"Because," said Peter, "I used my eyes." He was beginning to find the Colonel's Orderly Room manner irritating. "It was still sealed. I saw it. As a matter of fact, I believe I've still got it somewhere." He opened his briefcase and found the letter. He also saw, reproaching him, his unfinished and undispatched report to Arthur Troyte.

The Colonel took the envelope, handling it gently. He said, "You should have used your fingers, Mr. Manciple, not your eyes. This letter has certainly been read. It's a very old trick. You can do it with a wire. In India, servants who were interested in your correspondence often used a thin sliver of bamboo. Push it in here, at the top. See the hole? Wind the letter round the bamboo, and pull it out of the hole. It goes back the same way, in reverse. If you run your fingers over the envelope—feel it—you can always tell if it's been tampered with."

Peter thought about this, and then said, "I wonder if

139

you'd mind being a bit more explicit, about things in general. If I'm involved in something, surely I've the right to know what it is."

The Colonel sat for quite some time, smoothing his hand down over his splendid mustache. Then he said, "Intelligent chap like you, I should have thought you'd have guessed by now."

"A bit here and a bit there. For instance, I'm pretty certain that Professor Petros is a fraud."

"Oh, what makes you think that? You're not an archeologist yourself, by any chance?"

"No. But I've got friends who are."

He told him about this. When he had finished, he had the impression that the Colonel was looking at him with a little more respect. He said, "You're right and wrong. Petros *is* an archeologist. Not a very well-known one, but genuine enough for the purpose of the man who hired him."

"A man who calls himself Stephen?"

"Good," said the Colonel, as though he was examining an O.C.T.U. candidate. "I give you good marks for that. Spotted Stephen, did you? A very dangerous character. A high-class professional. We know a good deal about Mr. Stephen."

"I thought his English sounded a bit stilted. What nationality is he?"

"No nationality. A citizen of the world. His father was a French Jordanian. His mother came from South America. He's married to a Lebanese-Arab girl. And probably to half a dozen other girls in different parts of the globe. He was educated at the American University in Beirut. And very well educated, too. A charming man. He'd quote Thucydides while chopping your fingers off one by one."

"If he's a thug, why don't you pull him in? Him and his fellow thugs? And deport the Professor?"

"Lots of reasons. First, because we've nothing specific to charge them with. Second, because if you start deporting professors, you get half the parlor pinks in the country round your neck. And third, because the situation was nicely balanced, very nicely balanced."

"But why should anyone be watching Dr. Wolfe?"

"Because," said the Colonel, "he'd shot his mouth off in that unfortunate article he wrote. You heard about that?"

"I heard about it. And I thought that anyone in their senses would have realized that it was a joke."

"Nobody would think it a joke if there was even an outside possibility of having their water supply biologically attacked. A big country like Canada or Russia—it'd be unpleasant but not fatal. A small country with a limited water supply like Israel, it'd be a very different thing. They could be wiped out. No—they had to watch him. And we had to watch them. One party made a move, the other party would make a move. Like a game of chess. And then—are you a chess player, Mr. Manciple?"

"Yes."

"I had a feeling you might be. I know very little about it, myself. My children tried to teach me once, but they soon gave it up. However, I remember one move. I forget what the technical term is, but it's when the king changes places with one of the rooks."

"It's called castling. You're only allowed to do it once, because it changes the whole pattern."

"Right," said the Colonel. "And that's exactly what happened when the guard Lewis got knocked down by some hit-and-run hog and killed."

"It was an accident, then?"

"No reason to think otherwise. But it certainly pressed the button. Dr. Wolfe took fright. His car went over the cliff at Rackthorn Point. When I saw that happen, I knew the watching period was over. What I didn't anticipate"— the Colonel directed a bilious look at Peter—"was the arrival on the board of a new piece. A remarkable piece who seemed able to move in any direction he chose."

"All right," said Peter. "Analogy understood. I hope I haven't done any irreparable harm to your private game."

"Harm?" said the Colonel with a snort. "You damned nearly upset the board. When I heard that Petros had invited you up to the dig, I hoped he might be going to cut your throat and bury you in one of his trenches."

Peter looked at the Colonel. He seemed perfectly serious.

"I can tell you why he didn't," Peter said. "He had other plans for me. He tied a string to my tail. That way I could do his work for him. If I happened to find Dr. Wolfe, then he found both of us."

He explained about the device on his car.

"A bleeper," said the Colonel. "Sound move, that." Ten marks for the Professor this time. "Where did you go after you left the dig?"

"Into Exeter. To have a word with Dr. Wolfe's solicitor, Roland Highsmith."

"Yes," said the Colonel. "That explains a lot. A cautious man, Mr. Highsmith. The moment you left he gave his staff a fortnight's holiday, shut up the office, and took his family touring. Without leaving any forwarding address. Could be in England, more likely on the Continent by now."

Peter stared at him. The Colonel continued placidly, as though he had said nothing unusual.

"The opposition must have assumed he knew something *and* had passed it on to you. They couldn't get hold of him, so they followed you to Tiverton, with the idea of extracting it from you. Only you changed your mind at the last moment and spent the night at your old school. That's why poor old Birnie got duffed up instead of you." The idea seemed to amuse the Colonel, but only for a moment. He said, "After that you disconnected the bleeper, I suppose, and they lost track of you."

Peter realized that the moment of decision had been reached. Either he took the Colonel entirely into his confidence—Cryde Bay, the Chine, old Mr. Garland, the lot—or he didn't.

It was a close thing. If the Colonel himself had been a little more forthcoming, Peter might have done it. As it was, he seemed to have been offered a neat way out of his difficulties. He said, with hardly a pause for thought, "That's right, I've been cruising round for the last few days trying to forget all about it."

"I don't expect you'll be wanted for the inquest on Dr. Bishwas. I can probably fix the Coroner. Accidental death. Walking on the moor. Fell into the flooded river. If there's any trouble, we can get an adjournment for further inquiries."

Wrap up little Dr. Bishwas in a neat package and forget about him. Peter felt his dislike for the Colonel growing.

"And that being so, Mr. Manciple, I've one last piece of advice for you. Follow the excellent example set by Mr. Highsmith. Get into your car, making sure that no other illicit attachments have been made to it, and drive off into the blue. Keep on the move for a week. By that time we should have cleared up the mess."

"That sounds like very good advice," said Peter. And when the Colonel had stumped out and Peter had closed the door behind him, he added, "But it doesn't mean that I'm going to take it."

Instead, he sat down on the end of his bed and devoted himself to thought.

In the course of his business, at the conclusion of any important interview—and he was under no illusion as to the importance of the one which had just concluded—he had found it a rewarding exercise to go over what had been said and attempt to analyze the motives of the speaker.

It was clear that the Colonel had either told him too much or too little.

He had spoken quite freely about the Professor and his camp followers; but only *after* discovering that Peter suspected them already. He had spoken in ambiguous terms about Dr. Wolfe. "His car went over the cliff." Did he know that Wolfe was still alive, or didn't he? More curious still, he had not asked Peter what, if anything, Roland Highsmith had told him. The solicitor's action in running away made it clear that *he* knew something. The fact that the attack had promptly been switched to Peter made it equally clear that the opposition must have suspected this. What precise part had Roland Highsmith been playing, before he removed himself so hastily from the board?

No immediate answer presenting itself, Peter moved on to the next item on the agenda: his own course of action. He was as adept in examining his own motives as those of other people, and he now subjected them to critical analysis.

First, he hadn't liked the Colonel's manner. But this was a minor matter. Secondly, there was simple professional pride in completing a job which had been entrusted to him. There was no dodging the fact that if he brought it to a successful conclusion it would be a very large feather in his cap. Thirdly, and most important of all, he was the only person, apart from the vanished Mr. Highsmith, who knew where Dr. Wolfe was.

This produced a difficult conflict of interests. He had a duty to save his firm the payment of a six-figure claim based on fraud. At the same time, he had no desire to hand over Dr. Wolfe to the attentions of the sort of people who had tortured Dr. Bishwas.

It seemed to Peter that if he played his cards properly he might be able to pull off a sensational double. He would have to strike a bargain. If Dr. Wolfe would give him a written quittance for the insurance money, Peter would take no further step in exposing him. He would leave him free to continue such plans as he had made for evading his enemies. He felt sure that these plans existed. The house in the Chine was only a staging post. Dr. Wolfe had had years to prepare his careful exit. There must be a permanent hiding place, organized on those long motor trips which he had taken; trips which had started in France, but might have finished anywhere in Europe or Asia.

It was a logical plan, and not, surely, unduly dangerous. Cryde Bay was a safe house. Owing to the lucky chance of Peter's car breaking down and the obduracy of a garage mechanic, he had got there untraced. Stop a minute and think. Had he taken any step, while he was there, which could lead to him? He had made one telephone call, to his mother's house in London. Even if— and Peter could not help smiling at the thought that he was now taking her fantasies seriously—even if by any chance her telephone had been tapped, his call had been made by direct dialing and not through the exchange, and would not, therefore, have been traceable.

All he had to do was to make quite certain that he was not followed on his way back to Cryde Bay. Then make his way, unobtrusively, after dark, to the house in the Chine. He could be back in London on the following day with a clear conscience and a job well done— surely there was no danger?

The knock on his door which added a full stop to the sentence was soft but insistent.

There were policemen downstairs, the inn was under the protection of Colonel Hay and his soldiers. It was broad daylight. All the same, it was with an effort that Peter got himself off the bed, stalked across to the door, and opened it. Anna was standing in the passage. She said, "Can I come in, please?"

"Of course," said Peter.

"And do you mind locking the door?"

She sat down on the bed, and when he had locked the door Peter went over and sat beside her. He could feel that she was shaking. It seemed a natural thing to put an arm around her.

He said, "What's wrong, Anna, what is it?"

She said, "This horrible place."

"You heard about Dr. Bishwas?"

"I saw him." Her body was shaken with a fresh convulsion. "When they brought him in. And then they took Kevin."

"Took him? Who took him?"

"The police. For questioning."

"Why on earth—?"

"Because they found out. He was out that night. With the car. When he told them what he'd been doing, they didn't believe him." She managed a smile. "It was so silly that they ought to have known it was true. It was the first fine night we'd had for a week, and he wanted to see if he could find his way by the stars. He had a star chart showing all the constellations. You know what a Boy Scout he is. He was going to drive straight out onto the moor and see if he could plot his way back by the stars. It was what they used to do in the desert, in the war, he says."

"The police have got no imagination," said Peter. He still had his arm around her. His personal analyst told him that this was a case of the male exhibiting dominance because the female he wanted was frightened and

146

temporarily defenseless. He ordered his personal analyst to pipe down, and said, "What would you like to do?"

"What I want to do is get away somewhere. Anywhere, as long as it's away from here. But I don't want to ditch Kevin."

"It shouldn't be too difficult. Let me think for a moment. Have you paid your bill?"

"We paid each week in advance."

"Good. Then pack whatever you're going to need for the next few days into one suitcase and bring it in here. Then go for a walk. I'll pick you up in that lane behind the church in half an hour's time."

"What about Kevin?"

"Before you go out, write a note for him and ask Dave Brewer to hand it to him personally when he gets back. Tell him that we'll contact him tonight, if he's allowed away, or tomorrow at the latest, through the tourist office in Cryde. Whoever gets there first leaves a message for the other."

Anna said, "I think you're wonderful," kissed him quickly on the mouth, slipped out from under his arm when he would have held her, and disappeared. Ten minutes later she was back with a small brown bag. Peter was sorry to see that she looked a lot more in charge of herself.

She said, "I've given Dave the note. He said not to worry. One of the policemen told him that Kevin would be all right—it was just routine questioning. Do you think we're being silly, running away like this?"

"No," said Peter firmly. "I think we're being very sensible."

He finished his own packing and walked downstairs. There was a uniformed policeman in the hall, who looked at him curiously, but made no move to stop him. He threw the two cases into the back of the car, waved goodbye to Mr. Brewer, who had come out to see him off, and drove away down the sleepy main street. His first stop was the garage, where he found Mr. Key and arranged to keep the Savoia for a further week. He said, "I had a bit of trouble with the distributor, but that's fixed now, and she's going like a humming top. Better fill her up."

Anna was waiting for him, sitting on the low wall that surrounded the churchyard. She jumped in beside him without a word, and they drove off.

"'So light to the croupe the fair lady he swung,'" said Peter to himself. "'So light to the saddle before her he sprung,'" and added, as he accelerated down the road, "'They'll have fleet steeds that follow, quoth young Lochinvar.'"

He had worked out a roundabout route, leaving Bridgetown on the west, turning south to Exford, and cutting back to Wheddon Cross and then north again to Dunster and the coast. The sun shone. Earth and sky were empty of menace.

Captain Andy seemed unsurprised at the arrival of a second guest and the promise of a third on the following day.

"Lucky I've done up two more bedrooms," he said. "I'm afraid you'll all have to clear out at the end of the week when the Porters and the Moxhams come with their children."

Peter said, "We'll be away before then." He wasn't thinking about the end of the week. He was only thinking of that night.

When he had undressed, he sat on his bed, in his pajamas, and thought about Anna. He had carried her away across the crupper of his horse. She was in the room next door to his. He could hear the faint sounds as she moved about and, he presumed, undressed. It was his fatal lack of experience, not the wall between them, that was the barrier. How did one start? Would it answer if he rushed in, grabbed hold of her, rolled her over onto her back—?

At this moment the door of his own room opened softly and Anna came in. He saw that she was wearing a knee-length pajama coat and nothing else.

She said, "I thought it would be polite to wait five minutes in case you were coming in to say good night to me." And as Peter put his arms around her clumsily, "Is this the first time ever, little Peter?"

"The first time," said Peter thickly.

"It's not at all difficult. Like dancing, only nicer. Do you want me to teach you?"

This made Peter angry. He said, "No. I'll do the teaching."

Later Anna said, "Gently, Peter, please. When I said dancing, I meant a slow waltz, not a fox-trot."

15

When Peter woke up in the morning, Anna had gone. He dressed slowly and was halfway through breakfast when he saw her coming up the front path. She was wearing a macintosh, her hair was in a mess, and a towel over her shoulder made it clear that she had been swimming.

"You're a lazy pair of slugabeds," she said.

"I'm too old for early-morning bathes," said Captain Andy with a grin. "*You* ought to have been out, though."

"Tomorrow I will," said Peter.

"Tomorrow it mayn't be bathing weather. The barometer's down three points. Like I told you, there's something bad coming up."

After breakfast Peter drove Anna into Cryde and they called at the tourist office. It was the same girl who had helped Peter a week before. She said, "Your friend called in early this morning. He left a message. The car's in the station car-park. He'll be there every hour, on the hour, until you turn up."

Since it was ten past eleven, they spent some time strolling round the town. The sunshine during the last two days had cheered the visitors up and there were red arms and peeled faces everywhere. At midday they went back to the station and found Kevin sitting in the Land-Rover.

He said, "Discharged, without a stain on my character. But it took them hours to do it."

"What happened?"

"At first they didn't believe a word I said. Star-gazing indeed! Tell that to the marines! I told them exactly where I'd been, and said if they went to look they'd probably be able to find my tire tracks. I'd nearly got bogged several times. They said tire tracks didn't prove anything—they could have been made at any time. Then I remembered I did talk to one character. It was in the middle of nowhere, and I was beginning to think I was totally lost, stars or no stars, when I spotted this chap. He was some sort of sheep warden or cowkeeper, and he put me on the track back to Huntercombe. Then they did agree to go and check up, and since his story tallied with mine they apologized and let me go."

"They apologized?"

"Certainly."

"I think that's a bad sign," said Peter. "What did you do next?"

"I went back to the hotel and found you had flitted. Dave gave me your message, and I decided to pull out, too, and spend the rest of the night in the back of the car. Somehow I couldn't fancy the hotel any more."

"I know," said Anna. "It had got creepy. And it was so nice, to start with. Never mind. Peter's found a lovely place now. It's kept by a man who looks like a retired pirate. Not that he's very old, really."

"The best pirates retired young," said Kevin.

As the day went on, the heat increased. After a suitable pause to digest Captain Andy's lunch, the three of them went down to bathe. Peter was a good swimmer, but he couldn't keep up with Anna and Kevin, who went straight out to sea, using a lazy, effortless crawl which took them through the water like a pair of seals. After tea Kevin went into the town to do some shopping and Peter took Anna off in the other direction. He knew exactly what he wanted, and found it beyond the cliff top—a small dip, turf-covered and masked on three sides by bushes.

Now that the barriers were down, everything was relaxed and easy and totally absorbing. Peter unbuttoned the boy's shirt that Anna was wearing and found nothing under it except a warm and friendly brown body, which he explored gently.

After a period of shameless enjoyment, Anna said, sleepily, "Wasn't it lucky they did eat that apple?"

"What apple?"

"Adam and Eve. If they hadn't eaten it, they might never have found out about anything. Think how dull that would have been. And no descendants. The whole experiment would have been abortive."

"Looked at in that way," said Peter, "the serpent was one of the great benefactors of the human race."

They thought about the serpent for a few minutes. Then Anna, who had been lying on her back looking up at the sky, rolled over onto her side and put her face down onto Peter's until the tip of her nose was just touching his. Then she said, "What are you up to, Peter?"

Peter tried to focus on her face, but it was too close to see properly. She rubbed the tip of her nose against his and said, "That's how Polynesians kiss. Isn't it nice? Don't change the subject."

"I wasn't changing the subject," said Peter feebly. "You were."

"All right. What are you up to? And don't tell me you came to this place by mistake."

"Well—"

"The truth, the whole truth, and nothing but the truth."

"Very well," said Peter. He hadn't really considered not telling her. He was sorting matters out into some sort of logical sequence.

When he had told her everything, she was silent for a long time. Then she said, "You are the most extraordinary person I've ever met. Do you mean to say that you've worked all this out yourself, inside your own head, and told no one about it?"

"I did mean to tell the Colonel."

"Why didn't you?"

"He annoyed me."

"That's not a serious reason."

"No."

"Well, then?"

"It just occurred to me that I didn't really know much about him. He was watching Dr. Wolfe. He seems to be hand in glove with the police. But what's his real job? What's he a colonel in?"

"Some sort of intelligence outfit?"

"Does that make him someone I've got to trust? When I was talking to him, he said when he'd heard I'd gone up to see Professor Petros he'd hoped the Professor would cut my throat and bury me. And, by God, I believe he meant it."

"I expect he did. Professionals never like amateurs taking part in their games."

"Particularly as they sometimes win."

Anna thought about this. Then she said, "I don't think this is a game you can win, Peter. In fact, I don't think it's a game at all. It's a private war. Outsiders who get mixed up in a private war always end up by getting hurt."

"When I was at school," said Peter, "one of my reports said, 'Manciple has an enviable facility for getting round and out of difficulties."

"You're an eel," agreed Anna. "A great, long, slippery eel. But even eels get caught sometimes. What are you going to do next?"

"Talk to Dr. Wolfe. Try to make him see sense."

"When?"

"Tonight."

He could feel that she was frightened. The idea that she should be frightened for him was intoxicating.

"It's all right," he said. "I shall be all right."

"It's not all right." Anna sounded angry. "It's mad and it's stupid. You still think it's some sort of game. It's not a game. You'll get hurt. You may even get killed. Don't you care?"

"Getting hurt and getting killed are two quite different things. Yes to the first. I do mind about getting hurt. The thought that someone might treat me the way they treated Dr. Bishwas—it doesn't just scare me. It turns my stomach."

"Well, then."

"But the idea of being killed doesn't worry me in the same way at all."

Anna sat up. She said, "Either you're crazy or you're shooting a line. Of course you don't want to get killed."

"I didn't say I *wanted* to get killed. I said I didn't mind about it, one way or the other. My father died last year. He drove his car straight into a telegraph pole, at high speed, and was killed instantly. Officially, it was an accident. That was the verdict of the jury at the inquest. Nobody's likely to find the truth out now. It hit us all in different ways. My brother, Jonathan, who was the one I was closest to, simply ran away. He went to New Zealand, married the first girl he met there, and turned his back on the whole thing. He writes to us occasionally. My mother ran away, too. She ran away from the real

154

world. She lives a fantasy life of her own. I was the most cowardly of the lot. I decided to opt out altogether."

"To kill yourself?"

"Yes."

"For God's sake, why?"

"I reasoned it out logically. I'd had a very happy twenty-two years. From that point on, things were bound to get worse, not better. The wise guest knows how to leave the party. It's only the fool who stays on until the glasses are all empty and his host is longing to put the cat out and go to bed."

Anna was sitting bolt upright, staring at him. She said, "Having proclaimed all these platitudes and half-truths to yourself, just what did you do about it?"

"Oh, I had every last detail worked out. I went to my doctor and complained of insomnia. He gave me a small bottle of sleeping pills. Ten, to be exact. He warned me never to take more than two. I put them carefully away. A month later I went again. I said that the pills had been a great help. I got another ten. Two months later I got ten more. Then I booked a room in a quiet hotel in Surrey. I had a good dinner, retired to my room, locked the door, and sat down to write a note explaining what I was doing and why I was doing it. It covered six foolscap pages. While I was writing, I was drinking the half-bottle of whisky which I'd brought with me. Then I started to swallow the pills."

"All thirty of them?"

"All thirty. I got them down, too. Helped by what was left of the whisky."

"Then?"

"Then I lay down and blacked out completely. I must have been out for about six hours. It was just getting light when I woke up. My first idea was that I was in heaven. My next idea was that I was going to be sick. I just got to the basin in time. I spent the rest of the night

155

being sick and wondering whether the top of my head was going to come off."

"And that was all?"

"That was all."

"*Thirty* sleeping pills?"

"No. Only ten. My doctor had guessed what I was up to. The second and third bottles weren't sleeping pills at all. Compressed bread. He told me afterward."

"You really meant it, didn't you?"

"Certainly."

"And during all the time it took you to collect those pills—three months—it never once occurred to you that what you were doing was stupid and cowardly?"

"Certainly not. It was entirely my own business."

"You really think that? You think your life's given you, like a twopenny bar of chocolate that you can eat as slowly or as fast as you like and throw away the wrapper?"

The anger in her voice surprised Peter. He said, "If my own life doesn't belong to me, who the hell does it belong to?"

"It belongs to everyone in your world. You're given it so that you can do something for your people. You may have to expend it, yes. But you expend it in defense of them, as young men do in a just war."

There was a very long silence, in which the syllable "war" seemed to hang. It was Anna who broke the silence. She said, "I am being too serious. All that you told me is in the past. It is all forgotten now."

"If you mean," said Peter, "have I any present intention of killing myself, the answer is 'no.' But it remains a matter of total indifference to me if someone else chooses to do it. Provided they do it quickly, and reasonably painlessly. But I'm not going to pull the trigger myself. Not now that I've met you. How soon can we get married?"

Anna came up onto one elbow and said, "What on earth makes you think that I am going to marry you?"

"Instinct."

"Your instinct has let you down. You'd be a dead loss as a husband."

"Why?"

"Because you don't live your life at all. You play it, as if it was sort of a game where you throw dice and go on six squares or back three. And if you happened to land on a square which said, 'Commit suicide,' you'd probably do it. It'd be a hell of a consolation to your widow to know that you'd done it because the rules said so."

Peter looked at her in admiration. A new and formidable person was developing in front of his eyes. He said, "Like should never marry like. We'll make a terrific combination."

"I can see it's no use arguing with you." Anna started buttoning up her shirt. "And I suppose you're going on with this particular game."

"In reason," said Peter. "But only in reason. I don't want to get involved with what's going on behind the scenes. Colonel Hay and Professor Petros can get on with it, and the best of British luck to them. I just want to finish the business I was sent down here to do. Prove, beyond any argument, that Dr. Wolfe is alive. I can only do that by talking to him."

"And you're going to do that this evening?"

"Yes."

"When?"

"From what I saw of him last time, he doesn't seem to be the type who goes to bed early. Last time I visited the house it was eleven o'clock and he was just starting to cook supper. I thought I'd look in around midnight."

"I think you're mad," said Anna. "Let's go and swim."

After supper that night the four of them sat in the Captain's room and looked out over Cryde Bay as the sun went down behind the cliffs to the west of the town. No one made any move to turn the lights on. Afterward, Peter was able to remember almost every word that was said as they sat there in the dusk while the day died and the lights of the town came out.

Kevin, it appeared, had a theory about Mother Melldrum, and wanted to try it out on Captain Andy, who seemed to know almost as much about *Lorna Doone* as he did.

"You remember that she had two houses. Her summer one was inland, near Hawkridge, above Tarr Steps, at the crossing of the River Barle."

"But at the fall of the leaf," said Captain Andy, "she set her face to the Bristol Channel."

"Right. And made for the Valley of Rocks, which everyone now identifies with that dip in the cliff which local people call the Denes. Wrongly, I'm convinced."

"Blackmore located it quite precisely. As I remember it, he said it was westward a mile from Lynton. And there *is* such a place, with the Castle Crag on one side and the Devil's Cheese Ring on the other."

"Quite so. But what you have to remember is that both those places were identified and named *after* the book became famous. People looked for them and found them because they were in the book."

"Then what's your idea?"

"I think Blackmore deliberately misled people. He had a strong personal affection for the places he was describing. The last thing he would want was hordes of trippers climbing over them. The places existed, all right, but not just where he put them. Now, I've found a spot which fits in far more accurately with his description. It's not one mile west of Lynton at all. It's three miles east, between Kipscombe Hill and Countisbury Bay. There's a rock formation there which is exactly like his description of the Devil's Cheese Ring."

They wrangled about this for some minutes. Anna said, "Aren't you forgetting that he was writing a novel, not a guidebook? He could make things up and put them where he liked."

"I don't entirely go with that," said Captain Andy. "Blackmore was the first of the documentary novelists."

Kevin looked up sharply. Then he said, "The second, surely. Defoe was the first."

"Defoe was a journalist. Blackmore was a schoolmaster. At least, if he wasn't actually a schoolmaster, he wrote like one."

"And what do you mean by that?" said Anna.

"Nothing to his discredit. I've met good schoolmasters and bad ones. It's just that when they write, they seem to think they ought to work in a bit of instruction."

Peter said, "Matthew Arnold was a sort of schoolmaster. But he was a bloody good poet, too. 'The sea is calm tonight, the tide is full, the moon lies fair.'"

Everyone thought for a moment. Kevin said, "'The Forsaken Merman.'" Andy said, "No. It's 'Dover Beach.' There's a bit in it, I remember, about the grating roar of pebbles when the tide hurls them up the beach. Very graphic, I thought that when I read it. Most of the beaches round here are pebbles."

"If I remember rightly," said Kevin, "'Dover Beach' proves Andy's point. The first bit's description, but wasn't there a moral at the end of it?"

"'Ah, love,'" said Peter,

> "*let us be true*
> *To one another! for the world, which seems*
> *To lie before us like a land of dreams,*
> *So various, so beautiful, so new,*
> *Hath really neither joy, nor love, nor light,*
> *Nor certitude, nor peace, nor help for pain:*
> *And we are here as on a darkling plain*

Swept with confused alarms of struggle and flight,
Where ignorant armies clash by night."

"I wish I could remember poetry," said Andy. "I can do bits I learnt when I was a kid, but you seem to lose the knack as you grow up."

"I wonder what he meant by 'ignorant armies,'" said Anna.

"The armies of the night," said Kevin.

There was a long silence after that. It was so quiet that they could just hear the waves turning over the shingle at the foot of the cliff.

Kevin broke the silence by struggling to his feet out of the low chair where he was sitting and saying, "I'm for bed. I spent last night in the back of a Land-Rover. I can hardly keep my eyes open."

A little later Captain Andy, too, yawned and got up. He said, "I'll lock up now. But in case you two were planning to go out for a moonlight stroll, there's a spare back-door key in the drawer of the table in the hall. Barometer down two points more. We're in for a real blow."

"I wonder why he should think we might be going out for a moonlight stroll," said Peter.

"He's not blind," said Anna. They listened to the Captain pottering about, putting things away and locking doors. When they heard him going upstairs, Anna came over and shared Peter's chair with him. There wasn't much room in the chair, but in a way this made everything more agreeable.

When they had settled down, Anna said, "Say that bit again. About the ignorant armies."

Peter said it again.

"Poor old Arnold," said Anna. "He certainly had got the grumps. No joy, no love, no light, no peace. Everyone barging round in the dark, wondering who was going to hurt who next. I wonder what had upset him. Did he have an unhappy love life, perhaps?"

"I can't remember whether he had a love life at all. There was one chap he was very fond of, but he went off to Florence and died young."

"Homo, I suppose."

"You've got a filthy mind," said Peter. "This was strictly a spiritual friendship."

"I've got a very dirty mind," agreed Anna. Some time later she looked at her watch and said, "You'll have to be starting." Then she put both arms right around him and said, "Be careful."

The night was dark and heavy with the mounting pressure of the coming storm. Peter, who was wearing soft-soled shoes and a dark pullover, padded quietly through the empty streets. As he was turning into the road by the station, he caught sight of a policeman, and saw the glow of his flashlight as he examined the shop doors at the far end of the road. His first reaction was to dive into a doorway, but he realized that if he was caught there, it really would look suspicious. He switched to the opposite pavement and walked boldly on. The policeman ignored him.

Five minutes later he was slithering down the steep bank behind the house in the Chine. He had met no one. There was a light on in the kitchen. The end of the chase was in sight.

As he stood on the path outside the kitchen door, brushing the sand and leaves from his clothes, it occurred to him to wonder, for the first time, just exactly what he was going to say. Experience had taught him that when interviewing a stranger the opening gambit was most important. The traditional "Dr. Wolfe, I presume"? Or was that impertinent? Perhaps "I have been so looking forward to meeting you."

He knocked on the door, gently at first and then more firmly. Nothing happened. The house seemed to be completely silent. There were two possible explanations: either Dr. Wolfe had gone to bed and had forgotten to turn out the kitchen light, or he had gone out and was intending to return.

Peter tried the door and found that it was unlocked. He opened it gently and stepped in. The bearded owner of the house was seated in a tall-backed wooden chair at the head of the kitchen table. He was staring placidly at Peter, who thought for a moment that he was about to say something, but only for a moment. He had been shot, five or six times, in the chest. The heavy bullets which had nailed him to the chair had made a black puddle on his shirt front.

Peter wrenched his eyes away and felt for something to hold himself up. His fingers closed on a cold surface and he found he was clinging to the edge of the sink.

He began to think, painfully, as though the shock had affected the motor inside his head. He had told himself, a few minutes before, that the end of the chase was in sight. In sight? For God's sake, it was finished. Was there anything left for him to do? As his brain began to work again, his senses cleared and he heard the cars coming. There were more than one, and they were coming fast.

Peter went out through the kitchen door, leaving it half open, threw himself at the bank, and started to scrabble up it. Going up was more difficult than coming down. He had reached the wire when he heard the cars stop, heard doors opening and slamming shut, and footsteps running up the path. He jerked himself under the wire and lay flat in the deep bracken.

Someone was coming around the back of the house. He caught a glimpse of a policeman's helmet. The footsteps stopped. A voice which sounded quite close to him shouted, "In here, Sergeant, round the back." More footsteps hurrying. Peter turned over onto his front and started to wriggle.

By the time he reached the top of the bank, the tempo of the activity below him had slowed. People were talking, not shouting; walking, not running. Lights were being turned on in upstairs rooms. Peter crawled on hands and knees to the cinder path. When he got there, he tried to stand up, but his legs were unstable and his heart was beating double time. He was tempted to sit down, but realized that if he did so he might not get up in a hurry.

"Walk," he said. "Walk, and keep walking."

It took him five minutes to reach the station and another ten to get to the Seven Seas. He had seen no one, and, as far as he could tell, no one had seen him.

Anna was in his bed. She sat up when he came in, switched on the bedside light, and said, "Good lord, Peter, what's happened?"

Peter sat down on the end of the bed and started to giggle. There was an edge of hysteria behind the laughter.

Anna said coldly, "If there's a joke, you might share it."

"Not really a joke," said Peter. "Just a thought. Husband coming back late from the office. Wife waiting up for him, says, 'What have you been up to, dear? You look all in.'"

"You look as if you've been for a cross-country run."

Peter started to take off his trousers. "They don't look too good," he agreed.

"I'll brush them properly in the morning. Get un-

163

dressed and come into bed. Whatever's happened, don't worry about it."

With one of her arms around him and her body pressed up against his, it was easy to tell her everything, and when he had told her, it was easy to stop worrying; and easy to go to sleep.

16

When Peter woke up, the light was back in the sky. He lay still, for fear of waking Anna, who was sleeping peacefully beside him.

In the distance the clock of St. Barnabas' Church beat out four muffled strokes. A few hours' sleep had cleared his mind of the last dregs of shock and emotion.

He had started thinking again.

Most of his thoughts were on Anna and on Kevin. He had long since ceased to believe that they were at the Doone Valley Hotel by chance. Anna had said a lot of things to him, many of them loving and most of them probably lies. But on one occasion, provoked by him, she had spoken the truth. He was sure of that. It was when she said to him, "Your life belongs to everyone in your world." And more specifically, "You're given it so that you can do something for your people." Who were *her* own people? Surely not the wild Irish of the north among whom she claimed to have spent her youth. And to what cause was she wedded so passionately that she would give her life for it?

He looked down at the face on the pillow beside him. Sleep strips away the daytime mask. The stern tyrant becomes indecisive; the mild pedant becomes a stubborn fool. This was the face of a fighter, no question. But a fighter in what war?

Anna stirred in her sleep and muttered something unintelligible.

He thought about her last words to him: "Don't worry." *Was* there anything to worry about? It was with a feeling of liberation that he realized that his job was surely done. Sooner or later that bullet-riddled body would be identified as Dr. Wolfe. He had an idea that all workers in confidential government employment were fingerprinted. Once the identity of the body was firmly established, it would point only too clearly to Wolfe's killers.

Peter's own employers would be pleased, too. Since Dr. Wolfe had died on dry land, the insurers would not have to pay out on their policy. The only person to suffer would be his sister, Lavinia. She and her family of dogs.

He fell asleep again on this comfortable thought, and was awakened by an exclamation from Anna. She had got out of bed and was looking out of the front window. She said, "I'm beginning to think you shouldn't have run away. It would have been much more sensible to stay put."

"And let the police find me?"

"Why not? They could never have supposed that you shot him."

"I did what my instincts told me to do. They said, 'Scarper.' So I scarpered."

"Your instincts gave you bad advice."

"I didn't want to be involved in a murder case."

"How do you know you're not involved?"

"I'm only involved if they find out I was there."

"And suppose they do."

"How can they? No one saw me, going or coming back. I'm fairly sure of that."

"What about that policeman?"

"He didn't even turn round when I went past."

"He didn't need to turn round. He could see your reflection in the shopwindow."

Peter stared at her. He said, "You're full of uncomfortable thoughts this morning. Anything else?"

"When you went into the house, were you wearing gloves?"

"I haven't got any gloves."

"What did you touch?"

"The door handle, I suppose. And, oh, yes, when I saw Dr. Wolfe's body, I grabbed the edge of the sink."

"You'll have left plenty of prints behind."

"Suppose I did. How do you suggest they're going to identify them? My prints aren't on record. They'd have to suspect me first. And why should they?"

"I don't know *why* they should," said Anna. "But ten minutes ago a policeman walked up to the door and rang the bell. He's talking to Captain Andy now. No—he's finished. He's going."

Peter shot out of bed and across to the window. A solid blue-clad back was disappearing out of the front gate.

"Good God," said Peter. "I wonder what he wanted."

"Get dressed, and we'll find out."

They found Captain Andy finishing his breakfast. Kevin, it appeared, had departed in search of Mother Melldrum's cave.

"The policeman?" said Andy. "I sent for him. We had a burglary last night. You were in very late. You didn't hear anything, I suppose?"

"Nothing at all," said Peter. "How did he get in? What did he take?"

"He got in by busting open my office window. He turned all my papers upside down, and took nothing at all. There's an old cigarette case missing, but I might have lost that somewhere else."

"Why would a burglar want to look through your papers?"

"He might have been looking for money," said Anna.

"I keep my money in the bank," said Captain. "Too many bad types about these days. Did you hear what they did to Roland Highsmith?"

"Did to him?" said Peter with a sinking feeling.

"Not to him. He's away on holiday. To his office in Exeter. They burnt it down. It was on the eight o'clock news."

"Who on earth would do a thing like that?"

"Search me."

"It could have been an accident, I suppose."

"Not according to what they said on the news. The people who did it must have taken most of the night about it. They went through every room, including the strongroom. Turned all the papers out onto the floor and soaked them in petrol, then set light to the place. It went up like a Guy Fawkes bonfire. Lucky it was a corner house and the wind was the right way or it would have taken out half the street. According to what it said on the news, the inside was red hot."

"Poor Mr. Highsmith," said Anna. "Suppose he doesn't hear about it."

"Someone's sure to tell him. Never any shortage of people to give you the bad news. If you want a bathe you'd better grab one this morning. It'll be your last chance for a bit, I reckon. 'Build up slow, big blow.'"

A line of black clouds was forming out to sea, as solid and clear-cut as a range of hills, with a few dirty rags flying above the crest. The pressure of the coming storm and of his own uncertainties combined to keep Peter on edge. The news of Dr. Wolfe's killing must surely be out by now. The morning papers would have missed it, and the earliest London evening papers only got to Cryde Bay by teatime. There was not much conversation at lunch. Anna seemed to have her private worries.

At four o'clock Peter walked down to the station to see if the London evening papers had arrived. The solitary taxi driver in the forecourt aroused himself from slumber long enough to say, "No papers today. Strike or something." Peter walked back into the town. By the time he got there, the sky was black.

As he was passing Messrs. Highsmith and Westall, a police car drew up and Mr. Quarles got out of it and walked into the office. Peter caught a glimpse of his face as he crossed the pavement. He looked white and shaken. On a sudden impulse, Peter followed him in.

Mr. Quarles turned, recognized him, and said, "I'm sorry, I'm closing the office. I can't handle any business now." He collapsed into a chair and sat there, his mouth opening and shutting, as though he had more to say but someone had shut off the sound.

Peter slid home one of the bolts in the street door and came and sat down beside him. After a few minutes Mr. Quarles seemed to pull himself together a little. Peter said, "I wonder if you'd care to tell me what's happened. I can see you've had a shock."

"It's too much. My heart isn't strong. I shall have to go away. As soon as I can get hold of Mr. Highsmith. I shall have to ask him to find someone else. A younger man. You're not, by any chance, a qualified solicitor yourself?"

"No. But I'm an old friend of Mr. Highsmith's. I was talking to him only a day or two ago."

"Terrible," said Mr. Quarles. "You heard about the fire. It was on the wireless."

"Yes, I heard about the fire."

"And then this, on top of it."

"I'm not sure that I understand."

169

"His partner, Mr. Westall. Shot down. Murdered in cold blood. I had to see him. Mr. Highsmith being away, I was the only person they could turn to. I'm sorry to be making such a fuss about it, but you do understand, don't you? It was the one thing coming on top of the other."

Peter said, in a voice almost as shaken as Mr. Quarles', "Are you telling me that— Did Mr. Westall live at number eight, the Chine?"

"Certainly. Mr. Highsmith bought it for him when he had that nervous breakdown last month. He thought it would be a nice place for him to retire to. Peace and quiet." Mr. Quarles nearly choked on the thought. "And now this."

As he spoke, a violent gust of wind, coming straight from the sea, shook the flimsy framework of the house. It was the advance guard of the storm. Mr. Quarles seemed past caring. If the building had folded up around him, it would hardly have added to his sense of catastrophe.

Peter said, "I suppose you knew Mr. Westall well?"

"Oh, very well. He's only grown that beard since his illness, but I had no difficulty in recognizing him. None at all."

"When you say that Mr. Highsmith bought the house for him, I take it you mean that he did the legal work?"

"The conveyancing, yes. He handled it all himself from the Exeter office. He was a very considerate man. Look what I'm saying! He *was* a very considerate man. Wasn't that a stupid thing to say? It sounds as though I thought Mr. Highsmith was dead, too." When Peter said nothing, Mr. Quarles looked up, the panic clear in his eyes. "You don't think—"

"There's no reason to think that anything has happened to Mr. Highsmith at all. As soon as he hears the news, he'll be back."

170

"You really think so?"

"Certainly. And if you're shutting up for the day and have got your car here, I wonder if you'd mind running me back to my hotel. It's at the far end of the town, and I came out without a raincoat."

They could see and hear the rain coming down in flung sheets. Water was already trickling under the door.

"Of course I'll run you back. I see my secretary's gone already. Sensible girl. But I wonder— It's asking a lot of a comparative stranger, I know, but would you mind coming back with me to my place?" Peter stared at him. "It's a bungalow a little way outside the town, and it's rather isolated. I just don't fancy facing it alone." Before Peter had time to say anything, he hurried on, "It must be some gang who set fire to our office and killed Mr. Westall. I suppose we've offended them in some way. I thought the best thing would be if I went to stay with my married sister at Minehead. Until the police have— well—rounded them up."

Having delivered himself of this extraordinary statement, Mr. Quarles sat looking pleadingly at Peter.

"Of course," said Peter slowly. "I'll come with you if you like. I think you're exaggerating the danger."

"I'd be much happier if you would. Just until I can telephone my sister."

Mr. Quarles' car was parked behind the office. Although it was only a few paces from the door, they were soaked as they ran to it. It was like stepping under a shower bath. With wipers going and headlights blazing, they splashed off down the road.

No gang awaited them in Mr. Quarles' modest residence. Peter took off his coat and hung it up to dry in front of the electric fire while Mr. Quarles went off to telephone his sister in Minehead.

He came back looking worried. "They say the storm has affected the line. They're sure it will be through

171

again quite shortly. I'll put the kettle on and we'll have a cup of tea whilst your coat's drying."

His anxiety to keep Peter with him was apparent. Peter looked out of the window. The first fury of the storm had abated a little, but the rain was still sheeting down. He was going to need Mr. Quarles' car to get him home. His host bustled about getting tea ready, and after tea entertained him with a series of photograph albums. In more than one of them he was able to point out Mr. Westall. Any lingering doubts which Peter might have felt were dispelled. The man he had glimpsed through the window and whom he had later found shot was, without question, Roland Highsmith's partner.

But how, why, where had he gone wrong? There was a catch somewhere, if only he could put his finger on it.

"—a very happy family," said Mr. Quarles.

"Yes," said Peter. He was guiltily aware that it was some time since he had actually listened to what Mr. Quarles was saying.

"I imagine that it's much the same in your case?"

"Well—" said Peter. Was Mr. Quarles referring to his own family, or to the firm? He was saved by the telephone bell. The lines to Minehead had been restored. Mr. Quarles spoke to his sister, apparently with satisfactory results, and set about packing a bag. By seven o'clock they were heading back for Cryde Bay.

With an old raincoat, which Mr. Quarles had loaned him, over his head and shoulders, Peter splashed up the path of the Seven Seas Guest House and opened the front door. Anna was in the hall and had her back to him. She was speaking on the telephone, and the one sentence which Peter heard was certainly not in English.

As she turned and saw him standing there, there was a clatter of footsteps on the path and Captain Andy, also with a raincoat over his head, arrived at the double.

172

"God, what weather!" he said. "I'm soaked."

"You told us it was coming," said Anna. "Next time I'll believe you."

But while she spoke she was looking at Peter.

"I went out to get us something to eat for supper. Most of the shops shut up when they saw this packet coming. But I managed to get some sausages. We'll eat in the kitchen. It's on the sheltered side of the house, and we'll be able to hear ourselves speak."

"Is your brother back yet?" asked Peter.

"Not yet."

The Captain looked thoughtful. "If he's out on the open moor in this, he'd be well advised to stay put. It's too big to last. It'll be over before morning."

Anna said, "If I was out there, I'd certainly stay where I was. Marshes and bogs and quicksands terrify me. Can't I help you with the supper?"

"You can make the toast," said the Captain.

There was a flash of lightning, almost blue in its electrical menace. The Captain started counting: "—eight, nine, ten." Then the thunder.

"Still some miles away," he said, "but coming fast."

A second flash, and the hall light went out.

"Supper by candlelight," said the Captain. "Lucky I laid in a stock of them."

It was a difficult meal. Anna did her best, but it was clear that she was worried about Kevin. Peter was busy with his own thoughts. Fortunately, Captain Andy was in high spirits. The storm seemed to inspire him. Between the flashes of lightning and the answering crashes of the thunder he regaled them with reminiscences of other storms he had seen and suffered.

"The most comfortable place to be," he said, "is way out to sea. You can laugh at a thunderstorm when you're at sea." Peter had a mental picture of the Captain standing at the helm of his yacht laughing at the thunder. "The worst place to be is in an airplane. You've every excuse to be frightened if you run into an electric storm when you're flying."

"I can be frightened in an airplane even without a storm," said Peter.

After supper, when the vanguard of the storm had rolled away inland, the Captain armed himself with a torch and went down into the cellar to have a look at the fuses. He returned to report failure.

"It's not just us," he said. "The storm must have wrecked a pylon or something. I'll get us a cup of coffee. Then, little though I fancy the idea, I have to go out and attend a meeting of the Town Council. There's an ugly rumor that they intend to make me a councillor. I shall have to quash it."

"Why?" said Peter. "You'd make a very good councillor."

"I'm not civic-minded, and I'm only here four months in the year. By the way, there's quite a bit of water in the cellar, but I don't think it's doing any harm. If it gets a lot worse, send for the fire brigade. The number's one of the ones written up over the phone."

While he spoke he had been putting on waterproof leggings, a raincoat, and an outsize pair of boots. Now he clapped a sou'wester onto his head and plodded out into the hall.

Peter and Anna sat looking at each other. They heard the front door slam shut.

"Well," said Peter at last. He was glad of the candles. It would have been a lot more difficult in a blaze of electric light.

"So you heard?"

"Yes, I heard. What language was that?"

"I am a citizen of Israel. I was speaking to other Israelis. Naturally, we spoke in our own tongue."

"You and Kevin?"

174

"My husband is also an Israeli."

"Yes," said Peter. "I see."

There was a long silence, broken by the explosions of the thunder. At each thunderclap the candles flickered and their shadows danced in sympathy.

"You mustn't be angry," said Anna. "I tried to tell you once. This is war. In war, deceptions are necessary."

"And I was the dupe."

"But not an unwilling dupe."

"Not unwilling," agreed Peter, with a faint flicker of a smile. "Certainly not unwilling."

"You must not be angry with me, because I want your help. And I want it now. We have to find Kevin."

"Go out and look for him?"

"Yes."

"We should be much more likely to get bogged down than he is. He's got a Land-Rover with four-wheel drive."

"It's not a question of getting bogged down. I know where he is, and I am fearful for him. Since he has not returned, it seems likely that they have caught him."

"But," said Peter, "if that's right—Petros has five or six men with him. What could *we* hope to do?"

"There is no question of you doing anything. All I ask you to do is to drive me there in your car. If there is anything to be done, I will do it."

Peter had a feeling that he was hearing her real voice for the first time. It was the voice of a trained soldier speaking of duty. A voice which invites no argument, brooks no delay. He was far too intelligent not to understand what she was asking him to do. It was nonsense to suppose that he was going to sit in the car and let her go forward into danger on her own. If he agreed, this was the moment when he stepped across the sideline and onto the field. So far he had been a spectator in the secret, violent game that was being played across the wastes of Exmoor. From this point he would himself be a player. The thought filled him with equal measures of alarm and distaste.

He said, "We'd better rustle up what waterproof clothing we can."

Ten minutes later the Savoia was splashing down the road, headed southwest for Bridgetown and the open moor.

17

Anna had her head down over the map, which she was studying with the aid of a pencil torch. She said, "When we get to the next turning, we could be in sight of their huts. You will have to turn out your lights."

"If I turn out the lights, we'll end up in the ditch."

"Turn out your headlights, then, and go very slowly."

They crept along in low gear. After a few minutes Peter said, "I remember that farmhouse. We're pretty close to the turning up to the camp. We must find somewhere to put the car. Somewhere where it won't be bogged."

They found a place two hundred yards past the farm. It was a gateway leading into a field. Peter said, "Open the gate, if you can. I'll go past the opening and back the car in."

He managed this maneuver without disaster. The entrance to the gate felt solid, and sloped outward toward the road. Peter backed the big car far enough in for the gate to be shut again. The hedges on both sides gave cover. He turned out the side lights and locked the doors, and they started out. He noticed that nothing was now said about him staying in the car and Anna going forward alone.

The rain was lighter, hitting them in bursts as the wind blew it. They kept to the inside of the hedge and marched steadily forward. Peter counted their steps as they went. Four hundred, five hundred. They must be well past the turning up to the camp by now. Six hundred.

They had climbed two wire boundary fences and burst their way through one hedge. An opening showed on their right. Peter touched Anna on the arm.

She had found an old windcheater of Captain Andy's, and was wearing jeans tucked into her socks. Every stitch of her clothing was sodden with water and her feet must have been caked with mud, but she was moving easily, as though night was her element.

When she felt Peter's touch, she nodded. They turned through the opening, crossed the road and a deep ditch on the far side, and started to climb. Although uphill, it was easier going, over turf with patches of bracken and heather. Twice Peter put a foot into a rabbit hole and went forward onto his knees. Anna seemed to make her way by instinct.

When they nearly fell into the open excavation, Peter was able to pick up his bearings.

He said, speaking quietly, although the wind must have killed any sound at six paces, "This path leads back to the camp. There's a sharp lefthand turn by a tree just before you get there. Better stop there and have a look."

Anna nodded again. They moved quietly forward until they reached the tree. Both of them were seeing better now.

"That's the office hut. The barn is beyond it. That's where they keep the exhibits. And you can just see the caravans, at right angles to the barn."

Anna said, "I can see something else." She pointed. "There. Can you see it?"

"What are you looking at?"

"In the doorway of the barn. It's a man. There. Can you see now?"

A faint spark of light, quickly gone.

"He's a sentry. A bad and careless sentry. He's smoking a cigarette. Each time he turns his head—"

"Yes," said Peter, "I see him now. If they've taken the trouble to post a guard in weather like this, I know where Kevin is."

"In the barn?"

"Not just in the barn. As you go through the door, there's a smaller door on your right. Let me think about it for a moment. Yes. There's no lock on the inner door. It's shut by big, old-fashioned bolts at the top and bottom. I can't remember if the barn door had a lock or not. If anything, it would be a padlock."

"If it's a padlock, the sentry will have the key."

"I expect so."

"Then stay where you are. I shall not be long."

"Hadn't I better—"

Anna turned in the darkness and said, with her face close to his: "You have done very well so far, little Peter. Please do as I say. There is no time for arguments and discussions. I understand this work better than you do." Then she had gone.

Peter could follow her progress until she was almost up to the barn. Then the small blackness that was the girl melted into the greater blackness of the barn and was swallowed up.

Five slow minutes passed.

He thought he saw a flurry of movement in the barn doorway, but no sound reached him. Then, for further long minutes, nothing more. Peter strained his eyes, concentrating on the doorway. But the rain, as it eased, had thickened. It was almost a curtain of mist. He was blind as well as deaf.

He jumped as Anna loomed out of the darkness. Her

179

breath was coming in harsh gasps and she put a hand on his arm to steady herself. Peter said, "You couldn't open the door? Kevin wasn't there?"

"I opened the door. Kevin is there. You will have to come and help me. Quick, please."

Peter followed her down the path. The waiting had stiffened him up and he stumbled once or twice. Anna turned around and said in a venomous whisper, "Watch what you're doing. There are people very near."

Peter saw the man on the ground just in time to avoid stepping on him. He was sprawled flat with head twisted away from them toward the line of caravans parked beyond.

It was pitch black inside the barn, and the rain on the corrugated iron roof drowned all sounds. Anna flicked on her pencil flashlight once, to show him that the inner door was open, and once again when they were inside.

When the archeologists had taken over the barn, they had moved all the farmer's stuff into the inner room, which was jam-packed with rusty machinery, hurdles, and farm rubbish. Kevin was crouching on the floor, with his back against an iron drum. He looked up for a moment at the light, and then his head dropped again, as though there was no strength in his neck.

"He is not tied," said Anna, "but he cannot use his legs."

"I can walk if you help me," said Kevin. The words came out thickly.

They got an arm each under his arms and hoisted him to his feet. He was able to help them a little, but each time he put his feet to the ground they heard him draw his breath in. They had reached the outer door of the barn when the light in the nearest caravan went on, throwing a pale yellow beam through the dancing rain.

Someone was moving inside the caravan, but he was

moving without haste. Anna said, "Come on," and they stumbled up the track. Peter expected any moment to hear a door flung open, a shout, feet thundering in pursuit. Nothing happened. They moved away with maddening deliberation. "Faster," said Peter to himself, "for God's sake, faster."

They reached the tree. A few steps more and they were out of sight. Peter could feel the sweat mixing with the rain and running down his forehead and into his eyes.

The ascent of the path was a long agony. Anna said something to Kevin in their own tongue and he guessed she was encouraging him. When they reached the excavation, they would turn left and from that point onward it would be downhill and easier going.

Kevin was weakening. He was becoming more and more of a dead weight between them. Only by an unimaginable effort of courage and willpower had he kept his burned and twisted body moving at all.

"We shall have to stop," said Peter.

"When we get to the ditch," said Anna between her teeth.

How they covered the last nightmare stretch Peter never knew. Fortune must have been on their side. One foot in a rabbit hole, a single slip would have wrecked their frail convoy. When they slid into the deep ditch on the near side of the road, it was clear that they could go no farther. They were in harbor of a sort. They crouched together in the dark.

When they had got a little of their breath back, Peter said, "Did you kill that man?"

Anna was busy attending to Kevin. She said, "Yes," without looking up. Peter wanted to say, "How?" but it was not a question of immediate importance. He supposed that if you knew how to kill people and had the right sort of weapon, it was easy to come up behind a

181

man, in the night and the storm, and break his neck. What was puzzling him was that he was certain he had seen the dead man before. Then he remembered. It was one of the young men who had been in the car outside Miss Wolfe's house—the car which had followed him down to Sudbury, how many days, how many weeks, how many years ago?

When he told her, Anna seemed uninterested. "It is very likely," she said. "His name is Ramon. Stephen is his older brother. It is not important. I am trying to think what we shall do next."

"We stay here," said Peter. "It's not very comfortable, I agree, but it's safe. In a few hours it will be light. We'll stop the first car that comes along."

"If we do not get Kevin into shelter, he will be dead by morning. Also, as soon as it is light, they will follow our tracks down here and find us."

"Then I'd better fetch the car."

Anna, who had been looking back the way they had come, said, "No. It is too dangerous. If they have found Ramon, they may be guarding the road by now. I shall have to fetch help. I have friends not far from here. That farm we passed, had it a telephone?"

Peter thought about it. He had seen the farm by daylight. He said, "Yes. There was a line of wires going to it."

"Then wait here. I will not be too long."

She crossed the road and disappeared into the driving rain. Not too long? That might be anything from half an hour to three hours. Kevin was crouched with his knees up to his chin, as if he was trying to hold his damaged body together. From time to time he shook with some violent spasm of pain or shock. Apart from that, he was quite still. Peter wondered if there was anything he could do to make either of them more comfortable. There was already some water in the ditch, but, being under the overhang of the bank, they could avoid the worst of it, and it gave them some shelter from the driving rain. If Anna was not too long, Kevin might hold out. Who were her friends? And how could Kevin be so certain that they were not far away? Then he remembered the telephone call she had been making from Captain Andy's house. That was probably the answer.

Hours crawled by. Peter looked at his watch. He had noted the time when Anna left them. Two o'clock. It was now twenty-five minutes past two. Twenty-five minutes? His watch must be wrong.

Some time after this Peter became aware that a cold light was shining into the ditch. He scrambled to his feet. It was the moon. Captain Andy had been right. The storm had blown itself out. The rain had stopped, and the black clouds were scudding in full retreat across the sky. A sound made him look down. Kevin had raised his head off his chest.

"It's all right," said Peter. "Just hang on. Anna will be back soon."

"Anna," said Kevin.

"That's right. She's gone for help. She'll be back soon." Peter sat down again and put one arm round Kevin, who was shaking.

"Anna," said Kevin again, more urgently. He was fumbling in the pocket of his windcheater. After agonizing seconds he drew something out and pressed it into Peter's hand. It was too dark for Peter to make out what it was he was holding. It felt square and metallic. He stowed it away in his own pocket. Since Kevin seemed to be anxious about it, Peter said, "It's all right, Kevin. I'll give it to Anna as soon as she gets back."

The moon, which had been playing hide-and-seek behind the clouds, shone for a moment on Kevin's upturned face, and Peter saw the life going out of him. He saw the eyes glazing and the mouth coming open as the muscles slackened. Then Kevin gave a long and very gentle sigh, and his body, in Peter's arms, changed from something living to something without life in it.

Peter sat for long minutes unmoving. He had never seen death so close before. He had no idea what to do. He disengaged himself gently and stood up. As he did so, he noticed something so unexpected, and so grotesque, that it made his heart jump.

It looked as if someone, playing an obscene joke, had put a cigarette into Kevin's dead mouth.

It was a tiny roll of paper, in size and shape not unlike a cigarette. Kevin must have been holding it, hidden, inside his mouth. It looked so indecent that Peter got out his wallet and stowed the paper away in it. Then he got up, climbed out onto the road, and started to think again.

Kevin was dead. There was nothing more he could do. If Anna had friends, they could look after her. For himself, he wanted no further hand in the business. It was as he started to move that the men came through the gap in the hedge on the other side of the road. Two together, and then three more, and then Anna. They stood looking at him.

Peter said, "Kevin's dead."

Anna said nothing. She came forward and scrambled down into the ditch. One of the men went with her. He had a flashlight. Peter looked at the men standing on the road. Two were quite young. Two were a little older. They were waiting, patient and unexcited, as if standing about at three o'clock in the morning beside a dead man in a ditch was part of an understood routine.

The man with the flashlight climbed out. From the way he spoke, Peter knew that he was the leader. Then the others climbed down, one at a time, into the ditch. Anna spoke a few words to each of them. It seemed to

Peter like some form of ritual. When it was over, Anna came back onto the road. She said, her voice carefully under control, "Did he say anything to you? Before he died?"

"Yes," said Peter. He felt in his top pocket and got out the thing that Kevin had handed to him. It was a plain gunmetal cigarette case. "He wanted you to have this."

Anna turned the case over in her fingers. "Did he say why?"

"Just that he wanted you to have it. Perhaps there is something in it."

Anna opened the case. The other men watched her impassively. It was empty.

The leader said something. The men started to move across the ditch and up the hill. Peter said, "What are you going to do?"

Anna said, "We are going to teach these people a lesson they will not forget. I think it would be better if you stayed here. We shall not take long."

Then she was gone, leaving Peter standing beside the road. The incident had not lasted five minutes.

It was all very well, said Peter's monitor, coming sharply to life again, it was all very fine and large telling him that it would be better if he stayed where he was. Better for whom? Better than what? Better than following that savage commando up the hill, no doubt. But when they had finished their bloody business? He had seen their faces clearly in the moonlight. Might it not occur to them that he alone was in a position to identify them? No doubt Anna would tell them that he had helped her. But they were professional killers, men who would hardly allow sentiment to overrule considerations of their own safety. Also, they were the men who had killed Mr. Westall. Of that he felt an illogical but absolute conviction. The fact that they had wiped him out in error made the killing seem more, not less, horrible.

Ignorant armies clashing by night. No, his mind was made up. He was going while the going was good. For the second time he started to move. And for the second time he stopped.

Something was coming along the road. With a curse he slithered back into the ditch.

It was a five-ton Army truck, traveling slowly and without lights. It came to a halt ten yards short of where he was crouching. The door beside the driver's seat opened and a man jumped out. He was dressed in regulation combat dress, camouflage jacket, battle-dress trousers, and ankle boots, and was carrying what looked like a machine pistol slung over one shoulder.

He went around to the back of the truck and said, "All out, Sergeant."

There were sixteen men in the truck. Peter counted them as they dropped, one by one, onto the road. They made so little noise that he guessed their boots were studded or soled with rubber.

"All right," said the man who had first spoken. Peter could see him clearly in the moonlight and guessed him to be an officer. "Spread out as you go, but don't lose touch with the men on either side of you. Five yards should be about right. Straight up the hill, and stop when you reach the crest. When the covering party's in position, they'll give us a green over white. You stay with the truck, Sergeant. Run it down to the next turning and face it up the track to the camp. If anyone tries to break down that way, turn your lights on, give them *one* warning, and then shoot. Understood?"

"Understood, sir."

The Sergeant climbed in beside the driver, and the truck rolled off down the road.

"Right, then. Off we go, and for God's sake don't start shooting each other."

This produced a quiet laugh. The next moment the

road was empty. The nearest man crossed the ditch within two paces of where Peter crouched. Peter caught a glimpse of his face as he went by, very young and very solemn. Peter wondered whether this was the first time he had gone into action against an enemy who might shoot back.

"Third time must be lucky," said Peter. He tiptoed across the road and through the gap in the hedge. This time there was no opposition. He made his way back along the hedge, crouching low when he reached the turning up to the camp. He could see the lorry, but it was positioned with its back to him. No danger there. Five minutes more brought him to where his car was parked. Peter opened the gate, eased himself into the driving seat, and was careful to make no noise when he shut the door.

"Now for it," he said. "I know you're cold, old girl, I know you're wet, but please, please start first time."

The faithful Savoia did not fail him. One touch on the starter and the engine sprang to life. Roll down the short slope, out through the gate, swing right, and away. He thought he heard a shout behind him, but he ignored it. As soon as he was around the first corner, he switched on all the lights and put on speed.

It was only when he turned into the main road between Cryde and Cryde Bay that he realized how tired he was. His eyes were playing tricks. The section of road immediately beyond his headlights started to tilt. The illusion was so convincing that he changed gear to tackle a hill which disappeared when he came to it.

Better not drive too fast. Only two miles to go. Then he could go to bed and go to sleep.

This started a second train of thought. *Had he ever waked up?* Might the events of the last fantastic hours be no more than a dream, orchestrated by the storm? The sort of dream which aped realism by mixing the frightening with the fantastic: Mr. Quarles and his sister at Minehead, and Anna talking on the telephone; Captain Andy apprehensive that he might be elected a town councillor, and the body of the young man Ramon on the ground with his neck broken. Had Peter really stumbled through the rain and sat beside Kevin and watched him die? Were those solemn Israeli killers merely the creatures of his overblown imagination? These our actors, as I foretold you, were all spirits and are melted into air, into thin air. The cloud-capped towers, the gorgeous palaces. Watch it, for God's sake, keep your stupid eyes open.

And the soldiers? What was it the Colonel had said? A game of chess. They make a move, we make a move. He had certainly moved in force. How had he managed to time his move so well? It was a small mystery among greater mysteries.

Here was Cryde Bay at last. Park the car. Climb out. Shut the door. Fumbling for the keys to lock the car, he dropped them. It was an effort to pick them up. The moon was growing pale, defeated by the growing light of the morning. Peter remembered that they had left the back door unlocked when they went out. It was still unlocked. He crept upstairs through the silent house, managed to get most of his clothes off, and fell into bed and into a bottomless pit of sleep.

18

It was afternoon when Peter opened his eyes. Captain Andy was standing beside the bed.

He said, "It's gone half past two. I thought I'd better give you a nudge. I've brought you a cup of tea."

"Thanks awfully," said Peter. He propped himself on one elbow, conscious that he was still wearing his shirt and that there was, among other marks, a long, dark stain down the front of it.

"I didn't hear you come in last night."

"I'm afraid I was very late. I hope I didn't disturb you."

"I'm a sound sleeper," said the Captain. "What I was wondering about was what happened to those two friends of yours. They seem to have decamped."

The events of the previous night, blurred by sleep, came back to Peter with such brutal force that he jerked upright in bed, spilling some of the tea out of the cup.

"Better let me take charge of that," said the Captain.

"Look," said Peter, as soon as he felt able to speak. "I brought them here. I didn't know a lot about them. In fact, I only met them a day or two ago. I feel entirely responsible. Let me know what bill they've run up and I'll pay it."

"Do I gather from that that we shan't be seeing them again?"

Peter nearly choked, and said, "I don't think we will."

Now that he was sitting up, the stain on his shirt was glaringly obvious.

"It's blood, isn't it?" said the Captain. "Yours or someone else's?"

"Not mine," said Peter. "Kevin's. I'm afraid he's dead."

"Is he, now?" said the Captain calmly. "Then I think you'd better tell me about it." He sat down on the end of the bed. "I'm generally reckoned to be discreet."

"All right," said Peter. "Some of it isn't my story. I shall have to skip those bits. But I can tell you the main part of it. You may have read in the papers about Dr. Wolfe going over Rackthorn Point in his car."

"Certainly I read about it, and talked about it. Everyone seemed to think there was some sort of story behind it, but they didn't quite know what."

"It's the story behind it that I'm going to try to give you," said Peter.

The Captain was a good listener. At the end he said, "So I've been entertaining two killers."

"I don't think they were professional killers. I remember reading about the way the Israeli assassination squads work. They're divided into sections. There's an advance party, who make a reconnaissance and keep an eye on things. They usually pose as husband and wife or brother and sister or something like that. Then there's a communication party. They keep contact with the reconnaissance party and call up the actual killers at the right moment."

"Businesslike people, the Israelis. So Kevin and Anna were the advance party. A pity about Kevin. Do you think Anna is dead, too?"

"I don't know," said Peter miserably. "But I'm sure I shall never see her again."

The Captain said nothing immediately. There was a strength in him which Peter had sensed before. He fancied it must come from the roving life the Captain had led, and Peter was conscious of the reluctant envy which the young sometimes feel for older and more integrated people. When the Captain spoke, his mind had reverted to a different point. He said, "So you were actually in the house on the night poor old Westall was killed."

"I was indeed. And I got out seconds ahead of the police."

"I suppose you realize that you must have been there within minutes of the killing. According to the papers, it was an elderly couple in the next house down the Chine who heard the shots. They have a telephone beside their bed and rang through to the police at once. They reckon they got there in less than five minutes."

"Then I wonder I didn't hear the shots, too."

The Captain looked at him and said, "Yes. That is a bit odd. Maybe it's because you were up top and the sound was masked by the Chine. I think I better get you some breakfast. It's not the conventional hour for it, but you'll feel more able to face the world with something inside you."

When Peter had washed away most of the evidence of the night before, had put on a new shirt and finished dressing, he did feel ready to tackle a belated breakfast. While he ate it, he gave further thought to his own future.

Was there anything to prevent him from packing up and going back to London? It would be leaving a job half done, but it was now a job which could only be finished by professionals.

Thinking about his job reminded him that he had

still neither finished nor posted his report. It was four o'clock. With any luck he would find Arthur Troyte at his desk.

Mr. Troyte seemed only mildly surprised to hear from his errant employee. He said, "I didn't expect miracles, Peter. You've only been at it a few days. Give it to the end of the week, and if you haven't got any hard information by then, come back to base."

"As a matter of fact, I've got quite a lot of information."

"Which way is it looking?"

"I don't think Dr. Wolfe is dead."

This produced a short silence. Then Mr. Troyte, sounding like someone who has been presented with a large and unexpected sum of money, said, "Well—"

"Two days ago I was sure he was still alive. In fact, I thought I knew where he was hanging out. I was wrong about that, but it doesn't mean I was wrong altogether."

"If there's the slightest chance that you're right," said Mr. Troyte earnestly, "you can stay down there just as long as you like." He paused to think about it. "If it was a put-up job, it'll mean criminal proceedings against Wolfe."

"I realize that."

"Do you think his sister was in it with him?"

"I should think it most unlikely."

"Can I tell the underwriters about this?"

"For goodness' sake," said Peter, "don't say anything to anyone until you hear from me again. I'll ring you, or write, next Monday at the latest. Then we can make up our minds." He hung up.

Sam Phelps had been listening in on an extension line. He said, "I'm not sure we were right to send that young man down. It should have been someone older. Someone with a bit more ballast. He's probably dramatizing the whole thing. You know what young people are like."

"Could be," said Arthur Troyte. "But I don't think so. He's got his head screwed on all right, that boy. He won't get himself or us into any trouble. You'll see."

"I hope you're right," said Sam Phelps. "Because I can smell trouble coming."

It was after six o'clock when Captain Andy, who had gone out to do the shopping, came back with a basket of provisions and a serious look on his face.

He said, "I've been talking to an old friend of mine. Chap called Rayner. He runs the Esplanade. That big hotel on the front. I expect you saw it?"

Peter nodded. He knew from the Captain's manner that something else unpleasant was in the offing.

"The local bobby called on him this morning and asked to look through his register. He wanted to know who the current lot of guests were. He seemed particularly interested in the ones who had arrived in the last few days. Most of Rayner's people are regulars—old ladies, and mums and dads with young families. He wasn't interested in them. What he was looking for was a young man traveling solo."

"Did he say why?"

"Yes. When he'd satisfied himself that no one remotely resembling the man he was looking for was staying at the Esplanade, he accepted a quick half-pint in Rayner's office—off duty, they're old friends—and told him what the form was. There's an old character who runs a taxi and spends most of his time outside the station."

"I've seen him. He's always fast asleep."

"That's the impression he gives. But he sleeps with one eye open. He's a sort of unofficial police spy. I don't mean they pay him. He probably does it for sheer love of nosey-parkering. There *are* people like that."

"What did he tell them?"

"He said he'd noticed a young man, an exceptionally tall young man, arriving by train about midday, Friday. He knew he wasn't local, therefore he was a visitor. But an odd visitor, since he only seemed to have one very small bag with him. He didn't look like a commercial traveler. So what was he up to? If you'd hired his taxi, he would at least have known where you were staying, and that would have satisfied his curiosity. As it was, you were just a suspicious question mark."

"Nosey old bastard."

"That wasn't all. Later that day he noticed the same suspicious character prowling back along the path which leads from the Chine."

"I was *not* prowling. I was walking."

"He says you were prowling. He observed you carefully in the mirror of his cab. He says you were walking as if you wished to avoid attention. The upshot of it is that the police are making inquiries at every hotel and guesthouse in the town. It'll take them some time, but they'll get here in the end."

"Yes," said Peter, "I suppose they will."

"Taking the view," said the Captain, "that since I hadn't opened for the season, you and those friends of yours could hardly be described as guests—more unofficial lodgers, really—I haven't asked you to sign the register. If you were gone by the time they get here, I could say, without telling a lie, that you'd been staying here but I didn't know your address."

"Certainly not," said Peter. "It's good of you to suggest it, but I'm not going to get you into trouble. Besides, what about my car? It's been parked in your yard since Saturday night. Are you going to tell them you didn't even notice the number?"

"I could say that."

"No," said Peter. "Most certainly not."

194

He took out one of his professional cards. "This is who I am, and that's my business address. If the police want it, they can have it."

"Once they're after you," said the Captain, "it's not much use running away, I agree. Merely an idea. When you were telling me what happened last night, it sounded as if it was developing into a fair-sized battle. *Why wasn't there anything about it on the news today?*"

"Wasn't there?"

"Not a whisper. Nothing at all, on the morning or the midday news. Exmoor's a fairly empty sort of place, I agree, but it's not a desert. There are people about. If shooting started, on any sort of scale, they must have heard something and reported it. So why haven't we heard about it?"

"Because it's been suppressed."

"Right. But since the police weren't involved, doesn't it look as though the Army have got the last word in this show?"

Peter said slowly, "I had a talking-to from a Colonel Hay. He certainly implied that the Army was involved. Not necessarily the regular Army. He didn't say so, but I gathered that MI5, or MI6, or whatever the appropriate outfit might be, was involved."

"Do you know where Colonel Hay hangs out?"

"All I know is that he said in his report that he was staying in a farmhouse near by and actually saw Dr. Wolfe's car driving up the path toward Rackthorn Point and heard it go over."

The Captain got out a dog-eared sheet of the Ordinance Survey and they examined it together. The Captain said, "There's only one place it can be. There. On the other side of the River Culme. Rackthorn Farm. Give me five minutes on the telephone and I'll find out who it belongs to. Then we can locate their telephone number."

"I expect we can," agreed Peter. "And when we've done it, what then?"

"Then you ring up Colonel Hay and say you want to have a talk with him. I guess he won't say no. Tell him the whole story. If anyone can square the police, I guess it's him."

19

The telephone was answered by a male voice which sounded young and cheerful. The voice took Peter's name and invited him to hang on for a moment.

The moment became a minute, and the minute grew to nearly five minutes before Colonel Hay came on. He said, rather sharply, "Where are you speaking from, Mr. Manciple?"

"I'm at Cryde Bay."

"A pity. I hoped you'd have taken my advice and gone home by now."

"I wish I had. I'm afraid I'm in trouble. And I want your help."

"If you're the tall man who arrived at Cryde Bay by train just before lunch last Friday and was later seen strolling down the station path from the direction of the Chine, I should say you're in dead trouble."

"You've been in touch with the police."

"Naturally. We work together very closely. Superintendent Horne gave me a character sketch of you after he'd met you at Tiverton. He said you were an obstinate young bugger. Colonel Hollingum, at the Research Station, seems to have got the same impression."

"I'm sorry," said Peter humbly. "I wasn't trying to

upset people. I had a job to do, that was all. Now I'd be very happy to take the advice you've all been giving me, and go away and stay away. But I don't want to run off with half the police in England chasing after me. There'd be no point in it. That's why I want to have a word with you, and tell you everything that's happened." He paused for a moment and added, persuasively, "Everything. Then you'll be able to advise me."

"The trouble is," said the Colonel, "that you're rather a hot property at the moment. As I said, I've been working with the police, and if I start helping you behind their backs, they'll be apt to be upset. You see my point?"

"Then you think I ought to go straight to them?"

"I might be able to answer that question if I knew exactly what you had been up to. On the whole, I think we had better have a talk. The trouble is Rupert and I are anchored to the telephone here. We've got non-stop calls coming in from all over the place about—well, about a little trouble we had last night."

"If the trouble was what I imagine it was, I was involved in that, too."

This really did produce a pause. Peter got the impression that more than one person was listening to the conversation. Rupert? The report had mentioned an "Army friend" who was sharing the farm.

"I really think," said the Colonel at last, "that the sooner we have that talk, the better. I can't come to you, so you'll have to come here. Have you got a map handy?"

"I can get one. Hold on a minute. . . . All right."

"You'll be coming out on the main road from Cryde Bay. The normal way to reach this place is to go almost into Huntercombe. There's a track which leads up to Rackthorn Farm, just short of the village. Are you with me?"

"I can see a dotted line on the map."

"That's the way I *don't* want you to come. If you look again at the map, you'll notice the letters P.H. opposite to where the track turns off. And that, as you no doubt learned at school, means Public House. It's the Ram Inn. A very sociable little place. And a center of local gossip. But there's an alternative. About a hundred yards before your road crosses the Culme, there's another track. It isn't marked, because it was only made up when they opened the caravan site, but you can't miss it. It's exactly opposite the Bridgetown turning."

"If you mean the track that goes up to Rackthorn Point, I know it. I went up it to inspect the scene of the accident."

"That's the one. I suggest you leave your car actually in the caravan car-park. Don't start out until it's dark, and with any luck no one will notice you at all. Or if they do notice you, they'll think you're a caravaner."

"There's only one snag," said Peter. "I shall be on the wrong side of the river."

"You won't have to swim. Rupert will be there with the boat. Ten o'clock sharp. Goodbye."

Over supper Peter said to the Captain, "I'm sure it's all right. But he made such a point of my coming that way, after dark, and telling no one—I did begin to wonder."

"Some sort of booby-trap or ambush?" said the Captain. "Could be. I'm glad you're learning not to trust people. If you aren't back by morning, I'll raise a posse and come and look for you."

Feeling that the Colonel would appreciate punctuality, Peter took care to arrive at the caravan car-park at a few minutes before ten. He reached it without incident. It had been raining, on and off, for most of the afternoon, but, as often happened that provoking summer, it had stopped at dusk and the sky was now clear.

Rupert was waiting for him. He said, "I hope you're not afraid of boats. It's not quite as frail as it looks. It belongs to the farm, and since we can't stop the kids pinching the oars and the boathook, we have to make do."

It was an old-fashioned tub dinghy, and Peter looked at it with love. He said, "I'm not afraid of any river boat ever built. I was brought up in them and on them and off them. If you haven't got any oars or a boathook, what do you do? Paddle it with your hands?"

"We improvise." Rupert lifted the flat board which formed one footrest for the rower, invited Peter on board, loosed the rope, and took them across with half a dozen easy sweeps.

"They're sweet boats," said Peter. "I had one of my own when I was young. You can row them all day without feeling tired, and they turn on a penny."

"I could see you were a river man, from the way you stepped on and off the boat," said Rupert. "Last week I had to ferry a brigadier across, and he actually stepped *on* the gunwale. Can you believe it?"

"I hope he didn't get too wet," said Peter.

"There's a special providence looks after brigadiers," said Rupert. "Mind the step."

As he opened the door, the light fell on his face and Peter recognized him. He had seen him less than twenty-four hours before, jumping out of the front seat of an Army truck.

Colonel Hay was sitting on one side of a cheerful log fire. He got up as Peter came in, waved him to the chair on the other side of the fireplace, and poured out two generous tots from a bottle on the sideboard.

"It's a highland malt from the Isle of Skye," he said. "You can insult it with water or soda if you must, but I promise you it'll be much happier if you don't."

Peter agreed not to do anything which might make

the light-colored, innocent-looking liquid in his glass unhappy. It had a smokey taste, and went down sweetly.

"All right," said the Colonel, "let's have it. Everything you've been up to, from the beginning to the end, with nothing left out."

It was a history which covered ten days and the minute hand had gone once right around the grandfather clock in the corner and halfway around again before Peter had finished. He had, as he realized afterward, left out one detail, but it was not a conscious omission.

The Colonel punctuated his account with occasional grunted questions. He seemed more interested in times than in places. When had he first told Anna of his suspicions that Dr. Wolfe was not dead? When had he first translated the number on Roland Highsmith's pad into an address at Cryde Bay? Could that particular telephone call have been intercepted? (Peter thought it most unlikely. Why should anyone have wished, or been able, to intercept messages to a hotel in Tiverton? The Colonel agreed that it was improbable.) When had he reached Cryde Bay himself and located the man whom he thought to be Dr. Wolfe? When had he passed this news on to Anna?

He was interrupted twice. On the first occasion, the telephone started ringing. Since the Colonel ignored it and it soon stopped, Peter guessed that the call was being dealt with somewhere else in the house.

Five minutes later Rupert came in. He said, "Sorry to interrupt. That was Western Command. They want you at a conference. They're sending a chopper."

The Colonel said, "You'll have to represent me. You know as much about it as I do. More, really."

Rupert looked doubtful, but said, "I'll try to keep them happy," and went out.

When Peter had reached the end of his story, the Colonel got up and switched off the tape recorder which had been purring away on the table between them. He then poured out a second drink for both of them and sat down.

"That's that," said Peter. He felt the ease of the post-confessional. "I think the least you can do in return is to bring me up to date."

"Fair enough," said the Colonel. "I expect you realize that what you saw last night was the final stage of an operation which we've been preparing for very carefully. And, as far as these things ever do go, it went according to plan. The Israeli hit team and the Palestinians locked horns. It was brief and bloody. When we felt they'd done enough damage to each other, we stepped in and picked up the bits. The final score was two dead on each side. Five wounded—two Israelis, three Palestinians. Three prisoners in good condition. Oh, and one of our chaps got so excited he put a bullet through his own foot. That was the only casualty on our side. Very satisfactory, really."

The final score. It sounded, thought Peter, as though the Colonel was reporting the result of a rough game of rugby.

"Was Petros there?"

"The Professor? No, that crafty old character was safely tucked up in bed at the hotel. When we saw him this morning, you can't think how surprised and horrified he was. To think that he had been cherishing such a nest of vipers! Stephen had recruited them. He had told Petros they were Middle East students on vacation. Pleasant, hardworking boys. He'll be lucky if he gets away with it. I don't think the Home Office is very happy about the Professor."

"Is anyone going to be very happy about what happened last night?"

"I don't see any reason why anyone should know anything about it at all."

202

"Four dead. Five wounded."

"The dead will be buried. The wounded and the prisoners will be looked after in one of the private establishments we run for that purpose."

"I see," said Peter. The question had to be asked. The Colonel knew it as well as he did, and had been waiting for it.

"Did anyone get away?"

"Two people, as far as we know."

"Was—?"

"Yes. One was the girl. She'll be trying to make contact with her back-up party. They're operating from a private yacht at Plymouth. If she knows what's good for her, she'll get out of the country, and get out quick."

"Why do you say that?"

"Because the other one who got away was Stefan. Or Stephen, as he's been calling himself lately."

"Why should she be particularly afraid of Stephen?"

"If I were in her shoes, I should be afraid of him. Ramon was his brother."

"But he doesn't know Anna killed him."

"He'll have a pretty shrewd idea. He knows Kevin was got away before the attack came in, and the most likely person to have done that was Anna. He may not be certain about it, but it's the sort of conclusion he'll find it very easy to jump to."

"I hope—" said Peter, and stopped. What did he hope? That she was safe with her friends? That they would get her back to Israel? That he would never see her again?

"Remarkable girl," said the Colonel. "She led you on a bit, didn't she?"

"Yes," said Peter. "She led me on." He caught a sardonic flash from the Colonel's bulbous eyes and added defiantly, "She was very cooperative."

"Some people have all the luck," said the Colonel. "I

thought at one time she was going to try to seduce Rupert. Evidently she didn't consider him worth powder and shot. Disappointing for him. He's very seducible, that boy." He added, "Of course, there's always a chance her friends will get Stephen before he gets her. They've been after him for a long time. He had a very narrow escape in Stockholm last year."

Peter didn't want to think about Anna just then. He said, "I suppose last night finished the job, as far as you were concerned."

"Finished?" said the Colonel. "Certainly not. It's only just begun. It won't be finished until Wolfe is dead. Perhaps not even then. It all depends."

"Depends on what?"

"On how much of what's in his head has been put into those notes he took away in his briefcase. And how much anyone else could make of those notes without his help."

"Not very much, I imagine," said Peter, remembering what Dr. Bishwas had told him. "I gather they're in a sort of scientific shorthand. You'd have to be almost as far on as Dr. Wolfe was in that particular line to understand them at all."

"If that's right," said the Colonel, "he's a dead man as soon as anyone catches up with him. Not just the Israeli or Palestinian extremists who've been in the field so far. Anyone."

"You don't, I suppose," said Peter, "include the British government?"

The Colonel took out a clean white handkerchief from his pocket, unfolded it, blew his nose, replaced the handkerchief, and said, "You haven't really begun to grasp what this is about, have you? Let me lay it on the line for you. As long as Dr. Wolfe was working for us, his work belonged to us and we could control its use.

Also, he was under our protection. As soon as he moved out, he became an outlaw."

"Why?"

"Because, at that point, the information in his head and the notes in his briefcase stopped belonging to us and became the price he was prepared to pay for sanctuary somewhere else."

"Who was offering him sanctuary?"

"If we knew who they were, we'd know where to go and look for him. All we know about the country concerned is that it must have been the terminal point of those long, long trips which he used to make, starting on the other side of the Channel and ending God knows where."

Peter thought about it. Some pieces of the puzzle were falling into place. No more, yet, than a small part of the framework. The straight-edged blue bits which made up the sky.

He said, "You talked about him being under your protection. If he was as dangerous as all that, surely he could have been killed at any time during the last year or so."

"When?"

"When? Whenever he stepped outside the Research Establishment boundary fence."

"I should have been very much upset if anyone had succeeded in doing it. We had taken elaborate precautions to see that it didn't happen. When he went into Bridgetown for a drink, one of the guards went in his car with him and another car followed at a discreet distance. Dave Brewer was in our confidence. He'd have alerted us if there had been any suspicious characters hanging round the hotel. No, I don't think it would have been easy."

"What about his fishing expeditions?"

"More difficult still. They took place in daylight and

open country. We used a half-platoon on each occasion. Good practice for the men in fieldcraft. We had him ringed round so tight that no stranger could have got within half a mile of him without being intercepted. It's lucky for Wolfe he was an uncommonly truthful fisherman. We had a record of every trout he caught and its approximate size and weight."

"All right," said Peter. "But what about the times when he drove away in his car?"

"We couldn't do much about that, agreed. *But nor could the opposition.* It was the speed and unexpectedness of it which made it safe. He kept a bag packed in his car, drove straight out of the camp, and made for one of the half-dozen places you can cross the Channel from. A friend of his helped him."

"Roland Highsmith?"

"We think so. He seems to have been the one person who was fully in Wolfe's confidence. He'd buy the tickets in advance, probably in another name, and deposit them at a *poste restante* near the selected port. All Wolfe had to do was to drive straight there and pick them up. If he timed it properly, he could be out of the country within a few hours of leaving the camp."

"He might be out of the country now."

"Not this time. No. In the ordinary way, even if we did spot him leaving the country, we couldn't stop him. This time it was different. A faked suicide. Legitimate inquiries. We had the machinery ready. It only needed the signal to be given. No, he's still here, I'm sure of that. He wouldn't take a chance on it. He's lying up somewhere, waiting for the heat to come off."

"Where?"

"There's one man who could tell us that: Roland Highsmith. You say you saw him when you noted the house that first night; but he's very likely out of the country himself by now. If he's got any sense, he's having a quiet holiday with his family in the Black Forest. That's why you became such a prime object of interest. When you were seen leaving Highsmith's office, it was assumed that you'd found out from him the one fact everyone wanted to know: where Wolfe was hiding out."

"I thought I had," said Peter sadly.

"If you had the information, the Petros crowd assumed that Anna would have got it from you and passed it on to Kevin. That's what they tortured him to find out. Only the poor chap didn't know anything, so he'd nothing to tell them."

As the Colonel said this, a further small piece of the puzzle fell into place; a small but important piece.

Peter said, "It did surprise me that an experienced operator like Kevin should have let the opposition spot him so easily."

"To be quite frank with you, they didn't. It was our outer ring of scouts who saw him."

As the full import of what the Colonel had said sunk in, Peter stared at him in total disbelief.

Then he said, "Are you telling me that you—that your people—gave him away?"

"That's right."

"For God's sake!"

"Why not? We wanted things to come to a head that night. So it seemed a sound move."

"A sound move." Peter nearly choked on the words. "You handed him over, deliberately, knowing that he'd be tortured and killed."

"Tortured, yes. That's the sort of risk you have to run in this business. We didn't imagine they'd kill him."

"But they did."

"No," said the Colonel. "I'm afraid you've got it wrong. It wasn't them. It was you and Anna who killed him."

"What—what on earth—" Peter found that he was

beginning to splutter, and controlled himself by a strong effort of will. "What in the world are you talking about?"

"Kevin died of shock and exposure. If he'd been allowed to stay put where he was, the doctors could have pulled him through all right. He'd have been a bit bent, but he certainly wouldn't have died."

"You're lying."

"You can see the medical report, if you like. I've got it here."

"Even if that's true, you had no right— It was a vile thing to do."

"Lots of vile things get done in war," said the Colonel. "The thing was a planned sequence. We made one mistake. We thought that when Kevin didn't come back, Anna would whistle up her supports and move in straight away. We weren't to know she was going to try a solo rescue first. As a matter of fact, if it hadn't been for the storm, I don't think even she would have dared try it, though she's a very daring girl."

Peter had been conscious for some minutes of a growing fury. It was a bubbling up inside him, a hot and choking fire, stoked by each of the Colonel's carefully modulated remarks. Who *was* this—this white-mustached, pop-eyed little bastard who played with lives as though they were pieces on a board! Peter's monitor, who never slept for long, warned him of the stupidity of what he was doing. He realized that every word the Colonel uttered, every inflection in his voice, was programmed to a definite end. He knew that if he lost his self-control he might involve himself in a very dangerous situation. Yet no considerations of prudence could have stopped him at that point. He thought out exactly what he was going to say, and said it.

"Just now, you accused me of killing Kevin."

208

"Not deliberately, I appreciate that," said the Colonel kindly.

"Let me return the compliment. Not only did you kill a perfectly harmless person who was quite unconnected with your obscene games, *but you hadn't even got the guts to kill him yourself.*"

"I imagine you mean Mr. Westall. So far as I know, he was killed by the Israeli hit team, on mistaken information supplied by you and passed on to them by your young lady. I'm afraid any responsibility there must be yours, too."

"That's untrue. And you know it's untrue. Agreed that I told Anna about the house in the Chine whilst we were out together that afternoon. *But she was never out of my sight for a single moment between the time I told her and the time I myself left for the Chine.* So how is she supposed to have passed the information on? Certainly not by telephone. Perhaps by telepathy?"

The Colonel looked up once, and then dropped his eyes. It was a tiny movement. If Peter had been calmer, he would have noted the reaction and would have been doubly cautious. He had got inside the Colonel's guard. His point had scratched his opponent's skin.

"Well," said the Colonel at last, "it's a problem you'll have to solve for me. I'm afraid it's too difficult for my simple intelligence."

"There's no difficulty about it. I was the only person who ever suspected that Dr. Wolfe might be living in that particular house. I'd worked it out wrong, I agree. But I was the only person in possession of the answer."

"Quite so. And the only person you'd passed it on to was Anna."

"Wrong again. Two days before that I told an old schoolmaster. A Mr. Garland. I wanted him to come and help me identify Dr. Wolfe and talk to him. Mr. Garland worked for one of your organizations during the war and maybe kept in touch afterward. He must have felt in duty bound to pass the information on to his old employers. That's how you knew, or thought you knew, that Dr. Wolfe was at that house in the Chine. And that's the address you sent the Israeli killers to."

Peter hardly knew, by now, what reaction he expected. The Colonel, as usual, managed to surprise him. He hoisted himself to his feet, glanced at the clock, and said, "Do you know, it's after one o'clock. Another drink before you go?"

Peter shook his head angrily.

"You're quite sure? Well, I shall have to ask you to excuse me. I'm expecting a call from Western Command, and they should be coming through at any moment now."

Peter found himself on his feet. His legs were not entirely steady.

"I've enjoyed our talk. If there's any other help I can give you, please consider me entirely at your disposal. Can you manage the boat? Splendid. Then perhaps you'll be good enough to tie it up securely so that Rupert can use it when he comes back. Good night. Good night."

The door shut behind him, and Peter started off down the path, his mind in a state of total confusion. He was annoyed with himself, furious with the Colonel, puzzled and a bit frightened without being sure what he was frightened of. He was still trying to sort it out when he jumped into the boat, unhitched the mooring rope, and pushed out from the small landing stage.

A moment later he realized two things in quick succession.

The first was that the tide, which must have been one side or other of full when he had crossed three hours earlier, was now running out strongly. The second was that he had nothing to paddle the boat with. The footboard which he had planned to use was jammed.

He was too experienced to be unduly alarmed. There was a locker at the stern of the boat. He opened the lid and found that it contained nothing but a tin bailer with a wooden handle. It would make a paddle of sorts, but not a very effective one.

The current turned the boat broadside on, and Peter hastily shifted his weight across to preserve some sort of trim. The Culme, full from the rain of the previous night, had joined hands with the ebb tide and was racing for the open sea. It was only when he saw the tiny strip of sand at the foot of the trailer site flash past that Peter realized how fast it was running. It was too late to think of abandoning the boat and making for the bank. Even if he had been able to beat the current, he would have found himself among the crags and treacherous eddies at the foot of Rackthorn Point.

"What Rackthorn takes, Rackthorn keeps," he said to himself. Much better let the tide take him out to sea. It would be light in three or four hours, and the Bristol Channel was a highway for boats of all sorts. He'd be picked up before long. It was a stupid mischance, but nothing worse than that.

He put the bailer back in the locker and turned his attention to the jammed footboard. With that to help him, he could keep the boat bows forward and minimize the risk of being swamped. As he bent down, he saw, twenty yards ahead of him, the line of foam which marked the bar at the mouth of the river.

There was no time to do anything about it. The boat hit the white water sideways on, checked for a heartstopping moment, and then turned right over.

20

"When in doubt," his father had told them, "stick to the boat. People sink. Boats don't." As he surfaced, he could see the boat, upside down, bobbing along ahead of him. He spat out a mouthful of salt water and set out after it. They were both going with the current, and he caught up with it easily enough and heaved himself over it, grabbing at the upturned keel. When he had done that, he started to think.

At ten o'clock the tide must have been well past its high point, still just strong enough to check the current of the river, but no longer making against it. This would account for the ease with which Rupert had been able to take the boat across. That meant the tide would be due to turn soon after three. The tides in the Bristol Channel were strong and capricious. Given their head, they would probably carry him back close to the point from which he had started. The question was whether he could hang on for another three hours. He knew the bleak answer to that before he put the question. Cold, exhaustion, and his waterlogged clothes would have put him under long before.

There *was* a way out, if he was strong enough and clever enough to take it. His height would be a help. He remembered Anna saying, "You're an eel. A great, long, slippery eel." Eels didn't drown. Not if they remembered what they had been taught by their fathers.

The first step was to locate the mooring rope. He edged his way toward the bows, felt underwater, and found it. It was a fair length of rope. He passed it under the boat, from the near side to the far side, got both hands to the loose end, and exerted all the pressure he could while treading water.

For a moment the dead weight of the waterlogged boat resisted him. Then a wave, arriving from the far side at a fortunate moment, lent its help, and the boat turned over.

Peter felt his way back to the stern. It was easier now that he had the edge of the gunwale to hang on to. The locker was in the back seat of the dinghy. He had had no time to fasten the lid and it was more than possible that the bailer— No, thank God, it was still there. As his fingers touched it, he spat out another mouthful of salt water and said, "Don't hurry. Take it easy, you've done all this before."

He started, very gently, to bail. It was then that he realized the difference between the flat and friendly Thames and the dimpled sea. It was not rough. But there was a distinct lop on the surface, sufficient to put back any water he bailed out.

There must be an answer. Try to think. Ignore the cold, ignore the weight in your clothes and the ache in your wrist, and use your brains. All he had to do was get the thing started. He would have to do it by first tipping the boat slightly, and after that by speed.

The tipping was easy. He had only to press down on his side of the boat until it was level with the surface of the water and the other side rose a few inches. Then he hurled himself into the job of trying to scoop out as much water as possible before the next wave came along and canceled his efforts.

Twice he nearly lost the bailer. Then he saw the wave coming, released his side of the boat, and offered up a short prayer. The water lipped the few precious inches of freeboard which he had won. But it did not come over.

Carry on bailing. Ten, twenty, thirty, forty times. Hold the boat steady when a wave comes. This time there was a little more to spare.

As the level of water in the boat sank, he had to lean over, farther and farther, to scoop it out. Now a fresh decision had to be made. It was a matter of weighing up the failing strength in his arms and wrists with the desirability of getting as much water as possible out of the boat before he took the final step.

The boat was half empty and had recovered a lot of its buoyancy. Better to try it while he had a small reserve of energy left. He edged his way along to the flat stern of the boat. The bailer went back into the locker, and the locker was fastened. Then he grasped the stern in both hands, took a deep breath, and heaved himself forward.

The effort took his body over the thwart, but his center of gravity was still outside the boat, and he could feel the water coming in all around him. Only the knowledge that if he slipped back now he was finished gave him the strength for a final effort. Somehow he got his left knee over the edge of the stern, and that gave him the purchase for a last convulsive heave. Then he was lying in the boat, his face underwater and his heart going like a trip hammer.

But he was safe, and he knew it.

He turned over on his side and lay breathing deeply as his heart slowed down. Then he wriggled around, got hold of the bailer, and finished bailing out the boat. He stopped once to be sick. The muscles of his stomach were still knotted with the effort he had made, and vomiting was painful. After he had cleared the boat, he stripped off all of his clothes, wrung the water out of them, and sat naked, trying to make his mind up whether it was worth putting them on again. The night wind quickly told him that it was.

His watch showed the time as nearly half past two. It would be light in an hour or so, and if the tide had not carried him close enough to the shore for him to swim to land, he could expect help from other boats. He started to shiver in short, uncontrollable spasms.

This was the bleak hour before dawn, the hour which he had experienced before, when the last drops of confidence and hope had drained away and nothing was left but apprehension and emptiness and despair. It was the lowest circle in the Inferno, below the hot hells of anger and pain and lust, far down into the unsounded gray depths. It was the cavern of treachery and defeat.

The trance he fell into could hardly be called sleep. It was a temporary release, into the blackness of the nether pit. When he opened his eyes there was light in the sky. The morning breeze, blowing off the sea, had helped the tide, and he was quite close inshore, near to the opening of a small river. It was not the Culme. He thought for a moment that it might be the Lynn, but that would have been much bigger and there would have been buildings in sight. It might, he guessed, be the Widd, a small stream which ran out to sea on the other side of Culme Point.

Using the bailer as a paddle, Peter managed to turn the bows of the boat into the river. The tide was making strongly now, and he was carried upstream at a fair speed. When he had rounded the first bend and was out of sight of the sea, he edged the boat to the bank and managed to beach it on a patch of stones and gravel under overhanging trees.

He was so stiff and so clammed with cold that the simple action of stepping ashore was beyond him. He levered his long legs over the side, slid forward onto his knees, put one hand onto the boat, and started to organize the effort which would get him back onto his feet.

As he did so, his eye fell on the footboard which had so obstinately resisted all his efforts during the night to remove it and use it as a paddle.

The reason for its immobility was clear. The board had been fastened to the cleat at either end. He could see the bright heads of the new screws which were holding it down.

Peter remained on his knees for a full minute while his tired brain grappled with the shocking truth that was staring him in the face. He realized that all his future moves would have to be replanned. And before he could plan anything, he had to find warmth and security and sleep.

Work it out slowly. There was something to be done before he moved away. A premium to be paid on an insurance policy against further attacks.

He realized that he was not strong enough to turn the boat over. Instead, he leaned his weight on the near side until the water started to come in, and held it down until the boat was half full. Then, sitting and using his feet, he kicked it out into deeper water and watched it as it floated sluggishly away upstream.

Then he set his face to the bank, climbed it, and started inland. This was Exmoor. Tilted fields which had had their first mowing. Hedges of beech saplings planted as winter windbreaks. Patches of stony outcrop, knee deep in heather. Sheep, seagulls, and rabbits. Once, as he crossed the bottom of a small valley, he came face to face with a fox galloping home from a night of villainy. It looked at him for a long moment with unblinking yellow eyes, then slipped into the bracken and was gone.

It was near six o'clock, and the sun was already high, when he found what he needed. It was an isolated construction, set at the top of a fold in the hills, served by a single rutted track which ran up to it and stopped. It was no more than a framework of upright angle irons, with open sides and a corrugated iron roof, and it was packed with the baled hay which would be used that winter to feed the sheep he could see scattered, like confetti, down one side of the valley and up the other. There was a pump, too, which was rusty, but which looked as if it might work, and a trough made out of an iron cask cut in half lengthways.

Energetic use of the handle eventually brought up a spout of clear water. Peter washed the salt from his face and hands and drank his fill. Then, hoisting himself up by one of the girders, he wriggled onto the top of the hay, made a space for himself between two of the bales, and went to sleep.

It was past midday when he woke. The heat under the iron roof was considerable. His clothes had dried on him, and seemed to have shrunk as they dried. Peter wriggled into a cooler spot on the north side of the stack and looked out.

There was a road running along the crest on the far side of the valley. It could hardly be a busy road, for during the afternoon he saw only two cars and a girl on horseback. Beyond the crest, down in the next valley, he could hear a tractor working. He guessed that it was pulling a harrow. It never quite came into sight, but each time it got close enough to the summit he could see its tail of white dust. A kestrel, suspended on an invisible string, swung across the valley, quartering it for rabbits. The sun moved by imperceptible degrees toward the west.

At this point it occurred to Peter to examine the contents of his wallet which must have suffered from his immersion. He took out the banknotes which it contained, separated them with some difficulty, and laid them out on the straw to dry. It was while he was doing this that he found the scrap of paper which he had removed from Kevin's mouth. It was good-quality paper. Using his nails, he unpicked it and smoothed it out onto the palm of his hand.

It was a small piece torn off the top of a sheet of thick and expensive writing paper. The name and address had been engraved and were still quite legible.

M. Valentin Lasspinière,
Rue Belcourt 14,
Boulogne-sur-mer. 62200.

Boulogne! His mother's hometown. A place of memories. He had spent half the first fourteen years of his life there, and had visited it many times since. He thought he could even remember Rue Belcourt, a quiet street behind the cathedral. The name Valentin Lasspinière rang a faint bell. His mother would know it. He folded the paper carefully and put it in his notecase. What he had to consider was his next move.

His destination lay twenty miles or more to the south of him. With luck and judgment he should be able to cover that distance in the time available. On roads he could walk it in five hours. Across country he would have to allow eight. He had water to drink. The fact that he would have to go without food did not worry him. On other occasions, in order to test himself, he had gone without food for forty-eight hours, and on one occasion for sixty, and had found that it did not impair his physical capacity and actually sharpened his wits.

The first half of his journey would be across open

country. He was not clear exactly where he was, but Dunkery would be on his right and Croydon Hill on his left. At some point he would have to cross the main north-south road from Dunster. After that, if he kept steadily south with a little east in it, he must come out into an area of small roads and isolated villages and farms around Skilgate, Morebath, and Shillingford. Once he reached that area, there would be signposts to help him. He settled down to wait until dark.

A factor he had not reckoned on was the difficulty of crossing Exmoor in the dark. A hillside which was open going by day was full of traps by night. The heather was knee high, and under the heather lay sizable rocks. He nearly came to grief almost at once, when he put his left foot between two such rocks and pitched forward onto his face.

He thought, for a bad moment, that he had broken his ankle, but decided, after a few cautious experiments, that he had only twisted it slightly. It was painful, but it would support him. After that he went a lot more slowly.

He had started at ten o'clock. It was close on midnight when he slithered down a bank, waded through a stream, climbed another and much steeper bank, and found himself on the main road. A signpost told him that he was three miles from Dunster. So, coming diagonally across, he had covered barely four miles in two hours. That was not good enough. He realized that he would have to abandon any idea of a cross-country march and use minor roads. There would be few cars out at that time of night, and he should be able to see their lights in time to get under cover.

After an unpleasant traverse up a hillside of brambles and nettles, he struck a road which seemed to be going in the right direction. As he found when he looked at the map later, it was the small road which ran parallel to the main road and a mile or more to the east of it. It served his purpose well. On the only occasion that he met a car he had ample time to take cover.

Counting his paces and timing himself as he went, he reckoned he had covered the best part of ten miles when he realized that he was being edged back toward the main road. He could see the lights of the cars in the valley to his right. It was time to strike across country again.

The moon was hidden by clouds, but some light was filtering through. His night vision was now good and he could make out the general lie of the land. He had reached the terminal shoulder of a ridge, and the ground fell off in three directions. To the right, the road he was on swung down into the valley to meet the main road. The scattered lights beyond would be Dulverton. In front and to the left was an even sharper descent into a thick belt of trees. Down below the trees, hidden in the steep-sided valley, must run the Hadden stream, which joined the Exe at this point. It would not be difficult to cross, and beyond it lay open country.

It was when he was halfway down that he realized just how steep the valley was. It had started as open pasture with occasional outcrops of rock. As he got farther down, the hill shelved sharply. He found that an effective, if undignified, method of progress was sitting and sliding. When he reached the wood, he realized, from the fact that the top of a considerable tree was almost on a level with him, that what he had to negotiate was not a slope but a precipice. He wondered for a moment whether he ought to go back, but rejected the idea. He was committed to the descent, and would see it through.

There were saplings which gave him a handhold, and there were toeholds in the broken rock. Perhaps it was not going to be too difficult. He could already hear the river below him. At that moment the sapling he was holding came away in his hand. He rolled onto his face, grabbed for another handhold, missed, and started to slip. As he slipped, he felt something sharp dig into his stomach. The first thing he realized was that he had stopped slipping. Next, that he was gaffed. A pointed branch had hooked itself into the front of his trousers. While he was wondering what to do about it, a slow tearing indicated that the front of his trousers was giving way. He scrabbled wildly with his feet, found a foot-hold, lost it, and started to slip again. It was not a rapid descent, but it was horribly uncomfortable. It ended with a bump as his feet hit solid rock. He turned cautiously. A few feet away the River Hadden ran past, chuckling.

"There's nothing to bloody laugh about," he said sourly. "How am I going to walk through North Devon with no front to my trousers?"

While he was thinking about this, he sat down on the rock, took the shoe and sock off his left foot, and soaked his ankle in the ice-cold water. Although it was now, more than ever, essential for him to arrive before full daylight, he reckoned that he would be the better for a short break.

It was while he was sitting on that ledge of rock, with one foot in the River Hadden, that he finally grasped the truth.

There was no particular reason for it. Or was it fantastic to suppose that it was because he was doing what Dr. Wolfe had done, crossing Exmoor by night? Cutting, admittedly, a very different figure. He had so often visualized the scientist, neatly dressed, picking his way by the route he had mapped out months before, a brief-case in one hand, a rolled umbrella in the other, a small knapsack, perhaps, on his back containing food and drink for the day he was planning to spend in the barn at Watersmeet Farm. Perhaps it was simply because he had been thinking about it so long that the solution, which was bound to occur sooner or later, came to him then.

Reduced to its essentials, it was a very simple syllogism.

If the letter and number on the note pad in Roland Highsmith's office referred to a house which he had purchased in Cryde Bay for his ailing partner Mr. Westall, why had he taken such deliberate steps—first diverting Peter's attention and then quietly removing the page from the pad—to make sure that Peter did not catch sight of it?

Two possible solutions had already occurred to him. First, that it was some other note on the pad that Highsmith wished to conceal. Alternatively, that Mr. Westall himself was somehow involved in the affair. Peter had thought long and hard about both these possibilities, considering various permutations and combinations of them, without arriving at any useful result. Now a third explanation, simpler and more logical, presented itself. As soon as he thought of it, he knew that he was on the right track.

The key to the problem was Roland Highsmith. What did he really know about him?

Colonel Hay had suggested that Dr. Wolfe's plans, his holiday plans in Europe and his final evasion plans, had revolved around assistance from his old friend. Where exactly did the friend fit into the picture? Peter remembered Captain Andy telling him that Highsmith had been born and bred in Cryde Bay and had opened his first office there. The partnership was called Highsmith and Westall, but Miss Wolfe had described it as a one-man firm. The nervous Mr. Quarles, too, had made it clear that Highsmith was the lynch-pin. If he went, the firm would fall to pieces.

What followed from this? That Highsmith was an exceptional man and had a very close connection with Cryde Bay.

There, surely, lay the germ of truth. It explained such a lot. It answered most of the questions. Peter knew now where Dr. Wolfe had gone to on those motor trips through Europe. He knew how he had got the ugly scar on his face. He knew why Kevin had wanted him to give Anna an empty cigarette case. More than that, he not only knew where Dr. Wolfe was at that moment, he could even guess what his future plans were likely to be.

Having arrived at these conclusions, Peter solved his own more personal problem. It occurred to him that if he reversed his trousers, he would present a semblance of decency from the front. When he had done so, he replaced sock and shoe on his left foot, which was now quite numb, waded across the river, and set his face toward Morebath and Bampton. As he crossed the Bampton-Taunton road, the moon was finally blotted out and the rain came pelting down. He was not sorry about this. It was already four o'clock, and the overcast sky would win him another half-hour of darkness.

He plodded on. The rain worked its way into the back of his windcheater, down his back, and out at the gap which was now at the back of his trousers. His feet and legs were caked with rich red Devon loam.

For the last hour he was only half awake. One part of his mind was directing him through lanes which became increasingly familiar as the light grew. The other part was back at Blundell's. He was running in a cross-country race. The honor of his house demanded that he finish in the first fifty. It was a question of whether his lungs or his legs would give out first. His ankle had almost ceased to trouble him. It was amazing how much punishment the body would take without collapsing. From time to time he seemed to hear the cheers of a distant crowd.

It was six o'clock and the light was back in the sky when he crossed the big playing field, made his way into the garden of School House, and rang the bell.

Mr. French-Bisset answered the door himself. He was wearing a dressing gown and seemed wide awake and unsurprised at the scarecrow apparition on his doorstep.

"Well," he said, "you seem to have had a rough night, Manciple. Come in."

21

"You look as if what you need is a bath and breakfast."

"What I need," said Peter, "is a bath and bed."

"Been up all night, eh? You *have* picked an exciting job. You know your way to the bedroom, the one you used before. The bathroom's opposite. I'll bring you up a clean towel. I think you'd better leave your clothes on the bathroom floor, don't you?"

Washed, and wearing a pair of his housemaster's pajamas, Peter climbed into bed and fell straight into the dreamless sleep of exhaustion followed by tension released. He was recalled to consciousness by the rattle of a tray being put down on the table by his bed. It was a large black tin tray, and it seemed to have on it anything that anyone could want for breakfast. Peter sat up. He said, "You oughtn't to do this, sir. I could quite easily have got up."

"Just as easy to do it this way," said Mr. French-Bisset. "The boys went home yesterday, and I'm all alone here, except for old Sally. You remember Sally? When I told her you'd turned up out of the blue at six o'clock in the morning and would probably be ready for breakfast by four o'clock in the afternoon, do you know what she said? She said, 'Manciple. I remember him. Not surprised. Clever boy. No saying what he'd do next.'"

Peter said, "It really has been rather a—well, a curious sort of chain of events. I'm not sure—"

"No need to tell me anything. If you're involved in some hush-hush job for the government, less said, the better."

"Who did you get that idea from?"

"I was talking to Mr. Knight down at the Stanhope Arms."

"Oh, I see," said Peter. "Yes."

If Mr. French-Bisset assumed him to be working for the Secret Service, it was going to save him the trouble of answering a lot of unanswerable questions.

"Incidentally," continued Mr. French-Bisset with a splendid assumption of nonchalance, "I'm sorry to see that you're dead. Some sort of cover story, no doubt."

He threw a copy of the *Western Evening News* onto the bed and departed.

LONDON MAN MISSING
BOAT FOUND ABANDONED

A tragic outcome is feared to an evening visit made by Peter Manciple to Rackthorn Farm, on the Culme River between Cryde and Huntercombe. A fisherman this morning discovered a small boat, afloat but half submerged, at the point where the Widd stream runs out into Porlock Bay. He identified it as belonging to the owner of Rackthorn Farm. A Colonel Robert Hay, who is holidaying at the farm, told the police that Manciple had visited him on the previous evening, leaving his car at the caravan site on the far side of the stream. "We use the boat constantly for ferrying. It never occurred to me that there could be any possible danger," said the Colonel. "He left the house around midnight, and was to leave the boat on the other bank for a friend who is staying with me and was going to be back late. It's something we have done dozens of times ourselves without giving a thought to it. The Culme is less than thirty yards wide at that point." The Colonel agreed that the river was unusually full on account of the summer rainfall, but said that he was still puzzled how the boat could have been swept out to sea.

Mr. Manciple, who is employed by Messrs. Phelps, King and Troyte, Insurance Adjusters of St. Mary Axe, London, was in Cryde on business. His mother, Mrs. Marie Manciple of 16 Eckersley Gardens, Hampstead, has been informed.

He was finishing his breakfast when he noticed a second and smaller news item.

UNEXPLAINED RIFLE FIRE

Farmers in the Exford area reported hearing a number of bursts of rifle fire, single shots and what sounded like automatic fire in the direction of Dunkery at some time after midnight last Tuesday. An army spokesman said that he knew of no maneuvers which could have been taking place in that area at that time. The police have been alerted to the possibility that deer poachers have restarted the activities which plagued this district some years ago.

The Colonel, as Peter had noticed before, was a man who liked to tidy away loose ends.

"Clothes," said Mr. French-Bisset, reappearing with a selection of garments. "Your trousers, I am afraid, were beyond us. You must have reminded anyone you met of 'the poor Indian whose untutored mind clothed him in front and left him bare behind.'"

"Mercifully, I don't think anyone did see me. The rain kept them indoors."

"I have a selection here. It's a curious thing that growing boys seem to lose interest in their clothes the moment they grow out of them. Like snakes shedding their old skins. I find a quantity of miscellaneous garments abandoned at the close of every school year. We've no one of quite your height, but Garstone wasn't far off it." He displayed a pair of gray flannel trousers. "There's a blazer here which should go well with the trousers. It belonged, I fancy, to Whitmarsh. He was always a natty dresser. Sally has laundered your vest and pants. Your shirt, I'm afraid, was past redemption. I'm lending you one of mine. You can return it at your convenience."

"It's very good of you," said Peter, "but I can't possibly—"

"Your shoes," said Mr. French-Bisset firmly, "have come up quite nicely. And I suggest you take this light raincoat. I'm not sure who it came from. It might have been Kent-Blake's. I rather think it was. Shaving gear in the bathroom. I suggest you get dressed and we'll see what you look like."

Peter lowered the trousers to the full extent of his braces and decided that the shirt, which was several collar sizes too large, would have to be worn open at the neck. The blazer fitted perfectly. He descended to find his housemaster pouring out glasses of sherry.

"Do you think I could have a word with Sally?" he said. "I'd like to thank her."

"She'd be delighted," said Mr. French-Bisset. "Come with me."

He led him along familiar passages. They found the old lady ironing sheets. She looked at Peter out of the guileless blue eyes which had been curiously comforting to him when he had first arrived in that terrifying place.

"There was blood on your vest," she said. "Up to your tricks again."

"If it was blood, it was probably mine, Sally."

"I didn't suppose you'd been murdering somebody. Not that I'd have been greatly surprised. You were always a boy who went his own way."

She slapped another sheet onto the ironing board to signify that the audience was over.

Mr. French-Bisset said, "You'll be wanting to telephone your mother, I expect. She'll have been badly worried."

"If I'd thought I could do it safely," said Peter, "I'd have rung her the moment I saw that paragraph in the paper."

"Safely?"

"I'm afraid our telephone will certainly be tapped."

"Good heavens," said Mr. French-Bisset. He looked as though he would have liked to make some comment, but restrained himself with an effort. Peter's stock as a Secret Service agent was rising.

"I've been looking up trains to London. That is to say, if you're planning to go to London. Perhaps you haven't quite worked out your future moves yet."

Washington? Bonn? Moscow?

"I shall have to go to London," said Peter slowly. "But after that it depends on how things work out. I wonder whether I could regard this as my headquarters for the next few days. I mean, from the point of view of receiving and forwarding messages."

"Certainly. I shall be here myself until the middle of next week. Our idle governors have a habit of meeting in London from time to time and I may be called up to advise about appointments. We're faced with a bit of a crisis over last-minute resignations—but I needn't bother you with school politics. You must have much more serious things to worry about."

"Two or three days will be quite enough," said Peter. "If I or anyone else sends you a message, could you pass it on to this man at Cryde Bay? His name is Anderson. He's perfectly reliable, and I'm planning to keep in touch with him. I'll give you his telephone number. It might be better if you remember it and don't write it down."

"Certainly," said Mr. French-Bisset. "Certainly. Never write anything down. Much safer. Now, about getting up to London."

"I'd prefer to arrive after dark, and as inconspicuously as possible."

"No difficulty. I'll run you out to Tiverton Junction in my car and you can catch the six-thirty Cornishman. It gets to Paddington at nine. Should be getting dark by then. You'll pass muster as a young man who's been spending a short holiday in the West Country. But it did occur to me that you'd look more convincing if you had some luggage with you."

He went out into the hall and returned with a battered suitcase. From the initials on it Peter recognized it as having belonged to an oafish boy called Baker who had left School House the term that Peter had arrived.

"We'll put in a few books and newspapers to give it a convincing weight. You'll have time for a light supper before you go. Unless it's too soon after your breakfast."

"I've got a lot of leeway to make up," said Peter.

At half past six on the dot the Cornishman pulled up at Tiverton Junction, and Peter, wearing Garstone's trousers, Whitmarsh's blazer, and carrying Kent-Blake's raincoat and the oafish Baker's suitcase, now weighted with obsolete copies of Hall and Knight's Algebra and Kennedy's Latin Primer, joined a carriage full of returning holiday makers. He had planned a story of a walking tour on Dartmoor, but he had no need to use it. As soon as conversation became general, he found he had only to listen to other people's accounts of their holidays.

"Thank the Lord," said the woman in the corner, "that we decided to send the children abroad. Think what they'd have been like, sitting for a fortnight in a boardinghouse at St. Ives watching the rain coming down. Herbert spent most of *his* time drinking with the local fishermen."

Her husband said that it wasn't all drinking. They had managed to catch a few fish. A small man in the far corner said that all he'd caught was a cold. At nine o'clock on the dot the train rolled into the misty cavern of Paddington Station and Peter climbed out.

Having time yet to kill, he dumped his suitcase in the cloakroom and made his way to the station buffet, where he secured a meal of a sort and extended it with repeated cups of coffee until the time had crept around to half past ten. By now, so oddly had his hours become reversed, he was feeling wide awake and energetic. He decided to walk back to Hampstead.

He had not made the comment about his telephone being tapped solely in order to impress Mr. French-Bisset. It was a real possibility. He was beginning to feel an unwilling respect for Colonel Hay's devious mind. The Colonel might not have been convinced by that waterlogged boat. All the same, there was a limit. He could hardly tell the local police to put a twenty-four-hour cordon around Peter's mother's house. The most he could do, surely, was to ask that the man on the beat keep an eye on it.

There were several ways into the house. The quietest was the back gate, reached from a lane behind the house and leading through the garden to the kitchen door.

The moon was hidden and it was quite dark when Peter reached Eckersley Gardens. The lane produced no unpleasant surprises. He opened the garden gate quietly. His rubber-soled shoes made no noise on the paved path. The kitchen door, as he had expected, was locked. He had his own key, which he fitted quietly into the Yale lock. No bolts. The door opened with hardly a squeak. He stepped inside and shut it behind him. Then a voice from the darkness at the far end of the room said, "One more step and I shall shoot."

"Please don't shoot, Maman. It's only me."

He heard something which might have been a sob, quickly choked. Then his mother said, "Is it really you?"

"Flesh and blood," said Peter.

"They didn't succeed in killing you, then. I'm glad."

"I'm glad, too. Can we turn the light on?"

"Not in here. Come through to the front room."

The curtains in the front room were tightly drawn. His mother said, "Be careful not to walk between the curtains and the light. They will see your shadow."

"Then the house *is* watched?"

"Of course. But only in front. I do not think they will have seen you come in. If we are careful, they need not suspect that you are here."

"It'll only be for one night. I shall have to be away very early tomorrow. It will be a comfort to sleep in my own bed after some of the places I've slept in recently. Is that gun loaded?"

It was a small-bore sporting rifle.

"Certainly it is loaded. It is a twenty-bore shotgun which I bought from your Uncle Henry. I think he overcharged me. Also I have your father's Army pistol. And certain other weapons."

"Are you preparing for an attack on the house?"

A fortnight before, he would have asked the question wholly in fun. Now he was only half certain that it was a joke.

"I am prepared for anything. I have had an alarm system installed. It sounds a buzzer in here and in my bedroom if any of the house doors is opened. That was how I heard you come."

"If I had been an intruder, would you have shot me?"

"Most certainly. In the legs, for a start."

"For a start," said Peter. "Yes, I see." He got out his wallet and extracted the scrap of paper.

"Does this name mean anything to you?"

His mother put on her glasses and studied the paper.

"Certainly I know Valentin Lasspinière. He is in fact, a relation, though a distant one. His mother was the niece of my Great-uncle Charles on his mother's side. Thirty years ago his was the best-known name in Boulogne. You had but to speak it and the little boys in the streets would have known whom you meant."

"I thought it meant something when I read it. He was in the Resistance, wasn't he?"

"He was the leader of the Resistance in all the Pas-de-Calais. It was not only that he led it. He did it with such wit, such effrontery. You must have heard me tell the story of the young English Lieutenant. His name I forget. But he had been betrayed to the Germans. They knew he was in the old city, and they were combing through it. He went to Valentin, who is an expert at the make-up. He turned the Lieutenant into a girl, a ravishing girl. Another difficulty then arose. The head of the Gestapo was much attracted. The Lieutenant had great difficulty in resisting his attentions. Everyone on our side knew the truth and laughed about it. Laughter was precious in those days. Valentin Lasspinière—yes, he was a fine man. I did not know that he was still alive."

"I think he must be," said Peter. "I discovered this in circumstances which certainly suggest that he is alive. If he is a relative of ours, do you think you could write me a letter introducing me to him?"

"I could do that. I will post it tomorrow."

"Don't post it, give it to me."

"You are going to France?"

"To Boulogne."

"Might one ask why?"

"To find Dr. Wolfe," said Peter.

22

Peter set his alarm clock to wake him at five o'clock. He had selected his wardrobe and laid out the clothes before he went to bed. A pair of faded corduroy trousers, an open-necked shirt of bold green and white checks, a fawn-colored pullover, a respectable jacket, and a pair of brogue shoes. He completed the outfit with a cloth cap of the type worn by navvies at work and Tory prime ministers when out shooting, and a camera which was carried by a strap around his neck and bounced about on the middle of his stomach.

He took his passport with him, although it was probable that he would not need it, some money borrowed from his mother, and a letter which she had written for him. It was a quarter to six when he slipped out of the house by the side door. He examined the main road carefully. There was no apparent sign of life. He did not see the policeman standing in the entrance to a house farther up the road. The policeman saw him, but took no action beyond making a note in his book.

By half past six Peter was breakfasting at an all-night café in Shaftesbury Avenue, and an hour later he was at Charing Cross Station, occupying a corner seat in an empty carriage in the morning train to Deal and Rams-gate.

It was going to be a fine day. The day trip from Deal to Boulogne, which he had seen advertised, should be running. "Six hours in La Belle France. Back the same evening. No passports, no formalities." It had seemed to Peter to be exactly what he wanted.

The train sauntered through the orchards, hop gardens, and fields of Kent, green from the rain that had fallen on them and bright under the sun. It was not a fast train. It was ten o'clock before it pulled into Deal station. When Peter reached the Esplanade, a small crowd had already collected outside the hut from which tickets were being sold. Families with excited children. A hearty male quartet, three of whom, Peter noted, were also carrying cameras. Two middle-aged ladies who were assuring each other that the sea looked calm. A thin and serious-looking man with a guidebook. Peter joined the tail end of the queue.

At half past ten a young man with long blond hair and a book under one arm hurried up, gathered the party together, and directed them into a bus, which took them to Dover. Peter guessed he was a student. He had a squeaky voice which made the children laugh. The advertisement had been correct—there were no formalities of any sort.

On the boat Peter found a chair and placed it on the after deck next to the chair occupied by the serious man. He said, "I see you have the Michelin guidebook. I expect you travel a good deal in France."

"I think I might claim," said the man, "to be moderately well acquainted with the country. I make a point of visiting it each summer, and have been doing so for the last thirty years. No, I lie—thirty-one years. If you have never been before yourself, I think you will be greatly surprised."

He continued to surprise Peter, with scarcely a pause, for the ninety minutes which the boat took to reach Boulogne. As they approached the quay, the blond young man popped out from some private hiding place and said, "Do please remember that we start back at six o'clock. That means six o'clock by *our* time. If you haven't brought your passports, this is most important. Last week a young lady missed the return journey. I believe she's still in a French prison."

The audience assumed this to be a joke and laughed, but Peter noticed the middle-aged ladies checking their watches.

"Although this is only a day trip, you're allowed to bring back duty-free goods. Anything you do buy you'll have to declare. Enjoy yourselves."

The guide returned to his lair. Peter noticed that the book he was carrying was *Cheshire on Real Property.*

"Perhaps I could show you some of the sights," said the thin man. "I am tolerably well acquainted with the history of the town." They walked off onto the quay and past a pair of impassive gendarmes, chatting as though they were old friends. "The ecclesiastical architecture is not without interest."

"It's very good of you," said Peter. "I may have time for some sightseeing later. I really came over on business. I'm afraid I shall have to attend to it first."

He walked up the Rue des Pipots and made his way into the old town of Boulogne, the Ville Haute, which he knew and loved. It lies tightly enclosed, keeping itself to itself, caring nothing for the world which bustles and scurries outside. The narrowness of its gates and the steepness of its streets daunt passing motorists. They hurry past on their way to Calais in the north or Abbeville in the south, knowing nothing of the tall buildings, shadowed streets, and quiet squares inside those medieval walls.

The Rue Belcourt was a turning off the Rue de Lille, on the far side of the Basilisque de Notre Dame. Number fourteen was at the far end. It was a withdrawn house fenced with high iron railings in front and separated from the street by a paved court; a house of solid quality and dignity. Peter crossed the courtyard and climbed the six steps which led up to the front door. He did so with a feeling of almost breathless anticipation. Such a long, such a complicated path. So many twists, so many hazards and blind corners, to lead at last to this quiet house in the city of his birth.

He jerked the wrought-iron bellpull and waited. He could hear the jingling of the bell deep inside the house. Silence returned. He was on the point of pulling it again when he heard slow footsteps. A small door cut into the massive front door opened and a woman looked out. She was dressed in black and had a face like a good-natured monkey.

She said, "Monsieur?"

"I am looking," said Peter, "for Monsieur Valentin Lasspinière."

"This is his house."

"I have a letter for him."

"Yes?"

"He is at home?"

"Yes."

"Then perhaps I might be permitted—"

"You wish to hand the letter to him yourself?"

"I should prefer to do so."

"Then enter."

Feeling as nervous as any prince invited into an enchanted castle, Peter stepped up to the door. He had to duck his head to get through.

"You are very tall," said the lady. "You speak excellent French, but I surmise that you are English." She led the way down a shadowy hallway and pushed open a heavy door. "If you would have the kindness to wait here, I will inform Monsieur of your arrival."

Valentin Lasspinière was of middle height, his most noticeable feature a shock of snowy-white hair. He had the round and mobile face of a Gascon, a man who suspected life to be a joke and had spent a lifetime proving it so.

He read the letter carefully and said, "Tante Marie. I hope she is well. It is many years since I have seen her, but I remember her, of course. I even remember you. She brought you once to see me. You were then so high." M. Lasspinière bent forward and placed his hand six inches from the floor.

"Taller now."

"A little. This letter mentions my old friend Alexander Wolfe. I was sad to read of his death. The reports in our newspapers gave few details, but I gathered the impression—perhaps I was wrong?—that there was some mystery about it."

"You were not wrong," said Peter. "And you were aware, I think, that he went in some danger of his life."

"That I knew."

"And you helped him, as you have helped many men before, to evade his enemies."

"I gave him what help I could."

"If you could tell me about that," said Peter, "it might help us, in turn, to obtain the satisfaction of discomfiting his enemies."

M. Lasspinière looked at Peter thoughtfully. He said, "From your interest in the matter, do I deduce that you are of the police?"

"I am investigating the circumstances of his death."

"I see."

The silence which followed was broken by the arrival of the woman in black carrying a tray. There were two glasses and a bottle on it. M. Lasspinière filled the glasses and handed one to Peter. He said, "It is a local wine, but drinkable." They drank in silence.

Finally, M. Lasspinière said, "Dr. Wolfe is dead. What I am going to tell you cannot, therefore, harm him. But I will tell it to you on condition. It is for your ears alone. If it helps *you*, by enlightening you on certain points, so much the better. But it is for information, not for action. You will not repeat it. If I am asked about it, publicly or privately, I shall deny it totally. Do you accept those conditions?"

"Certainly," said Peter. "You understand that I had surmised certain points, but they were guesses only. What I required was the confirmation which I realized that you alone could give me."

M. Lasspinière refilled both glasses and said, "I had known Dr. Wolfe for many years. I am myself interested in the science of genetics—as an amateur, you understand. Dr. Wolfe, out of his great learning, and even greater kindness, assisted me. He stayed in this house more than once. With his help I was able to follow, at a respectful distance, the path he was mapping out for himself, into the unknown. It soon became apparent to me that it was a path which must lead him into personal danger. I am now, Mr. Manciple, as you see me, a most respectable and peace-loving old personage. But in my youth I was not unacquainted with violence and danger. You might say that I lived hand in glove with them for four years. I am not boasting of it. Many Frenchmen did the same. I simply state it as a fact. Five years ago, in this room, Dr. Wolfe and I examined his problem. We examined it dispassionately, as scientists should. And we came to certain conclusions."

"Which were?"

"Which I will now explain to you," said M. Lasspinière. "Bearing always in mind the conditions I have laid down."

240

Detective Sergeant Fred Dawlish, Peter's snooker-playing friend from the local police station, was selected as the man to follow up the report which had been made earlier that morning by Police Constable Roberts. The matter had first to be referred back through Division and Central to Special Branch, who had asked for the watch on the house. Special Branch had been cautious. Their own interest in the matter stemmed from a request from the Home Office. It hardly amounted, they pointed out, to an authorization for positive action.

"Everyone's passing the buck," said Inspector Lowcock. "What that means is, if anything goes wrong, *we* carry the can."

"What I can't make out," said Dawlish, "is exactly what I'm meant to do."

"Exactly what you're meant to do is make an inquiry. We've had this report about young Manciple being drowned. Right? Now we've had another report saying he may be alive. Right? *You* know the family. It's natural you should be the one to go along."

"I know Peter," agreed Dawlish, "but I've never met his mother, not to talk to. From what he told me, she's nutty as a fruitcake."

"If *she's* a fruitcake," said Inspector Lowcock, who was given to making remarks of this sort, "*you'd* better use your loaf, hadn't you? But don't stir things up."

Armed with these helpful instructions, Dawlish approached the house and rang the bell. In the silence that followed, he heard a sound as of a chair or a table being shifted, and one of the curtains in the front window stirred.

"She's there, all right," he said. "What's the old coot playing at?"

He rang the bell again. Nothing happened. He rang

it a third time and tried a sharp rat-tat on the knocker. This did provoke a reaction.

There were footsteps in the hall. Dawlish switched on a cheerful smile and waited for the door to be opened.

The letter-box flap was lifted and Mrs. Manciple said, "I'm warning you. If you don't get off my property, I shall shoot you."

"Come, now, ma'am," said Dawlish.

"I shall count three. One—"

"Peter wouldn't want you to do a thing like that."

"Two—"

"Be reasonable."

The word "Three" was followed by a spurt of flame through the letter box and a loud crack. Dawlish switched off his smile and leaped for the gate. As he did so, the door half opened. There was a second loud crack, and something burned the leg of his trousers. He dodged behind the garden wall and raced for the telephone kiosk at the corner.

A third and louder explosion followed him.

"I thought I told you not to stir things up," said Inspector Lowcock.

"For God's sake, she's been shooting at me. She damn nearly hit me."

He looked down at the leg of his trousers. There was a brown singe mark, but no bullet hole.

"All right. I'll send a couple of cars round. Just keep your head down."

"You're telling me!"

When the reinforcements arrived, their first job was to clear the spectators from the road.

"We'll need another car," said Lowcock. "Block both ends of the street. When we've got these silly buggers out of range, we'll have to rush it."

"There's a path at the back. And a gate into the garden. I've been in that way before."

A second loud crack from the front garden had the effect of hastening the departure of the spectators. Lowcock got busy on his car wireless.

"Here comes the press," said Dawlish.

A young man in the shabby raincoat which is the uniform of reporters in all weathers was coming up the street, taking care to keep his head down.

Lowcock, who was backing his car, waved him away angrily. The young man took this as an invitation to come up to the car.

"What's up, skipper? I.R.A.?"

"I don't know what the hell's up," said Lowcock. "And if you're not out of the street in one minute flat, I'm running you in, for a start."

There was a curious sighing noise and a loud explosion at the far end of the street.

"For God's sake," said the reporter, "they're using mortars." He contemplated the telephone box, decided it was too dangerous, and took off up the street to find a resident who would let him use the telephone.

The third car had now arrived. Lowcock gave out his orders. For five minutes there had been no sign of life from the house. He was trying to remember a standing instruction, which had been circulated to all metropolitan stations, dealing with situations of this sort.

He said, "You've all got to remember that psychology is more important than force. The great thing is to keep them talking and rush them when they're off their guard. Everyone got that? Right. I'll do the talking, you do the rushing."

There was a murmur of what might have been gratification from his force, which now comprised five uniformed policemen and three detectives.

"You, Lowry, and Rooke, go round the back. When I open up on the loudhailer, you make your way up the garden path, keeping under cover, and see if you can effect an entrance through the kitchen door."

"What do we do when we get inside, skipper?"

"You use your initiative. Any more questions? Right."

Minutes later Lowry and Rooke were peering over the garden fence.

"What does he mean, keep under cover?" said Rooke. "There isn't any cover."

"There's a row of runner beans on the right," said Lowry. "You can have them. I'm going to use the tomato frame."

This was a small structure of wood and glass halfway up the path on the left. They neither of them noticed that one of the back bedroom windows was being very cautiously raised.

"This is the police," said a booming voice from the front. "The house is surrounded. You are advised to come out quietly. So far no damage has been done."

"Except to my trousers," said Dawlish.

"If you come out peacefully, no one will get hurt. But I have to warn you that force will be met by force."

"Over we go," said Lowry. They vaulted the fence. Rooke hurled himself onto the ground behind the beans, and Lowry raced for the inadequate cover afforded by the tomato frame. As he reached it, there was a long streak of light from the window, something thudded into the frame, and the glass disintegrated. Before he could move, there was a second flash. This time the missile rose high into the air and exploded in a galaxy of colored stars.

For all except those public figures who feature regularly in the press, there must be an element of shock when one's name appears unexpectedly in print. Peter, who had arrived back in Deal with as little formality as he had left it, bought an evening paper to read on the train. The headline "RED FACES FOR HAMP-STEAD POLICE" meant nothing. The subhead, "THE SIEGE OF ECKERSLEY GARDENS," brought him up all standing.

A modern version of the Siege of Sydney Street was enacted this morning, this time not in the sleazy purlieus of Whitechapel but in the respectable location of Eckersley Gardens, Hampstead. The owner of Number 16 Eckersley Gardens, Mrs. Marie Manciple, resenting the arrival of Detective Sergeant Fred Dawlish, drove him from her front door with a powerful barrage of fire. The Sergeant, concluding that he had stumbled on a nest of I.R.A. saboteurs, retreated and sent for help, which soon arrived in the form of Inspector Lowcock from the local station and half a dozen of our stalwart boys in blue. The house was surrounded and Mrs. Manciple was commanded to come forth. Instead she continued her fusillade, this time from the back of the house, unfortunately destroying a valuable tomato frame. It was only then realized that the weapons she was using were those more traditionally associated with the annual celebrations of the fifth of November. She had equipped herself with a projector which threw squibs and crackers with considerable accuracy, and supplemented this with a few well-aimed rockets. It was when one of these burst into a multicolored display of shooting stars that the police realized that they were not, in fact, faced by a gang of armed desperadoes. Mrs. Manciple is French and, according to her neighbors, has frequently expressed strong feelings on the subject of police surveillance. She lost her husband last year, and recently received news that her son had been the subject of a boating fatality in Devonshire. The police, when asked whether any charge would be made, were not prepared to commit themselves.

Peter said, "Good God," and then, "Thank the Lord she didn't actually shoot anyone." Then he started to laugh. It was a long time since he had had anything to laugh at, and once he had started he found it difficult to stop. A middle-aged lady sitting opposite said, "I'm so glad you have found something to amuse you. The papers these days seem to be exclusively devoted to the propagation of gloom."

"Shooting rockets at the police," said Peter.

"I read about it," said the lady. "Of course, she was French. That explains a lot."

"I suppose it does," said Peter.

One thing was clear. He could not now do as he had planned and spend a second night at home. He might be able to find a room in a hotel, but London that summer was packed with foreign tourists, and registration would be tricky. The longer he remained off the map, the better. On the other hand, if he gave a false name and the hotel asked to look at his passport, he would be in trouble.

It was as his train was pulling into Charing Cross that the solution occurred to him. Having consumed a late supper, he walked across London toward the area of Bayswater which lies behind Paddington Station. Here he found what he wanted: one of the few remaining all-night Turkish baths. There was a pleasant anonymity in nudity and steam. Wrapped in towels and prostrate on a couch, he dozed away the central hours of the night, emerging at six o'clock in the morning to what promised to be a fine day. It was not until he had walked for half a mile without meeting a single soul that he realized that it was Sunday. Since he was not planning to arrive back at Cryde Bay until after dark, he had a day to kill.

Having considered the matter, he decided to visit the Zoo, and spent much of his time in the dim quietness of the reptile house watching the snakes—sensible creatures who did not waste a particle of energy and made the most of the comforts of captivity.

At four o'clock he emerged into the sunlight, walked across Regent's Park, and took a Bakerloo Line train to Paddington. He had calculated that no one attempting to forecast his movements would imagine that he would return to Devonshire.

The five o'clock train got him to Cryde Junction at half past eight, where he changed onto the local switch-line train for Cryde Bay. He was glad to find the train full of family parties. When he arrived at Cryde Bay, he was careful to be among the last to dismount. By the time he reached the forecourt, all the taxis had been snapped up. Excellent. He wandered out into the town. The wind was steady from the southwest, and there was a feel of more fine weather to come.

Peter felt a lifting of his spirits. The end of the long chase was in sight. It was by no means clear to him how things would fall out, but he had a conviction that Fortune, which had played such a surprising game on his behalf, was not going to desert him on the final lap.

Captain Andy opened the door to him. His shirt sleeves were rolled back to the elbow and he was carrying a paintbrush in his left hand. His right hand was in his pocket. He said, "Well, this is a nice surprise. You've timed your return to the minute. I've just finished the last piece of touching up. I trust that the paint smell will be out by teatime tomorrow when the first of my guests arrive. I was about to celebrate with a solitary supper, but I can easily stretch it for two."

"Thank you," said Peter.

The Captain looked at him, with his head cocked to one side. He said, "You look as though there was something very important that you had to say and were finding some difficulty in saying it."

Peter said, "I was wondering whether you were really planning to be here at teatime tomorrow when your guests arrive. Or whether you would have moved on, one stage further, in the journey which started when you manhandled your car over Rackthorn Point."

23

"In fact," said Dr. Wolfe, "I shall be moving on." Supper was over, and they were sitting in the room which served as an office. "I ought to have pulled out at once when I discovered that my cigarette case had been taken. I wasn't deceived by that fake burglary. Not for a minute. I knew Kevin had taken it, and it wasn't hard to guess why."

"Because it had your fingerprints on it."

"Inside and out. It was the case I used most. Kevin's people would have a record of my prints. As soon as he'd had a chance of comparing them, he'd have been certain."

"He wasn't certain before?"

"Suspicious. But not certain."

"It must have been a shock for you when Anna and Kevin turned up here."

"It was a bad moment. But I don't believe either of them recognized me. Not to start with. There was no reason they should. They'd seen me before, on a couple of occasions, in the dim lighting of Dave Brewer's saloon bar. I don't believe they would have tumbled to it if I hadn't made a stupid mistake. Do you remember, that evening, when we were talking about Blackmore?

Kevin said something, and, like a fool and without stopping to think about it, I trotted out the comment that Blackmore was the first of the documentary novelists. The moment I said it I knew that I'd given myself away."

"I tuned in to Kevin's reaction," said Peter, "but I couldn't construe it."

"A few weeks ago, in the Doone Valley Hotel, the conversation had taken the same turn *and I'd made exactly the same remark*. The same words, the same tone of voice. That was what Kevin recognized. Not my face. My voice. But he wasn't totally convinced. That's why he wanted my prints."

"He took this, too," said Peter. He smoothed out the scrap of paper on the table.

Dr. Wolfe said, "I had a number of letters from Valentin Lasspinière. I suppose he recognized the name. It's well known in certain circles. It would have been an extra piece of confirmation, but the prints were what really mattered."

He was sorting out papers and stowing them away in the pigeonholes of the desk. "Must leave the place shipshape."

"Who's going to look after it?"

"Roland Highsmith. I spoke to him on the phone yesterday. He's fixing up a manager to take charge for the rest of the season. Then he'll probably close it down. It belongs to him."

"He organized the whole thing for you?"

"He and Valentin. We worked it all out five years ago. Essentially, it was a very simple substitution. Once Roland had got me a passport in my new name, the rest followed automatically. I took my car across to Boulogne, drove round the countryside a bit until I was sure no one was following me, brought the car back, and stowed it away in Valentin's garage. He made a few changes in my appearance. Contact lenses to replace the glasses I normally wore at the Biological Warfare place. A bald patch, which I could cover with a toupee when I got back to work. A touch of sunburn. A completely new outfit. That was really all that was necessary. On the last occasion, since things seemed to be hotting up, he added the scar. And a bloody nuisance it was. I had to take it off each morning to shave, and put it back again. But it was basically a good idea, because when I did leave, people would be looking either for a man with a scar or someone who'd grown a beard to hide it."

"Too true," said Peter. "Then when M. Lasspinière had worked his magic, you came straight back here, I take it, and opened up the guesthouse for the summer."

"Right. And you'd be surprised how easy it was. I needed Roland's help, opening an account at the bank and getting the different licenses and permits for this place. He was so well known round here that all those sort of arrangements went through smoothly. He'd bought this house for me. We chose Anderson as my new name because the old lady it used to belong to happened to have been called Anderson. Once I'd elected her as my Aunt Selina, quite a few people claimed to have met me as a small boy. One of them even produced a photograph of a repulsive young person in a sailor suit and said how little I'd changed."

Dr. Wolfe laughed with genuine amusement.

"It was astonishing how quickly everyone, including myself, adopted my new persona. Good old Captain Andy. It helped that I'd done a bit of sailing and flying and was able to talk the jargon. My only fear was that one of my summer guests would come from Luton and start asking questions about my alleged business there. It didn't arise, but I expect I could have ridden them off. Luton's a large place."

"Plenty of factories round Luton," agreed Peter. One

thing which was fascinating him was the way that Captain Andy, now that the masquerade was over, was turning back into Dr. Wolfe. Even his choice of words was changing. "A repulsive young person." Captain Andy would have said "a frightful kid."

"You've no idea what a status it gives you in the community when you become a rate payer and get on the roll of the Parochial Church Council. As you know, there was even a move to get me onto the Town Council. I had to stop that. Suppose they'd made me mayor! Picture in all the local papers."

"What were you planning to do eventually?"

"I was going to announce that I'd given up my business in Luton and decided to retire here permanently. And then," said Dr. Wolfe sadly, "you came along."

"I know," said Peter. "I'm very sorry. Really I am."

"I never asked how you did it."

"It was when I was in Mr. Highsmith's office. He must just have completed the purchase of that house in the Chine for his partner. The Land Registry number happened to be written on the memo pad on his desk. He knew I was looking for you, and the very last thing he wanted was for me to be nosing round Cryde Bay, so he distracted my attention for a moment, tore that sheet off the pad, and threw it away. It was a natural precaution to take. But quite fatal. Of course, he couldn't have known that I've got a photographically retentive memory."

"I knew as soon as I met you that you were a remarkable young man," said Dr. Wolfe. "What are you going to do next?"

"It depends on your plans."

"I'm getting out. If I hadn't had some rather complicated arrangements to make, I'd have been gone before now. I gathered from what I read in the newspapers that the two opposition factions had become embroiled with

252

each other, and I thought that might give me a breathing space. But I can assure you it's been an anxious two days. I'm a man of peace, but I've had a gun under my hand every hour of the day and night. I'm ready to go now. Next stop, Ireland. I've got good friends there. After that—"

"You'd better not tell me."

"I was only going to say somewhere in the Mediterranean. After that, maybe the Pacific."

"The world his parish," thought Peter. He added, "If you would be prepared to give me a statement saying that you had no claim to the insurance money, I'd hold it up until you were safely away."

Dr. Wolfe thought about it. He said, "Yes, I suppose that's the least I can do. Lavinia doesn't really need the money. She's totally self-supporting. Any money she has got is spent on those dogs. All the same, I've had a better idea. You're not married, are you?"

"No."

"No one in mind?"

"No," said Peter harshly. "No one at all."

"Pity about that girl," said Dr. Wolfe, replying to the thoughts rather than the words. "A very good-looking girl indeed. But hard as steel. Purified and refined in the fire. They are the new Joan of Arcs, twice as fierce and ten times as clever as that deluded peasant girl. What I was going to say was, why don't you come with me?"

"Come with you? Now, tonight?"

"Why not? I'll promise to post off a clearance to your company as soon as we're away. You're a free agent. When you get tired of travel, you can come back. Make your fortune by writing a book about it—*My Travels with a Mad Geneticist.*"

"Well—" said Peter.

"Don't you sometimes get an urge to cut your painter

and sail away? Like Ulysses, when he got bored with Ithaca? The lights begin to twinkle from the rocks. 'The long day wanes: the slow moon climbs: the deep moans round with many voices.' Do you know, I've heard just that sound when I've been alone on a boat. The sea begins to talk to you. It's when you start talking back that you have to watch it. That's when you need a friend along with you."

For a minute Peter was tempted, but he knew that he was going to say no.

"To lead the life of Ulysses," he said, "you've got to have the character and temperament of Ulysses. I'm not like that. I'm hopelessly unadventurous. I've got no stamina. I give up easily. I got so depressed once that I tried to kill myself. I don't want to talk about that, but I really did try."

"How right the ancients were," said Dr. Wolfe, "when they accounted hopelessness as one of the seven deadly sins." He took a piece of paper out of the desk drawer. "I'll write you a full quittance. And I'll send you a letter, from wherever I am, a fortnight from now. Hang on to the envelope, then you can tell your people this document came in it. That'll cover you for not having produced it before."

The idea of going away was working on Peter. To sail away, to see something of the wide world, beyond the western stars. The man he still thought of as Captain Andy would be an ideal companion for such a venture. After all, what had Peter got to keep him in England? He had almost made his mind up to say yes, but somehow the words would not come.

"I've a little more packing to do," said Dr. Wolfe. "I plan to be away by midnight. Here's your letter."

As he said this, he had picked up his briefcase from the desk. Catching Peter's eye, he smiled, opened the briefcase, and held it upside down. Nothing came out.

Then he pointed to the open grate, where Peter could see a small pile of gray dust. Peter said, "You mean you've burnt them? All the microfilm records of your work? Six years' work?"

"I did it last night. There are not more than three people in the world who would have understood them, but that was three too many. There's a bottle of Scotch in that corner cupboard. Help yourself, and pour one out for me. I won't be long."

When Dr. Wolfe was ready, Peter helped him carry his luggage down to the boat. A kit bag, a suitcase, and a knapsack. As soon as they were stowed on board, Dr. Wolfe got ready to cast off. He went about the business with the neatness and speed of a man who knew exactly what he was doing.

Peter went back to the house and climbed the stairs to his bedroom. By the time he got there, the boat was moving. He saw the red port light as it swung around to clear the end of the jetty and set off down the Channel.

The boat was about a quarter of a mile from the shore when it happened. First a flash of white light, then the crumps of the explosion, then the shock waves which blew the curtains in at the open window where Peter was sitting. He could see the boat clearly in the moonlight. It was on fire at one end. As he jumped to his feet, the boat seemed to stand on its head. Then, quite slowly, it disappeared, and there was nothing to be seen but a cloud of white smoke or steam drifting across the smooth surface of the sea.

Peter sat down again. There was nothing he could do. He sat there while boats put out to the scene of the explosion and came back again. One of them was a police launch. He saw the men lean over the side and pull something into the boat, and thought for a moment that it was a body; but as the launch swung sideways, he saw that it was a piece of wreckage.

He thought, "If they identify the boat, they'll come here and start asking questions. What am I going to say?" Perhaps he ought to remove himself out of the house and hide somewhere. His dulled brain refused to grapple with the problem. He sat still.

He heard two o'clock and then three o'clock strike from the church tower of St. Barnabas', and it was while the chimes of three o'clock were still sounding that he heard another sound.

Someone had opened the side door of the house and was coming up the stairs.

The newcomer was walking softly, but with an occasional drag and stumble which suggested tiredness. The footsteps passed his door and went on toward the end of the passage. Peter guessed the truth then, and called out. The footsteps stopped, then came back down the passage. The door opened and Anna came in.

The full moon, shining directly through the open window, lit her up as though she had made an entrance onto the stage. She was dressed as he had seen her before, in windbreaker and jeans, and she was soaking wet. Her drenched hair was lying in straight lines down the side of her face, which showed white in its dark frame.

She said, "I didn't expect you to be here. I came to pick up some dry clothes and a few other things."

Whenever she had spoken before, even in times of stress, her voice had had a lift and a lilt in it. Now it was as lifeless as the voice of a ventriloquist's dummy.

He said, "Was it you—?"

"I was on board fixing it when I heard you and Dr. Wolfe coming down to the boat. I had to stay on board to finish the job. When I had done it, I swam ashore. I bungled the setting of the time fuse. It wasn't meant to go off until the boat was much further from the shore."

From the lack of emotion in her voice, she might

256

have been apologizing to her partner for bungling a short putt.

Peter said, "Why?" and then, when Anna said nothing, "Why *you*?"

"I did it because it had to be done. And because I was the only person left to do it. Yesterday morning, before it was light, Stefan and a friend swam out to our boat in Plymouth Sound and blew it to pieces with limpet mines. I was on shore, in the house of a friend. That was why I escaped. Four of our people were on the boat, sleeping, just above the point where one of the mines exploded. Three of them were killed. The fourth is in hospital. He will probably die."

Peter could think of nothing to say.

Anna continued in the same flat voice. "Fortunately, some of our stores were on shore. Enough for what I had to do. The friend brought me here in his car this evening. He is waiting for me now."

"And then?"

"Either Stefan will kill me or I will kill him. I think he will kill me. He is very clever."

"And then your friend will kill Stefan, or Stefan will kill him."

"It's possible."

"In God's name," said Peter, "is your life for nothing more than killing and being killed?"

"*We* do not throw our lives away."

Peter could feel the anger inside him, bubbling up, overmastering all other emotions.

He said, "You're children. Stupid, cruel, arrogant children. If the games you play weren't so deadly, they'd be a joke. A bad, bloody, crimson joke. Have you any real idea what you've done? Just for a moment, can you stop seeing it as a move in a game and look at it as it really is? You've wiped out a man. Not only a great

257

man, but a decent, kindly man. A man who was particularly kind to you."

"He had to die."

Peter jumped to his feet, took two steps forward, grabbed the front of her windcheater, and shook her. She made no attempt to get away. After a minute the fury drained out of Peter and he let his hands drop. They were wet from the drenched material and he wiped them against his legs.

Anna said, "He was your friend, too. Do you plan to do something about it? Perhaps you would like to kill me? I don't think you have the skill, but you could try."

Peter sat down. He said, "I don't want to kill you. I just don't want to see you again."

Anna said, "I'm sorry for you. You are feeble. You were prepared to throw your own life away for nothing, but you think it wrong to spend it in defense of what you believe in. I am sorry for your country, because it is made up of people like you. You have lost the spirit and the will to fight. It is sad because you had that spirit once, and taught it to other people. If you could see yourselves as the fighting nations of the world see you now, you would be ashamed."

She went out softly and shut the door. He heard her moving about in the next room. Some time later he heard her going down the stairs; then the door shutting behind her. He sat there for a very long time.

When at last he stirred himself, it was to go across to the writing desk in the corner and switch on the table lamp which stood on it. He was stiff and cold. He lit the gas fire in the grate, and then sat down at the desk, opened his briefcase, and took the half-finished report out of the envelope which was already stamped and addressed to Messrs. Phelps, King and Troyte, Insurance Adjusters of St. Mary Axe. He wrote steadily, covering page after page.

The empty house was quiet. The street outside was quiet. Even the sea was quiet. As Peter wrote, the light grew and the sounds of day began to steal back. Away down the road a door slammed and footsteps clattered on the pavement. A boy came past on a bicycle, whistling. A car started up.

By the time he reached the last page of his report, the sun was over the horizon in the east. The first long, slanting rays were reflected off the sea and threw a pattern of dancing light onto the ceiling. He switched off the table lamp.

It was customary to end a long report with a summary of its conclusions. In this case, it presented no difficulty. Peter wrote: "Total certainty can only be achieved if the body is recovered and fingerprints and dental details are matched. But in view of the facts which have now come to light, there cannot be any further room for doubt that Dr. Wolfe is dead, and that one of the causes of his death was drowning. The sum secured by the policy will therefore have to be paid to his sister, Lavinia."

A tiny piece salvaged from the wreckage.

He blotted the last page, shuffled all the pages together, inserted them in the envelope, and sealed it.

He noticed that the gas fire was starting to pop and realized that another coin would have to go into the meter. He leaned back in his chair, flexed his fingers to get the cramp of writing out of them, and closed his eyes. To make any further decisions, even to move, seemed an intolerable effort.

Downstairs, in the hall, a telephone started ringing.

24

The three cars came quietly up the road and drew in to the side twenty yards short of the Seven Seas Guest House. Colonel Hay and Rupert climbed out of the leading car. Men got out of each of the other cars. Two of them went around to the back of the house. A third took up his post outside the front gate. The fourth accompanied the Colonel and Rupert up the front path. All this was done without any word being spoken.

The man with the Colonel had a look at the lock on the door, selected a bunch of keys from a haversack he was carrying, and set to work. It took him less than a minute to find the key he wanted. As the front door swung open, he stood to one side, and the Colonel walked in, with Rupert behind him.

The sun was well up by now. The light through the open door reflected from the barometer which hung in the hall beside a blown-up photograph of a boat under sail and a neatly framed notice which said, "Guests will oblige by *not* bringing too much sand into the house. Spades, buckets and prawning nets should be left in the porch at the side."

The Colonel stood still for so long that he seemed to

be reading the notice carefully. Then he sniffed. The smell was unmistakable.

His lips formed the words "Fried bacon." Rupert nodded. They went down the hall, still walking quietly, and opened the kitchen door.

Peter had his back to them. He was holding a frying pan in one hand and a bacon slice in the other. When he heard the door opening, he turned his head and said, "Good morning, Colonel. You're just in time for breakfast."

"I had breakfast," said the Colonel. He made a sign to Rupert, who went out, shutting the door.

"You must have got up very early. Would you care for a cup of coffee?"

"I've been up all night," said the Colonel. "Yes, I'd like some coffee. Perhaps you could manage a cup for Rupert as well. He'll be down in a moment."

"If he's searching the house, I can save you the trouble. There's no one here except me."

"I didn't expect there would be," said the Colonel. "To tell you the truth, I'm surprised to find you here. You know what happened last night?"

"If you mean the destruction of Dr. Wolfe and his boat, yes. I saw it happen. You didn't arrange that as well, did you?"

"You mustn't credit me with supernatural powers. I suppose his records went down with him?"

"No. He burned them before he left. You'll find the ashes in the grate."

"Did the girl come back here afterwards?"

"Yes."

"She'd have needed clothes and money. Not that they did her a lot of good. The car she was in was ambushed outside the town by Stefan and his friend. They killed the girl and the driver. Stefan's friend was badly wounded. Stefan got away scot-free."

Peter visualized the polite, controlled, athletic young man who had shown him around the dig—how long ago? He said, "He seems to be very lucky. A born escaper."

"I could name another," said the Colonel, looking at Peter. "Do you realize that you are the only man, the only outsider, left alive who has any idea of what has been going on in the last two weeks?"

Rupert had come in quietly and closed the door. The Colonel looked at him, and he shook his head. Peter could see the two men in the garden outside. They seemed to be examining one of the fruit cages. He said, "Am I to understand from that remark that it would suit your book to finish me off and bury me in the back garden?"

"My dear chap!"

"After all, you did try to drown me."

"All we planned for you was a cold night at sea. To cool your ardor a little. We never thought you'd be so clumsy as to turn the boat over. Right, Rupert?"

"Certainly not."

"In fact, when we heard about it, our first idea was that you'd done it deliberately. After all, you did try to commit suicide once before."

"How do you know that?"

"We've investigated you in depth. Naturally, we talked to your doctor."

"I see," said Peter. He got up and went over to the stove, where the kettle was now boiling. He put a spoonful of coffee into each of the three china mugs, poured boiling water on them, and brought them back to the table. The Colonel and Rupert watched him impassively. He said, "But just in case you were contemplating stopping my mouth, I ought to tell you that I have written out a very full account of everything that has happened and that I posted it early this morning. It's addressed to my employers. You might prevent its publication, but you can't stop it. Unless, of course, you have the power to interfere with Her Majesty's Mails. Milk and sugar?"

"Neither," said Rupert.

"Both," said the Colonel. "You know, Mr. Manciple, you really are a most unusual person. You're wasted in your present job. I can think of a much more sensible and permanent way of shutting your mouth than burying you in the vegetable garden. Why don't you join us?"

Peter stared at him.

"It's a perfectly serious offer. You have exactly the sort of talents we could use. And in addition you seem to enjoy, almost to excess, what Napoleon counted as the most important attribute in a soldier. Amazing luck."

Peter started to laugh. It was not hysterical laughter. It was the genuine laughter of release, the sort of laughter which clears away fears and inhibitions and leaves the laugher as relaxed and happy as if he had achieved a successful orgasm.

It was so infectious that Rupert started to laugh as well. The Colonel said stuffily. "You might share the joke."

"I'm sorry," said Peter. "It was you offering me a job. As it happens, you're just too late. At half past six this morning I had a telephone call from my old housemaster at Blundell's. He apologized for telephoning me so early, but he'd been summoned up to London by the school governors. They'd told him that one of his jobs was going to be to find an assistant housemaster to work under him. The matter was urgent, as the man had to start next term. He proposed to recommend me. I have the necessary qualifications and they like to give preference to an Old Boy if they can. He said he was certain I would get the job, if it appealed to me."

"And you think that would be more exciting than the job I offered you?"

"Oh, I think so. Yes."

"Nonsense," said the Colonel crossly. "What you're doing is running away. It's what a man in the Middle Ages used to do when he found life too much for him. He joined a monastery. Right, Rupert?"

But Rupert was beyond speech.

27 million Americans can't read a bedtime story to a child.

It's because 27 million adults in this country simply can't read.

Functional illiteracy has reached one out of five Americans. It robs them of even the simplest of human pleasures, like reading a fairy tale to a child.

You can change all this by joining the fight against illiteracy.

Call the Coalition for Literacy at toll-free **1-800-228-8813** and volunteer.

**Volunteer
Against Illiteracy.
The only degree you need
is a degree of caring.**

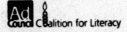

Ad Council Coalition for Literacy